THE LAST SOLDIER

In a remote corner of Arabia the Sheikhdom of Hassan has survived from the Middle Ages. It is corrupt, cruel and newly independent. The Ruler, Hajji Kassim, is a man of reputed wickedness; his brothers are men of devious ambition.

Colonel Clive Masterman, DSO, the commander of the Ruler's army, is required to keep the peace in this land of turbulent loyalties, under the inspired but erratic counsel of the former Political Agent, Charles Peachy. Late one evening the Colonel is startled by a shot in the desert, an incident followed by a brutal assault upon a native soldier by one of the white officers under his command. And from these strange beginnings a story of mutiny, revolution and war develops, leading to tragic conclusions.

This novel is both a remarkable study of a professional soldier faced with problems beyond his strength, and a beautifully drawn picture, sketched with a wry humour, of an Arab sheikhdom in the first days of self-government. Although Colonel Masterman is independent of military authority, he still tries to preserve British traditions in his native Levy. But events unfold that force him into attitudes and actions for which he has no gift or sympathy, and finally, against his deepest convictions, he is compelled to an act of supreme disloyalty.

Patrick Raymond's previous novels have been notable for his superb evocation of the remoter parts of the old British Empire in the process of change. For this novel he has chosen a more dramatic theme in which violence abounds, yet one which is under-played with outstanding effect, and the desert itself becomes as sinister an element as the ageing Emir, Hajji Kassim.

THE LAST SOLDIER

PATRICK RAYMOND

CASSELL · LONDON

CASSELL & COMPANY
35 Red Lion Square, London WC1R 4SG
*Sydney, Auckland, Toronto,
Johannesburg*

First published 1974

I.S.B.N. 0 304 29307 5

Printed in Great Britain by
Northumberland Press Limited,
Gateshead
F.1173

FOR MICHAEL MEYEROWITZ

NOTE

This story is fiction. The Emirate of Hassan, as described in these pages, has no place on the map, and clearly it is not a portrait of any one of the desert emirates of Arabia, each of which is now improving the lot of its people. No modern ruler has the devilish heart of Hajji Kassim bin Mahomet Al Farahid. No British official has acted in the manner of Charles Peachy. In particular, I give my assurance that the character and actions of Colonel Clive Masterman are not based on those of any British officer, past or present, who may have served in Arabia, and certainly he in no way resembles any of the distinguished officer-arabists who have done so much for the advancement of the region in recent years.—P.R.

I

The English soldiers were leaving the desert Emirate after a hundred years. No one could say quite what would happen when they had gone. The Political Agent at the capital was obliged to show a confident face; he could not issue a prognosis of disaster foretelling every dark stratagem and murder that might result from the disappearance of the regiments; this would not have pleased the Emir, nor the perplexed and elderly members of his court. And plainly it would not have pleased the merchants, smugglers and fishermen who found their livelihood in the town of Bir-el-Shama and along the muddy shore line. In fact he did not know what would happen, although his contemporaries in service had a fear amounting to terror of the native state from which military power had been withdrawn—then the process of corruption was swift and the dissolution complete. Through his mind, though it was resilient, passed the phantoms of abominable licence that would arise in the desert and destroy the political structure of the sheikhdoms when the soldiers' authority was removed. They would murder the rulers and their servants; they would fill the oil wells with sand. However, the decision had been made and the merchant transports lay off the jetty waiting to embark the heavy equipment; the ships lay on the blue waters of the Gulf where they were reduced in size and importance by the fierce sunbeams; but they marked the last vestige of attention the English would pay to this rotten place. Thereafter the phantoms would occupy the state and the great desert, the Rub al Khali, would reclaim the towns and villages up to the edge of the Gulf.

The last ten years had shown a slow advance in the amenities of the Emirate of Hassan—ten years of progress following three thousand of neglect. It was a tiny improvement in the face of a vast lack of interest, a tiny light in a

1

great dark. Under British direction, and financed from the oil revenues, the Ruler had built a primary school and a clinic, and the fact that both were empty did not disprove that an advance of some sort had been made. The capital was cleared of litter and dead creatures and a fine new highway, metalled and of twin carriage, struck out into the desert where it came to an abrupt end in the dunes, the product of a grand intention which had succumbed to the heat or to the wayward alteration of aim which was the plague of local development.

The Emir of Hassan, His Highness Hajji Kassim bin Mahomet Al Farahid, had succeeded his uncle as ruler only twelve years before in circumstances of some obscurity. The previous ruler had been found at the foot of a flight of steps, with terrible injuries, dead: it was possible he had slipped. Hajji Kassim had the grudging confidence of the British in that, twenty years earlier, he had attended a military academy and served for a short time in a cavalry regiment; he was therefore confirmed in appointment as the most eligible of a short list of candidates notable for their lack of suitability. With guidance he might succeed; if he did not it would be just another smudge in a record a century old and black with failure. He was tutored in the means of government and economic development and he granted concessions for the exploitation of the oil which lay at a slight depth under his kingdom and the shallow off-shore waters. He invested the large income from the oil royalties in British stock and undertook a few building projects in the capital. For once in the millennium something in the state was going up rather than falling down, and his English advisers were gratified.

At the time of his accession the Emir's palace was a pleasant old house of mud brick some miles inland. As his income increased, so walls of white lattice enclosed further acres of garden and terraces of flowers. Flights of steps led upwards to strange new pavilions. At the centre, dominating the desert thereabouts, rose domes and towers of gold. To anyone who caught sight of the Emir's palace at dusk, when the sky flamed with amber, it seemed a place of marvellous beauty, an image of paradise marred only by the stories of vile ritual taking place inside. The walls and gateways were guarded by men of the Hassan Levy; the Emir himself was escorted by a body-guard and falconers.

Now the lorries bumped through the streets on their way to the jetty where their loads were transferred to lighters and ferried out to the merchantmen. English voices were alive in the town for the last time; thereafter the silence of the desert would smother the Emirate, the phantoms of disorder would promenade in the empty streets, and the houses would all fall down. The ships disappeared into the haze one by one; the soldiers moved out of the Gulf and into the obscure records of imperial history. Then the sea was as empty as it had been in the long centuries before the English came.

Colonel Clive Masterman, the officer commanding the Hassan Levy, and his officers, stayed in the Emirate. So did the Political Agent and his staff. They were seconded from their departments in London and they remained at the request of the Emir and as hostages to fortune, to fall prey to whatever forces of evil took possession of the state. The Colonel and his wife lived in a married quarter at Warboys Camp, where the Levy was resident. The other officers had single quarters there. The Colonel now found himself independent of all British military connections and in sole command of the Emir's army; a disquieting experience. He liked the silence and space of the desert, but he shared the opinion of the officers that the Emirate could not survive in a military vacuum and that dark forces must shortly occupy the state. He did not define these forces; he had simply a sense of impending disaster, one that would consume the habit of order and restraint the English had left behind them.

The Political Agent had no wife but lived with a step-daughter of outrageous beauty in a small compound on the edge of the town. When his country surrendered all local responsibility, the Agent, Mr Peachy, had become simply an adviser to the Emir, drawing his salary from the palace; but in the first days of independence the work of the former Agency continued, in a twilight of obligation, chiefly because no other office had appeared to accept the burden. Mr Peachy was still called 'the Agent' though this title should have lapsed with the transfer of power: the state took its first steps into the sunlight of independence on the arm of its former guardian and the illegality of such a thing was overlooked.

From Warboys Camp the towers of the Ruler's palace were visible across a shoulder of desert, and when Colonel Masterman turned towards them, as if towards an indisputable wrong, he wondered if the Emir would rule wisely now that the restraints had been lifted. 'A strange, dissolute man,' he muttered. 'God knows what he will do. Nothing that's good, I'll be bound.'

Nothing that was good: it seemed very likely.

The indisciplined spirits that attend upon a military withdrawal came to life in Bir-el-Shama. In the first weeks the state was visited not by revolution but by an abject want of seriousness. The only filling station in the town, made unsafe by lack of maintenance, blew up in a flash of orange, white and gold. The beachmaster's office from which the evacuation had been controlled fell into its original sections, the four walls opening to the compass cardinals and the roof falling centrally. As a result of some disorder (what it was no one could tell) the flow of drainage was reversed and basins in the lower town filled from the waste vents upward. But the increase in wickedness was not of a dramatic kind; the shadows deepened only a little; after all, this was a country where the torment of the individual soul was not, in any case, of particular note.

Only one incident caught the attention of Colonel Masterman and the remaining British residents. About a month after the soldiers left, at night time, a girl of pleasure escaped from the Emir's palace and fled into the desert, impelled by what fears it was not possible to say, and there disappeared among the dunes. A man of the Hassan Levy on guard at the palace had seen her figure running away in the moonlight, and he had laughed, supposing she would come back; but the girl had continued into the vast desert where, next morning, they had heard her voice but could not find her. She was not seen again; she was consumed by the sun. Colonel Masterman was disturbed by the incident which added to the sum of wretchedness prevailing in this sad place but he did not think about it for long. He tended to the opinion that the girl had paid the penalty of shamelessness, which was to be taken into the scorching sunbeams.

The event, with its sharp pain, diminished as the days passed. It was a lapse from dignity better forgotten because the Emirate depended upon the legend of a stern yet just authority. Soon it was barely recalled, nothing more than a sensation of unease, a tiny guilt not persuasive enough for definition. Now the name of the girl, if it had ever been known, was forgotten; her life was fixed only in the memory of a native soldier who had watched her running away in the moonlight.

That was all. There was no eruption of foul politics in Bir-el-Shama, and the phantoms walking the desert were not new but figures from the past—the sick shadows of poverty and superstition which had occupied the coast for centuries before the British intruded a small enlightenment. The palm gardens in the centre of the town, where once English ladies had grown pansies of fragile colour, and stocks and forget-me-nots, in defiance of the climate, now contained their afrits of diabolical temper, their night shades and demons. The Kabina Gardens on the outskirts of the town were the haunt of vile creatures. There was no rebellion, no fighting in the market place. None the less, if only by a little, the Emirate had moved back towards the age of the giant, the monster and the cockatrice.

2

Colonel Clive Masterman was seated on the roof of his quarter at Warboys Camp. There was a shine upon the desert as if the strong daylight had left an incandescence in the sand. He could just hear the voices of the soldiers in the barracks a hundred yards away. Elsewhere a mule stamped in a bedding of straw. A large acacia tree grew at the side of the house and the upper branches swelled over the roof giving him a sense of shelter in an otherwise empty scene. The boy Abu Bekr had brought him a chilled fruit drink which stood untouched on a wicker table. Colonel Masterman took pleasure in the silence of the place; for a time he might suppose that silence was the natural condition of Arabia; silence and peace. But he said aloud, with an ironic emphasis unusual for him, 'Hassan, Hassan—what will become of you? I really don't know.'

The long low coast was in sight from the roof. The land rose so gradually it was difficult to see where the Gulf ended and the shore began. The squat houses of Bir-el-Shama stood on higher ground. A light, two lights appeared there as the dusk advanced. The barrenness of the land, which rose only a few feet above the sea, left him with the impression that this was a place where human beings should not be required to live. Not a soldier, not a thief, no one. It was a debased land whose very existence was shameful. The town of Bir-el-Shama, mud-coloured and without pattern, looked like a form of life that had struggled ashore from the Gulf and there expired in the sun. Miles down the coast a tiny red flame showed where the oil men were burning surplus gases from an off-shore well. They perhaps should inherit the Emirate as they alone could make it pay.

He heard the fall of his wife's stick as she mounted the first steps of the interior stairway leading to the roof. He would not go to help her; she would not wish him to do that. He heard the deeply-taken breath as she mounted the second step and stood there resting. He said aloud, keeping the concern from his voice, 'You can see to Faleh-la. The sea's like glass. Everything is redeemed by the evening!'

In the same moment he was aware that the Quartermaster, Captain Sloan, was crossing the empty space between the headquarters and the house, but him he hardly noticed at that time.

His wife continued step by step until her head came into his sight where the stair reached the flat roof and here she paused, again resting. He brought a second chair to the table and waited for her to reach him.

Captain Sloan had meanwhile stopped under the roof, waiting respectfully for the Colonel to see him. 'Ah, Sloan. Come up by all means,' the Colonel said. 'Tell the boy to bring you a beer.'

Dorothy Masterman stood at the end of the roof, holding his attention. The dusk had blackened her features; he could see only the tall figure and the stick. 'Sit down, my dear. I can bring the chair nearer, if you prefer.'

'Leave it, leave it. I can manage for myself.'

He watched with admiration as his wife crossed the roof to the table and there seated herself. 'Well done,' he said, which she ignored.

Captain Sloan had in the interim climbed the outside stair to the roof. Masterman barely saw him. Sloan had served for many years in the ranks of the Service Corps and the habit of reticence had made him easy to ignore. Even now the Colonel found it hard to remember that Sloan was an officer.

'My dear fellow, I beg your pardon!' the Colonel said suddenly. 'Come and join my wife and me in a drink.'

Sloan still wore his uniform, which was stained with sweat. The Colonel noticed the ribbon of the British Empire Medal, another for long service in the ranks, and he was disconcerted by these trappings of the non-commissioned officer. Sloan was heavily built, his eyes dull. His years in the sergeants' mess had made him stubborn; his deference to authority had made him silent. He would not look directly at the Colonel. Masterman said, 'It's good to see you, Sloan. The boy is bringing you a beer, yes? Please make yourself comfortable.'

Sloan took a chair awkwardly, without speaking.

'I'm always happy to see my officers at this time; so, of course, is my wife.'

Stiff with pain, Dorothy Masterman paid no attention to the Quartermaster. Sloan must have come for some purpose, as a soldier of his type would be unlikely to call socially, and the Colonel felt uneasy, as if the news he brought must necessarily be bad.

To keep their voices moving, Masterman said, 'What a view! See how the sky turns to orange at sunset!' But the air moving off the town was dry and hot and sharp-smelling. The country was incapable of good; it was shaped for wretchedness. 'Moments like this are the reward of expatriate service. I can recall many similar moments from my service as a younger man. In the Far East, in India. Now the whole thing seems worth-while.'

Sloan's foreign service ribbons showed that he had been in more theatres than Colonel Masterman, but he said only, 'I'm sure you are right, sir.'

A dull fellow, the Colonel thought, but dogged.

'Kashmir I remember best. The mountains rose out of valleys filled with flowers. I can't conceive of a more beautiful place.' It was certainly better than Hassan, which was nothing at all, a zero, whose product was poverty and death. I wonder what the devil wants, Colonel Masterman thought; but he did not like to ask directly when Sloan was his guest.

Without moving the direction of her gaze, Mrs Masterman said, 'The loss of authority is already showing in the streets. The people are impolite; yesterday I was pushed into the gutter. I do not see how the present situation can continue.'

Captain Sloan said, to no one, to himself perhaps, 'It was never much of a place. There was always trouble here.'

Masterman blushed at this difference between his wife and his guest. Junior officers should not express opinions of this sort. How on earth could Sloan know the truth of Arabia, which had puzzled better minds than his? 'The Levy will keep order,' the Colonel snapped. 'There is nothing to fear.'

Sloan smiled grimly, as if at some private vision of disaster, but he said nothing.

8

'Hassan has no natural shape or centre,' Mrs Masterman said, giving not the smallest weight to Sloan's opinion. 'The country has only been kept in being by British influence.'

'Hassan,' said Sloan, as though the name had a meaning for him, one hidden from the Colonel. 'It's no different from the other states. Hadraif, Khoiram—they're all cruel places.'

'Yes, cruel,' said Mrs Masterman. 'Hassan is cruel.'

For a moment they had acknowledged one another; each seemed to recognize the other's immovable opinion; it was almost an exchange of respect.

Abu Bekr brought glasses on a tray. The army glasses were far from elegant but the Colonel had not thought it wise to bring his own from England; they would get broken when his command dissolved in mutiny. He looked at the first stars. I cannot think what the fellow wants, he thought again; and he ran through the possibilities of mishaps which might have brought Captain Sloan to the Commanding Officer's residence.

This morning, to her disgust, there had been a donkey lying dead in the soukh, Mrs Masterman said then. She wasn't so much absorbed in the deficiencies of Hassan as keeping complete the tally of frightfulness, as if honesty required no less.

'They lack sensitivity,' the Colonel said sharply.

Sloan nodded. He did not seem disturbed. He gave a fitful laugh, it might have been at the death and decay of things in the Emirate, and the Colonel shifted in his chair, vexed at the sense of rapture at the dissolution of life in Hassan that seemed to be affecting the old Quartermaster. They might be going to the devil but there was no point in taking pleasure in the fact.

The greater dark fell swiftly and only the edge of the desert showed against the fading sky. The nearer ground, where Bir-el-Shama displayed a few lights, was mercifully concealed by the darkness. In the evening the manifest disgrace of Hassan lost some of its point. Now one might imagine the state to be administered with less than total ineffectiveness, that the gutters were not choked with filth, that the gardens were in leaf and not in a brown decay; the darkness gave scope to the imagination which the daylight had dulled; and now the soldiers might think their purpose here to be other than absurd; for the moment it was possible to believe they defended something of value, that Hassan had its own peculiar merit. In the warm dark Colonel Masterman looked back on his long service as if at something worth-while. He forgot the abominable parts of it—he forgot his protection of corrupt and squabbling potentates against their outraged people, his defence of meaningless frontiers, the heat, the dust, the long pointless vigil at the limits of empire.

'My God, in Kashmir the air blowing off the mountains was clean!' he said. 'I recall it had always a scent of flowers. The balcony of the club faced the mountains, and in the evening you could watch the changing colours of the sunset reflected in the snows. I never saw a more beautiful place.'

'Yes, it was beautiful,' said Mrs Masterman; 'it was not like Hassan.'

'Oh, Hassan,' said the Colonel absently; then with contempt, 'Hassan—it is not a favoured place; people do not behave well here.'

Perhaps now he could ask Captain Sloan why he had come. He felt uneasy; there was something he did not know; the news brought by the Quartermaster must add fractionally to the sum of danger in the Emirate—it would bring a little nearer that moment, feared by all soldiers, when discipline would be lost.

He turned to Captain Sloan. 'You are the duty officer, yes? You have something to say to me?'

Sloan did not like to discuss regimental affairs in this setting. He could find no comfort in the wicker chair. He cleared his throat noisily. Then he told Colonel Masterman that a native soldier was missing, he hadn't been seen since midday, they couldn't be certain where he had gone.

So *that* was it. The Colonel was annoyed. It could surely have waited until morning. 'My dear fellow, what of it? There's always a native soldier missing. Put him on the absentee report and the company commander can deal with him when he returns.' He felt relieved, it was nothing more than a missing soldier, he had thought it mattered. Captain Sloan could not distinguish between the trivial incident and the one with far-reaching consequences, a fault common amongst officers who had served many years as NCOs.

Sloan was silent. He had something more to say.

'Well, what is it?'

'He took his rifle with him.'

'Damn,' said the Colonel.

'Sergeant Major Ramadi thinks he went into the desert.'

'Very probably. They usually do.'

Still, he would not concern himself with the thought of a native soldier at large in the desert with a rifle and perhaps sixty rounds. The fringes of the desert abounded with such armed men. For a hundred years the ball and tracer fired at British soldiers had been of British stock, and the assassins had lain concealed as their British instructors had taught them. Colonel Masterman put the matter from him; he would not let the evening be spoiled by an absentee.

Sloan said, 'The man was Hamid.'

'Who? Hamid? My dear Captain, there must be twenty soldiers called Hamid.'

Captain Sloan did not answer. He had nothing more to say.

'Well, there it is—another failure of imperial discipline,' the Colonel said cheerfully. 'I doubt if we shall see him again. Turn in the usual report in the morning, Captain, if you please.'

Sloan left soon afterwards, going down by the outside stairs, and they listened to his footsteps as he went back to headquarters.

He had left his message with them and it was commonplace enough.

They sat in the obliterating darkness as the air cooled and the smell of Bir-el-Shama grew less distinct. The stars thickened.

The Colonel said excitedly, 'Do you remember Kerela, Dorothy? Or Mangalore? Do you remember how the wind off the sea made the palm trees flash with silver? There the sea was so clear you could look down fifty feet to the corals.'

A while later, somewhere in the hills beyond the town, a shot was fired and Colonel Masterman turned instinctively towards the quarter from which the sound had come. The whiplash echo told him it had been a rifle but there was nothing remarkable in that. A bedouin might have fired at a rival.

Perhaps it was the missing soldier firing into the air to celebrate his release from restraint. More likely it was some squalid wretch who had turned a weapon into his chest. In this place of turbulent motives one couldn't tell and inquiry would lead to nothing. Still, a shot had been fired; there was a change in circumstances. He heard the sergeant of the guard calling for increased watchfulness and the cries of the sentries as they answered him from all down the wire. The Colonel was cheered by the voices and the evidence of order they implied; at least within the camp there was the composure of discipline.

I wonder if that was Hamid, he thought. It might have been, as these men did strange things; he might have shot at the rising moon.

Damn the man, the Colonel thought. Soldiers had deserted before but Hamid was the first since the British withdrawal and his action marked a break in authority. The shot was not repeated and in a minute the memory of it was erased by the silence.

His wife, who had paid no attention to the shot, said then, 'Hamid? Did Captain Sloan say it was Hamid?'

'A very common name in the regiment, of course.'

She said nothing more and Colonel Masterman was disturbed. 'What does it matter?' he asked irritably. 'There's nothing to choose between one soldier and another. It really makes no difference which one has deserted.'

'Hamid was the soldier who watched the girl running away.'

'Girl? Which girl?' It was a moment or two before he remembered the incident at the palace when a girl ran into the desert and there died. 'Really? Hamid? It could surely have been one of the other soldiers called Hamid? It doesn't have to be the same one, does it?'

His wife didn't reply and the Colonel was annoyed with her for making such a suggestion. 'I really can't see that it matters. There was no significance in that affair. It was stupid, meaningless—just a part of the rotten life here in Hassan.'

The air stilled; there was no further sound from the hills. Far down the coast the flame at the oil well stained the horizon. It varied in height, sometimes sinking to a tiny mark, at others springing up to form a long red scar which lighted the surface of the desert. The oil men paid no heed to the shabby life of the Emirate; they pursued their vulgar profit with a singleness of purpose unmatched by any other people in the Middle East. The Colonel put them out of his mind. The soldiers had been first in the desert; they had drawn the maps, subdued the people, kept the uneasy peace; and now they had to watch over the bitter end with the same attention to the needs of others.

His task was simple, necessary and without much glory. It could not be modified or changed. He must keep the peace as long as possible. He could not tell when the indiscipline would begin; he could not be certain it had not begun already. Sometime, no doubt, he would be killed and his command would be dispersed; and then there would be no order in the state but instead the horror of mutiny and of minds gone mad.

Now the air was cold and in a minute they must go down. The Colonel put his hands on his knees; he meant to rise.

His wife said, 'Of course, Clive, you could go home. You owe nothing to Hassan.'

A stupid thing to say. How could he explain his resignation to his officers? And in any case he had a job here.

'You cannot tell me the place is worth saving,' Mrs Masterman said.

'That isn't the point. I have a duty here.'

'Once before you ignored your duty, I recall.'

She was seeking payment for an injury long passed. It was a merciless stroke. He was hurt, angry, silent. 'You know very well that I cannot leave the Levy,' he said after a time.

Colonel Masterman held his wife in deep respect. She had strength he could not match and her present cruelty was no more than her regard for the truth. He sat with his hands on his knees, his mind disordered. 'I don't know why you said that,' he continued. 'My life in Hong Kong has no bearing on our present difficulties.'

Mrs Masterman had made her point and saw no need of argument.

He said, 'Needless to say, the circumstances were quite different then——'

But she had broken his confidence. He was weakened at a time when he must show no weakness. Sooner or later there would be war in Hassan. He remembered his failure in duty in painful detail.

He had fallen in love. It was twenty years ago. He had not expected to love then, or indeed at all; he had thought the private disappointment of his marriage had dulled for ever his power to love; yet at that time, when the main elements of his life were brought into harmony, when the places and people, the scents and the airs had merged, it seemed, into a universal conspiracy, he had loved, without thought, without reserve. For a while the perfect order in nature had continued; he remembered how the Hong Kong outlines had been consumed in the endless summer light; he recalled them now from a part of his memory he never spoke of and which had advanced a long way towards decent mystery. Her name was Sarah; she was dark, low-voiced. To this day he could not say the name aloud. He was charmed, rapt, deeply disturbed at his own want of caution. He saw the workings of his love as a leaping flame which destroyed even loyalty.

Now he was angered to the point where, inevitably, the evening at Warboys was spoilt. 'There are things better left in the past,' he said.

'It is not in the past,' Mrs Masterman said.

Of course, at that time, he had taken no account of the way his life pursued ordinary ends. The conspiring influences had moved into disarray. Her love turned to embarrassment, to a sort of contempt, and she told him without much gentleness, 'It's no good, Clive. It's got to stop.' And he had felt the appalling loss of love; his life had entered the void of the dispossessed when even his restored loyalty had no value for him. He had not seen her again but she had reappeared in the faces, the voices, the movements of others; each dark woman contained some relic of her, each was her ghostly representative; and in time she had become just a voice and an infusion of colour at the centre of his mind. Every once in a while she returned with new clarity—she returned nearly whole, in the person of someone else, and then he was frightened and vulnerable and wary of hurt....

He rose from his chair, ready to go downstairs; there was nothing more to stay for. He had resumed the part of military commander in a turbulent sheikhdom, a soldier bound to optimism. He had still to win in Hassan.

'Plainly, my dear, I cannot leave my job until some sort of stability is achieved.' He stood at the head of the stairs, facing his wife. 'I can't consider resignation. I am confident the Levy can keep some sort of order and that the Ruler will behave wisely. After all, it's a month since the British left and nothing has happened yet.'

3

Charles Peachy, the Political Agent, whose duties were now advisory and poorly defined, looked up sharply from his papers and called for his chief clerk. 'Zamil? Are you there?' The ceiling fan was moving the papers on his desk and already they were muddled. The sun was at midday strength, and were he to turn the fan off his hands would stick to the papers; this was one of the minor penalties of working in a place like Hassan. 'Zamil. Where are you?'

The Agency seemed deserted. The sunlight streaming between the blinds and lying in a bright swathe across the tiles was his only companion. He was uncomfortable; the sweat ran down his back and gathered at his waist-band; but were he to increase the speed of the fan his papers would fly to the corners of the room. 'God damn the bloody place,' he said without stress.

Through the blinds he could see the courtyard where the sun whitened the ground and nearly obliterated the walls and pillars of the small pavilion which stood at the end of the lawn. There was no movement but for the slight progress of the shadows as the sun passed the meridian, no sound other than the rhythmic thrash of the fan and the rustle of papers lifting and falling on the desk. He felt as if he were the last person on earth—time had come to an end, the world had died, and only he had lived through the momentous change in condition. He got up from the desk and walked flat-footedly to the window where he looked at the hard, brilliant sky. Hassan, that insult to human kind, lay in the eye of the sun; it had been a departure from sanity to place a town at this latitude where the only feature was a slight indentation of the coast. A crow, like a ragged clergyman, fell down the sky and disappeared behind the compound wall, and he was reminded that life continued in the state, that evil prospered, that the end of organized life was brought closer as the shadows edged across the courtyard.

'Well,' he said loudly, complacently, to no one but himself, 'I really don't care; it matters not a jot to me. They can give Hassan to the jackals and that devious potentate Hajji Kassim bin Mahomet Al Farahid can beg for a living.' He chuckled; despite the heat and the threat of social disaster he found himself in a good humour. There would be a splendid rightness in the collapse of the House of Al Farahid which deserved nothing better than extinction. He extemporized further, 'O my sly master, listen! There are twenty brothers each with a loathing for you: there is Abdullah the Wicked, Abdullah the Wise and Abdullah the Half-wit; there is Saud the Fair and Saud the Fat and Saud the Fatter; and believe me, Hajji Kassim, one of these gentlemen will disembowel you because that is the manner of Hassan.'

The recitation pleased him and he raised his plump figure three inches by standing on his toes. He laughed, it might have been the last laughter in Hassan; but then he subsided on to the flat of his feet and looked gravely into the garden.

He could not deny that the nearest British frigate was seven thousand miles away in the English Channel and the nearest regular battalion was encamped in Wiltshire. Colonel Masterman and his white officers still commanded the obedience of the Levy, of course, but the regiment would be of doubtful value if the political structure of the state should break; then tribal sympathies would cut across regimental loyalty and the Levy would fall to pieces. The bedouin was not made for disciplined service. And the Agent did not care for the dullness he detected in the Colonel's mind; Masterman had already conceded defeat, he could not believe that the rule of law would survive, across his mind lay the pallor of his own demise. The Agent would have preferred an officer less dedicated, less rational, one better able to master the absurdities of politics in Arabia, where to follow the course of affairs one needed to be both poet and criminal and to understand besides the romantic fatalism which underlay each new cruelty.

Charles Peachy was himself without fear. He saw his own squat figure as too squalid to deserve special protection. When they came for him he would beat them with his bare hands, and were they to make an end of him then at least he would not have to return to the English rains.

The sky laid a tremendous light across the garden and flattened the pavilion until it had no dimension of depth and lay in the same plane as the sky. A dark girl stood there, clothed in scarlet. He started because he had not seen her appear. He could not say if she had seen him but within her glance there was an outraged criticism which might have been for him—or perhaps for the sunlight or for Hassan; he tapped on the window, saying 'Sarita, Sarita', but the girl moved away towards the gates, out of his sight, and then the brash sunlight filled the place where she had stood. A car started in the courtyard and he heard the watchman opening the main gate. The girl had gone to Faleh-la, where the oil men were giving a party.

He fretted at the window. He had lost his good humour and become instead anguished and morose. 'O God,' he said, and cried. He walked up and down the office trying not to think of the girl—trying not to remember the dangerous state of Arabian politics and the drive towards violent solutions which might already have begun. He developed a temper so explosive that when Zamil came in sideways from the outer office the Agent greeted him harshly.

'Damn you, Zamil. You're an habitual absentee.'

Zamil was timid, querulous, filled with tiny spites.

'Shut up,' said Peachy, though Zamil had not spoken.

He disliked the chief clerk with his fraudulent degree from a university in Iraq, with his scholar's brow and hollow cheek. He disliked all clerks who could see no further than their records. Zamil's documentation of the small sins of Hassan was ably done, exactly indexed, and worthless; it took no account of the great indisciplines which plagued this part of Arabia and which could not be described. He began an account of recent disorders but Peachy waved him to silence.

The Agent walked to the end of the office and came back at twice the pace, truculently. 'Zamil, Zamil—it makes not the smallest difference how many injuries have been done. You cannot start from detail; you must start from principle.'

But the clerkly mind of Zamil was not engaged in principles, which passed above his head like skeins of wild geese. He was recording the evidence of wrong for the Emir, and for the old blind magistrate who dealt out the fearful penalties prescribed by the Emirate.

'Very well, then—very well, my dear Zamil!—sever the hands of the thief, poke out the eyes of the Peeping Tom, deprive the fornicator of his power to make love—torment every man jack for his vile passion—and, let me tell you, it will not stop the violence of the people. Why? You ask me why? Because the mind of the Arab was fixed for ever in the Middle Ages. Because Hajji Kassim bin Mahomet Al Farahid, like all his tribe, is consumed with the spirit of corruption and decadence and can no more lead the state into the twentieth century than he can fly in the air.'

The Agent beamed at his chief clerk, feeling the better for these exaggerations, but Zamil had paid him no attention. He raised his ledger and continued his account. Since yesterday noon there had been an incursion of tribesmen from Ras Al Hadraif, a stabbing in the old town, the abduction of a minor for purposes undisclosed——

'Spare me the details,' the Agent said.

——a rifle had been discharged at the Emir's palace, without casualty.

'What? A rifle?'

Conceivably this could matter. A threat to the life of the Ruler could set off a widespread disturbance. One of those murderous brothers, I'll be bound, the Agent thought.

'The shot seems to have come from the desert, at about half past eight o'clock in the evening. The time was marked by the Colonel.'

'But it didn't hit anybody, of course.'

'It went into the roof, doing no damage. The Emir was on a lower balcony.'

'I suppose the guards saw nothing.'

'Nothing.'

'Then what was the point of it?'

Zamil frowned; he was not given to an examination of causes. 'An accident, perhaps——'

'It might be,' the Agent said reflectively. But to hit the palace roof the gunman would need to have been within a thousand yards and close to the area patrolled by the guards.

Still, in the Emirate a search for motives was usually disappointed; a bedouin could have fired at the golden roof for no reason in the world but that it took his fancy. 'Yes, an accident. Who can say? Was His Highness disturbed?'

'I don't think so. He did not notice the shot until his attention was drawn to it. He has punished the guard.'

The Agent grimaced; that would mean trouble with Colonel Masterman who did not like the indiscriminate punishment of men of the Levy, for whose chastisement only he held the warrant. 'I see. Perhaps it doesn't matter. What is a rifle shot in Hassan?'

'I suggest it is without meaning, sir. There are many such incidents; they have seldom any point.'

'Quite,' said the Agent. 'There is no point.'

Zamil went away. He had no news to tell but that Arabia continued on its wayward course towards those unwritten ends the mind could not contemplate. Today is as yesterday, Peachy thought; and he tried to convince himself that it was true. Nothing is changed in Hassan, he told himself; the townsmen still cheat, the bedouin have the same diseases. He would try not to think about the girl, nor about a breakdown of order in the Emirate, and certainly he would not think about the consequences for Sarita if the Levy mutinied and the tribes attacked the town.

'Sarita,' he said suddenly, to no one.

But she had gone half an hour ago to Faleh-la. There was nothing in the garden but the violent sunlight.

Things will improve, he said inwardly; but he recognized his weakness in thinking so. The Emir will rule with justice, the Colonel will keep the peace—the Emirate of Hassan will move into a period of unequalled calm and charity.

The first for a thousand years.

O God, he thought. O God.

4

The great desert, the Rub al Khali, which lay inland from Bir-el-Shama and extended a thousand miles towards the Red Sea, began where the metalled road ended. The first miles were crossed by tracks and scattered with camel grass and thorn, but beyond this narrow fringe there was no feature but the wind-driven sand. Here the sun destroyed any movement towards life; it was a place of unequivocal death. Every country, every town, every dwelling on the borders of the desert faced outward to the sea, and accordingly the Rub al Khali, the Empty Quarter, the greatest feature in Arabia, was the feature least regarded.

The neighbouring states and kingdoms, all to the seaward of the desert, drew their spirit from the Rub al Khali even as they ignored it. Hassan and Ras Al Hadraif, no matter that the ruling families were both Al Farahid, robbed each other of sheep and grazing and placed explosive charges in the disputed wells. The boundaries moved backwards and forwards between the many states as the tribes shifted their grounds; wars flared between them so often they were nearly continuous. No heroes had their origin in the Empty Quarter; there were only the ragged partisans of haphazard causes, or of no cause at all, who roamed the edges of the desert and whose lives ended violently between the dunes.

The sheikhdoms were unanimous only in their dislike of one another. In government the Sheikhs adopted the styles of the desert, conferring the same harsh judgements. They spent their leisure in the pursuit of exotic responses. The great profit from the oil wells was disbursed to an international harlotry and to the Hindu boys of golden complexion whose skills were marked at a still higher price. The capitals of Arabia were worked by a sisterhood from Scandinavia whose gains were substantial, as were those of the agent in Beirut who exchanged art photographs for contracts. The people did not think it strange and the oil men did not care at all. It was the way of the sheikhdoms to find the greatest value in the cheapest dross.

The Rub al Khali, then, was dead and disregarded, and no one went there, not even the wildest of the bedouin. In the daylight the shadows between the dunes swung with the movement of the sun; at dusk they deepened and extended until they joined. There was no change in habit at night. At moon-rise the dunes showed whitely and the shadows between them continued their movement in a faint parody of the daytime shadows. But despite these things the great desert, the Empty Quarter, was nothing: it was an oblivion, a mockery, a fatuous error to which no one in his senses would give a moment of his time.

Along the outer wire at Warboys Camp, which was the first defence against the desert, the Levy kept watch at night. Once every hour the guard commander walked from post to post striking the inattentive with the back of his hand. The soldiers watched the line of wire and the rising desert beyond with failing concentration; they were wrapped in the boredom known to soldiers when the habit of obedience, the starch of the uniform alone kept them upright. They passed in and out of that waking dream in which their fears were magnified and they saw shadows, phantoms at the defensive wire. Sometimes a soldier raised his rifle and sighted into the darkness as a shadow moved without sound at the corner of his vision. At this hour, this post, the native sentries stood at the division between reality and dream, between the present day and the Dark Ages, and each shadow, each intrusion from the remote past, each pagan image made them stiffen and search with their eyes until the shadow vanished and there was nothing to their front but the strands of wire and the empty desert.

At a time after midnight some months after the British withdrawal a sentry gave a warning cry. A figure moved at the outer wire, lit by the starlight, one that did not vanish but instead loitered along the edge of the defences towards the entrance where the picket challenged him. The other sentries joined savagely in the call. The man laughed, called foul insults at the soldiers, and did not go away; he stood outside the gate beyond the guard post despite the snap of a rifle bolt as a sentry sent a round into the chamber.

What did he want? the guard commander called.

He did not say; he simply laughed at them and sat down behind the barrier.

'Go away!' the guard commander said.

'Foul thyself,' the man replied.

'You will be punished.'

'As ever, as ever.'

Other voices shouted all along the wire. Someone, God only knew who, had challenged the restraints of discipline, and in this there was sharp dismay. The sounds brought the duty officer, Captain Sloan, down to the gate. He walked slowly and carried a stock whip in his hand. The guard commander raised the barrier and Sloan passed through, walking heavily, intent upon his duty.

The sentries watched in the starlight as the officer spun the whip in the air and brought the lash down across the intruder's shoulders with a sound that was heard a mile down the wire. They saw the wretched man leap and fall and lie submissively in the dust. They heard the repeated whine of the lash as the officer delivered his punishment with an intensity of purpose they had not seen before in a white superior. The man lying in the dust made no sound, and he did not attempt to avoid the appalling penalty his fault had earned for him. The sentries were silent now. When Sloan had finished his task he coiled the whip into his palm, passed back through the barrier which was lowered behind him, and without a glance across his shoulder walked back into the headquarters.

The man who had suffered punishment rose to his knees, to his feet, fell, rose again and disappeared into the darkness.

They had met and separated. An appointment had been kept. A purpose of the Rub al Khali had been served. Only after an hour did anyone send for the Levy commander to acquaint him with what had happened.

'It was an extraordinary thing,' Colonel Masterman said

angrily; 'without precedent in my experience. I do not know how an officer under my command, and with a considerable length of service, could give himself to such brutality. What can have got into him? The man—who was it? Hamid, no doubt—was only absent without leave; he had not even been posted as a deserter. I must have it known that I will not tolerate the indiscriminate punishment of accused soldiers. Punishments must be warded in the accepted manner and conform to the scales laid down in regulations. And now of course, we have lost the soldier for ever. I really do not see how I can avoid bringing Captain Sloan before a court martial.'

The Colonel was deeply disturbed by the incident outside the wire. He had placed Captain Sloan under arrest. It was a departure from discipline which arose not amongst the local soldiery but in a white officer trained in the obligations of service. An officer must never lose his nerve; no matter that he was beaten or stoned, he must retain the composure of authority and issue his decisions from a clear head. Nothing else was acceptable in those places where he must face the extremes of madness. Of course, Captain Sloan was not an officer in the real sense as he had been commissioned from the ranks, a procedure the Colonel accepted but did not care for. Once a man had been a sergeant for many years he would be a sergeant for ever and he could not be expected to make dispassionate judgements under stress. 'I shall order a summary of evidence,' the Colonel said. 'It is the only means I have of reaching the truth in this senseless affair.'

To establish his displeasure beyond all doubt, Colonel Masterman called a conference of his senior officers. The three company commanders, Major Tillotson, Major Graves and Major Kirkbride, and the adjutant Captain Lovelace, showed a proper concern at Sloan's departure from normal conduct. 'I must have it known I won't accept any reduction in our standards, gentlemen, whether in punishment or in any other part of our duty. Our value to the Emirate lies in our restraint, our fair-mindedness. On no account must we become affected by local hysteria or we shall quickly lose the respect of the bedouin.'

An officer senior to Sloan, Captain Barrie, a bloom from

the cavalry, was detailed to take the summary, and the Colonel felt he had done what he could to restore the habit of obedience. He waited impatiently for the tiresome business of trial and punishment to be over. Captain Barrie reported to him when he had made his first investigations into the case against the old Quartermaster.

Sloan was fifty and unmarried. He ran the stores with a womanish tyranny: abrupt, unresponsive, occasionally violent towards the native storekeepers, it seemed he was regarded with contempt. How could they regard him otherwise when he struck them with the force of his arm? Masterman did not like petty violence towards native soldiers, though he accepted that it might sometimes be necessary; it was unbecoming in a serving officer whose word alone should be enough for the reinforcement of order. What else? he asked; what other defects of character had Captain Sloan, who had cruelly whipped a defaulting soldier? Well, Barrie could not be sure, he did not want to make unsupported judgements, but Sloan was believed to find his relaxation in the massage parlours of Bir-el-Shama where the Armenian sluts had skilful hands. The Colonel grimaced; it was what he would have expected of Sloan who plainly had a dirty side. He did not care to think of the scented parlours and the slimy-skinned masseuses who were naked under their overalls; they belonged to Hassan's degradation, and any decent society would have suppressed them long ago.

'It's exactly as I would have expected,' Masterman said. 'The man has a narrow, spiteful mind which is passing into corruption, and I am glad we have had this opportunity of putting a stop to his activities. He's not suitable for service in Hassan with its squalid temptations. A punishment will be salutary, not only for the officer but for life in Hassan. It will be seen that the laws of decency can still apply.'

Captain Barrie was seconded from a fashionable regiment. His well-cut uniform obeyed his every movement. He believed that engagement with a problem was vulgar, that ignorance was the only real virtue. He had not the slightest interest in Captain Sloan.

'I am sure you are right, Colonel,' he said; but he hadn't listened.

'You will see that I am,' the Colonel replied.

A whipping at Warboys Camp, no matter what the circumstances, was unlikely to engage the attention of the civil power in Hassan to whom such things were hardly novel. The magistrate would think it apt a defaulting soldier should be beaten; in his own hands there were penalties far more terrible than anything inflicted by a dour old officer within a military establishment. In the past soldiers had always been flogged. Fierce punishment was the style of the Emirate. Along the borders of the desert that same night there had been violence enough to make Sloan's action trivial, and a single cruelty could not add much to the great delinquency of Arabia. In the desert there was a lack of concern, of judgement—a lack even of moral definition that allowed the individual to take his natural shape; the Rub al Khali set no limit upon the devilry, or the charity, of those who lived there. Here there were no commandments, no unalterable truths. In this vast desert there was nothing but a drive to separateness in which the denizen must find his own solutions.

5

Before the grant of independence, the Political Agent had entertained the civil and military leaders of Hassan on the last Friday of each month. He saw no reason to change this arrangement now that the sheikhdom had full liberty; as an adviser to the Emir, he liked to keep the ruling family in sight, where his ear might catch the nuances of rivalry. The minor Sheikhs were given to ambition and Peachy's years in Arabia had taught him to detect an ugly thought almost as soon as it was entertained. In the garden of the Agency, which was surrounded by a high white wall topped with radial spikes, and where the grass could not be made to grow, the servants stretched a hessian carpet over the dust and put up a coloured awning. They fixed lanterns in the palm trees. Along the wall a weak growth of oleander gave some colour to the garden but there was little else to show. Today, as in the past, the guests would come at six o'clock, when the sun was sinking into the desert and the orange light lay across the walls—when it did not seem too mean a place in which to hold a party.

Ali Kadir, the head servant, knew that he must keep a full glass in Mr Peachy's hand. From the corner of his eye the servant watched his master as he made an irritable inspection of the garden waiting for the girl to join him. Ali Kadir, like all the household staff, knew of the Agent's infatuation for the dark girl who was the daughter of his dead wife, but not his own, and whose mood veered between the chill of Europe and the raucous engagement of Asia. For himself, Ali Kadir disliked Sarita with a quiet loathing that never disturbed his houseboy's smile but which gave his attention to her, his bow, his movements behind her chair, the emphasis of parody. Now before the start of the party Ali Kadir offered Mr Peachy a drink in which he had increased the strength of the spirit to an absurd degree.

'Thank you,' said the Agent, who saw no need for complaint.

This evening, waiting for his guests, Peachy felt pleasantly detached from the stress of entertainment. The mood might not last. As the best interpreter in the state it would be his job to help the exchange of ideas, making skilful alterations where necessary; he must take the spite out of politics and blunt the edge of insult. It was a task he undertook with relish and to such good effect his evenings ended usually in only partial discord. Zamil could offer only literal translations, and as these appalling truths helped no one the Agent usually shut him up. The secretary joined him now, a shadow along the wall.

'Zamil, Zamil, speak little or not at all,' the Agent said amiably.

'As you will,' the secretary said, shrinking from sight.

Under the harsh direction of Ali Kadir the servants set the tables with nuts and sweet things, and they laid trays with the foul soft drinks preferred by the Arabs—with peppermint, citronade and sarsaparilla. Temperance was the one great obedience of Islam, but to set against this restraint there were marvellous liberties.

'Sarita!' the Agent said.

The girl was at the end of the garden, behind the oleanders, in white; to the Agent's eye she looked lovely in this poor place.

'I am here,' she said softly, darkly; then, with the shrill plaintiveness of Anglo-Asia, 'What is it? What do you want?'

'To see you, my dearest, as ever.'

She moved towards him in the half light and her shoulders made a tiny flourish of welcome, but she said coldly, 'Don't waste your time with me, Father. The sheikhs won't like it if you give me your attention.'

Zamil giggled in the shadows.

'Go to the devil, Zamil,' the Agent said in Arabic.

'If it pleases you, master. My lady is beautiful, is she not? But her race is indeterminate.'

Ali Kadir was opening the gate to admit the first of the guests. It would be the party from Warboys, for only the soldiers would have this regard for punctuality, but the Agent did not take his eyes from the girl. 'You look very nice,' he said in English. And then in Arabic, 'You shine like the stars, my daughter, and you touch my heart.'

Sarita said irritably, 'The guests are here. They're standing in the drive. I don't like it when you make fun of me.'

'I never make fun of you.'

'Then speak in a language I understand.'

'I said only that you have my affection.'

The girl moved towards him mysteriously and with her fingers pressed a crease from his collar. She said warmly, intimately, 'Go to your guests, my father. The Colonel is waiting.'

In the increasing dusk the Agency garden held a small enchantment that would last until it was quite dark. The soft light showed the grass and the flowers in less than their true impoverishment: here as elsewhere in the Gulf there was a movement away from reality, from hardship, which the Agent accepted as one of the consolations of Arabia. There were scents, dull and fugitive, along the beds and the creeper-covered walls. The open faces of the flowers seemed to emit their own pale light.

The Colonel loomed large under the awning; the Agent marvelled at his height. 'Colonel, Colonel, it is always a pleasure to see you,' he said now with total conviction to the man who could destroy them. It would not be possible to find a man better fitted to lead them into disaster, to lend grace to the last sickening minutes. In the vulgarity of massacre they would be saved by the decorum of Colonel Masterman, and they would die not horribly but with manifest style.

Peachy said abruptly, 'Ali Kadir, the officer must have whatever he wants. At once, do you hear?'

The servant bowed and shuffled backwards. 'The master shall have every service, as befits his station.'

Mrs Masterman made dogged progress across the lawn, using her stick. The Agent was struck by the courage that carried her so painfully towards him, and at once he halved the distance between them and took her thin dry hand. Ali Kadir brought a chair at his urgent signal. 'Sit down, dear lady. A footstool would help, yes?'

'Thank you. It would not.'

'Or a cushion?'

'Don't fuss me, Mr Peachy, please. I am well enough as it is.'

The Agent beamed with admiration. Sometimes the ultimate in strength was achieved by a middle-aged lady with a disability: Mrs Masterman was invulnerable to kindness, to the good opinion of others.

In the late dusk the parakeets rose from the palm gardens nearer the shore and flew brokenly to higher ground inland. They crossed the Agency garden, where the guests turned to watch them. Many reached the Emir's palace where they flew blindly about the roofs and between the minarets. The Agent fretted from one guest to the next. As it grew dark, as the blessing of dusk was withdrawn, there was a small increase in wickedness in the Agent's garden. The impulse to cruelty was magnified. There was a hardening of every unkind intention. Where is the Emir? the Agent thought.

The servants turned on the lamps along the veranda.

The Colonel had a most gracious smile when his fancy was taken. Peachy watched him now as he talked to Sarita on the lawn. He bent over her with courtly attention and his face lit up when she spoke to him. His smile puzzled the Agent, causing him to pause with his lips parted; the smile was one of sympathy, of recognition, yet the Colonel hardly knew her at all. A new, strange thought entered his mind and held it for a second or two.

'His Highness the Emir will join us soon,' he said, suddenly awake. 'Sarita, you will make him welcome. He will probably take fruit juice with a dash of cinnamon. Ali Kadir, you will attend to the bodyguard. And if they decline to leave their weapons at the gate, then don't insist upon it; that would be imprudent.'

The Agent stood moodily on the lawn, deficient of his principal guest. The officers and minor officials roaming the dusk-covered garden or standing in small groups under the date palms were a random gathering without point: they lacked the cohesion of kingship, they needed the justification only royalty could give. It didn't matter what sort of king it was, a lion in strength or a despot of insane cruelty; there was a necessity for kingship, here as elsewhere. Oh, where *are* you, Hajji Kassim? the Agent thought desperately. I don't care that your titles to the state are in question, your descent from the Prophet doubtful; I don't care that you are a diseased bag of guts without a redeeming feature; you are King and I will say nothing.

At his side, Sarita said, 'I don't like the Emir. Do you? His breath is stale——'

'Be quiet, girl. He is the Ruler, now and for as long as his life continues.'

'The Emir, the Emir?' asked Mrs Masterman. 'Did you say the Emir was coming?'

'The Levy are covering the road and the neighbouring gardens,' said the Colonel. 'There shouldn't be any trouble.'

They waited restively for the King as the last of the parakeets flew insanely across the sky and vanished inland. They waited more than half an hour.

When the Ruler came, the watchman opened the main gate as far as it would go, and the Agent and Colonel Masterman stood just inside the garden to greet him. Two askaris of the palace guard in purple robes crossed with cartridge belts took post on either side of the gate. The men of the bodyguard and the falconers loitered in the road outside or sat under the wall in the manner of the bedouin. The Ruler's car, finished in silver and with ermine along the facia board, carried the chief burden of kingship: the Ruler himself was dressed in a grubby white robe and broken sandals.

'Your Highness does the Agency great honour,' the Agent said with less than perfect truth as Hajji Kassim entered the gate.

The Emir nodded. He was short, undistinguished, with the face of a black weasel. The Sheikhs of minor degree, robed in white, tumbled out of the back of the car and moved like ghosts in the road outside: the Agent caught sight of Abdullah the Wicked, Abdullah the Wise and Saud the Fat, the murderous brothers upon whom he looked with such sharp concern.

The Colonel stepped forward and bowed smartly. He said in his soldier's Arabic, 'I am happy to see your Highness well. Your health and safety are of course matters of concern to the state.'

The Emir spoke in a thin, cold voice. 'Thank you, Colonel Masterman, I am well,' he said. 'And I am safe, I am sure, in the protection of such a distinguished soldier.'

'Who is this lady?' asked Abudllah the Wicked a while later. 'What is the matter with her legs? Is she unable to walk like the other English ladies?' He was tall, of superlative grace, and his eyes were alight with interest.

'Mrs Masterman, let me present Sheikh Abdullah bin Mahomet Al Farahid,' the Agent said, 'half-brother to the Emir. He presents his duty.'

'The Sheikh is kind, I am much honoured,' said Mrs Masterman. 'Try to take him away if you can, Mr Peachy.'

'The lady is touched by your greeting, Excellency. She has a disablement of the spine which prevents her from moving freely.'

'It is of no consequence to me; I ask for no blessing from this lady. Please make my excuses, Mr Peachy.'

'My Lady will understand,' the Agent said gravely. 'Mrs Masterman, His Excellency is charmed at meeting you, but he has to go.'

'What did you say his name was?' asked Mrs Masterman. 'I can't remember all the Sheikhs. He has a most disagreeable face.'

The voices within the walls were low and good-humoured and the Agent was happy enough. No one was actually being harmed—no one was being abused or threatened or held at gun-point no matter what devious forces were at work in the garden.

Sarita tugged at his arm, angrily. 'Abdullah the Wicked pinched me. He has no right to be offensive.'

'The Sheikhs are restive,' the Agent said. 'It arises from their political impotence. Abdullah is in charge of public sanitation, which is the Emir's way of showing disfavour, and it leaves him rebellious.'

But Sarita's face was frozen in complaint. She gave him a small, vanishing smile and went away.

But not far. She stayed on the lawn, her figure softly drawn by the lamps, and Peachy wondered if he had ever seen a girl so beautiful. O Sarita, he thought, you are all things, big and little!

At his elbow, Abdullah the Wise said, 'Who is that trollop? I may approach her, with your leave?'

'Do so, Excellency, and I shall kill you.'

Abdullah the Wise nodded and disappeared among the white robes on the lawn. The message was allowed in the sheikhdoms and Abdullah didn't really care.

Now the Agent could not distinguish the Emir from among the other robed figures in the garden. There was nothing to mark his royalty. On the other hand the figure of Colonel Masterman was never lost to his eyes.

'A very fine soldier,' said Saud the Fat, crossing to the Agent. 'He has, shall we say, the executive instinct; he is not troubled by the refinements of argument. I would be disquieted if he were.'

As usual, Peachy was alarmed at the intelligence of Saud the Fat, who had had the benefit of a Swiss education; the Sheikh stood squarely, openly before him, like a jovial monk, and it was a matter of regret to the Agent that Saud had the conscience of a rattlesnake. 'I mean to say,' Saud continued brightly, 'already there are too many dangerous romantics in Hassan. Our protector must be a man whose actions can be predicted and whose sense of justice is wholly impartial. I am sure the Emir can put his trust in Colonel Masterman.'

'As Your Excellency says, he is an admirable soldier.'

'He has perhaps too great a trust, too little understanding of our monarchical system, of the need for expedients....'

Saud let the sentence die, inviting argument, but Peachy would not be drawn by so perilous an exchange; he could not say what world of shifting loyalties lay behind this gentle provocation, or which of the robed figures had his ear turned towards them.

'Your Excellency will have another fruit juice? Or a marshmallow? These lollies were a gift from the Emir....'

Saud the Fat bowed in recognition of this dexterity; and Peachy left him and mixed with his guests under the palms. The stars were appearing above the courtyard walls, each marking, so they said, a potentate long dead.

Zamil walked sideways across the grass, bringing with him a

fitful indignation. 'The bodyguard have slaughtered a goat in the kitchen recess. They did not care for the cold chicken.'

'As they please,' the Agent said.

'I did not think it right, but I could not prevent them. Cook has gone into the desert.'

'As cook will.'

The light from the french windows cut a path across the garden to the farther wall. Here the Colonel stood with the Emir. The Agent felt concerned, but he could not say why; the Colonel's courtesy was complete and it was unlikely he would say anything to upset the Ruler. Perhaps it was the difference in height, the soldier much overshadowing the Emir, which disturbed Peachy as he watched them from a pool of darkness. No ruler should be less than seven feet high and then there might be peace in Arabia. Or perhaps it was nothing at all—just the suspicions of a drunken political officer who had spent too long in the sunlight of the desert to be of use to anybody.

'It will soon be the summer holiday,' the Colonel said, a statement beyond all contradiction. His Arabic lacked refinement. The language needed to be spoken with rapture if an impact was to be made; it was a language of superlatives, in which falsehood looked better than truth.

'I shall go to Bahrain for my leave,' the Colonel said (an unmistakable truth).

'There you will find everything you want, and in abundance,' the Emir replied (in manifest falsehood).

'Might I suggest that Your Highness takes leave in Ras Al Hadraif, where your uncle is Ruler? You would be sure of a welcome there.'

'That is a possibility I will ask my staff to consider.'

Peachy saw the need to intervene: the Sheikh of Ras Al Hadraif, as black an Al Farahid as any other, had threatened to feed his nephew to the peregrine falcons if he should enter the state.

'A charming suggestion,' the Agent said, interposing his squat figure between Colonel Masterman and the Emir, 'which I am sure His Highness will one day take up. There is, of course, the question of the disputed boundary, where the

Sheikh has resisted our just claim with some asperity.'

'A trivial matter,' the Colonel said.

'Quite so; but problematical.'

'He would kill me,' said the Emir without emphasis.

The Agent said, 'I am sure His Highness would prefer to holiday in England, where the climate is more agreeable. Brighton, perhaps——'

But the Colonel would not be deflected. 'The palace at Hadraif is comfortable and close to the shore. I know the Sheikh would make a suite of rooms available.'

The Emir's voice never betrayed his true feelings; he spoke always softly, as if the matter had no weight, even when announcing his most earnest decisions. Now his voice was mincing and effeminate. 'The state of Ras Al Hadraif was conceived outside the law and it lives now by no recognizable right. It is a rank cesspit, consumed by corruption. The Sheikh is not related to the house of Al Farahid, even remotely, neither are the people related to the Hassanites; they are an alien, devilish tribe without creed or charity. I will not take my summer holiday in Ras Al Hadraif.'

There had been some change of emphasis since the preceding week, the Agent noted with alarm. This probably arose from an incursion of tribesmen into the Maledifah desert where they were said to have destroyed two wells traditionally Hassanite. The boundary had been drawn seventy years ago by a colonel of Sappers and with no regard for topography or tribal divisions: with a soldier's liking for simple solutions he had ruled a line midway between the capital cities; and since this division had no local support the boundary had remained in movement.

The radiant face of Saud the Fat swung out of the darkness like the moon. 'Notwithstanding our difficulties with Hadraif, My Lord Emir, there is much in the Colonel's suggestion. The beaches there are touched by the south-east monsoon and the palm trees make admirable shade.'

What did he say that for? the Agent wondered; and his mind ran through all the unworthy motives that might be moving the heart of Saud the Fat.

'I shall go to Brighton,' said the Emir, who had no such intention.

'A wise decision,' said the Agent. 'I will send a brochure to the palace.'

'If My Lord is concerned about the Hadraifi boundary, I will have the Levy patrol the area,' the Colonel suggested.

But the Emir had lapsed into silence. What fancies passed through his mind the Agent could not guess—what visions of danger, of sudden death. He was disturbed at the sight of a man without passion.

Saud the Fat spoke again and the Agent could not at first make out his words.

'I congratulate my brother on surviving the attempt upon his life. We must, I suppose, take the matter seriously, no matter that it appears to have been without motive. I do not know what can have possessed the rifleman.'

Rifleman? What rifleman? The Agent felt the panic of ignorance.

The Emir disengaged himself from his dreams. 'The guard was at fault; he should have returned the shot. I have cut off the finger he might have used to discharge his rifle.'

'My Lord,' said the Agent, 'I do not understand.' He was lost in a dangerous sea and he turned instinctively to the tall figure of Colonel Masterman.

The Colonel spoke in English. 'A wretched affair, Peachy. It appears that a soldier of the Levy may have discharged a shot at the palace when the Emir was on a lower balcony. I can't say why; he was wrong in the head, I shouldn't wonder. It disturbs me that the Ruler should himself have punished the guard because, as you know, I hold the court martial warrant for all military personnel.'

The Agent breathed again, recalling that Zamil had told him of the incident; on the face of it there was no danger arising from this stupid affair.

'Of course the shot was meant to intimidate His Highness,' said Mrs Masterman, who had joined her husband in the light from the doorway.

At that, Peachy was angered, and he wished the wretched woman, who paid not the smallest attention to diplomatic nicety, would stop making unsupported judgements. He said, 'We cannot know anything of the sort. We cannot even be certain who fired the shot.'

'Of course not,' Colonel Masterman said awkwardly.

'It was the missing soldier,' said Saud the Fat complacently.

'I don't know, I cannot say,' the Colonel replied. 'There are many armed men in the desert. It need not have been Hamid.'

'Who else?' asked Mrs Masterman. 'Captain Sloan did right to punish him.'

Why doesn't she shut up? Peachy thought.

They were adrift on a perilous tide. Under a lamp by the wall Sarita was talking to Abdullah the Wicked. She laughed, she was happy. The Agent shuffled from guest to guest with a plate of canapés. 'A crayfish tail will delight My Lord Abdullah,' he said without enthusiasm.

In a voice empty of interest the Emir asked where Brighton was.

Zamil, at the Agent's back, said peevishly, 'The kitchen recess is swimming in blood. I don't know what to think. Such manners——'

The Agent smiled, laughed loudly, and became deeply serious. 'O Zamil, there are many abiding mercies, many blessings and small favours; but they are not here.'

Zamil went away: he didn't understand.

The Emir never sought the company of his public servants. If they were close to him he would sometimes speak as if continuing a train of thought, but he didn't look at them, and he didn't notice particularly when they went away. His mind was independent of outside influence, it might have been on a more lofty plane or at the behest of an old royal instinct which did not argue or discuss but simply made known his wishes. He paid no attention to praise or insult, though a subsequent edict, generous or cruel, might show that the words had been recalled; he gave not the slightest hint of the course of action he proposed, which life was to be enriched, which ended in pain; his voice was always level and soft and imperative.

He said now, startling the Colonel, 'Who is this Captain Sloan? Why is he being held prisoner at Warboys Camp?'

'I did not know Your Highness was aware of the matter,' the Colonel replied weakly.

The Emir said nothing; he hadn't been answered.

'I arrested him for an offence against regimental discipline. I have ordered the evidence written down.'

'But what was his offence?'

The Agent slid close to Colonel Masterman, disliking this line of questioning. 'I will let My Lord have a written account, which is the best method of giving an exact report,' he said, knowing this to be absurd, as the Emir could not read.

The Colonel said, 'He administered an illegal punishment which I could not tolerate.'

The Emir was puzzled. 'But the soldier was guilty; the whipping was just.'

'How can Your Highness be certain?'

'He fired a shot at his ruler. Where is the doubt?'

'We do not know that it was the same man, and even if it was I would have to convene a court and have the evidence properly presented. An officer may not take the law into his own hands.'

Peachy heard laughter, which was surely the laughter of Saud the Fat, and he wondered what interest the Sheikh could have in an illegal whipping outside the wire at Warboys Camp; this shabby little affair could hardly be turned to political ends.

'It was only an illiterate soldier with a rifle,' the Sheikh said softly in English. 'My dear Peachy, you are white with anxiety! After all, it was nothing to be concerned about.'

'Your Excellency is no doubt speaking the complete truth,' whispered Peachy, wondering if in fact he was lying.

The Emir kept to his point, showing not the smallest irritation with Colonel Masterman. He said, 'Captain Sloan is to be released.'

'But, My Lord, he was gravely at fault! I must insist that I be allowed to discipline my officers as seems fit to me. I cannot admit that this is a matter within civil jurisdiction.'

The Agent was flustered, distressed at this confrontation between Masterman and the Emir, and for once he did not know what to say. The Emir gave a shallow nod, as if to say he recognized the Colonel's point, and did not speak again. He never gave his orders twice.

'I am sure Your Highness understands,' the Colonel said.

*   *   *

The guests were leaving by the gate, saying how much they had enjoyed the party. Charles Peachy bowed to the Emir and showed him into his car, and the bodyguard meanwhile leapt into a pair of Land-Rovers parked alongside. The Sheikhs dived into the palace car and sat in an untidy jumble on the back seat.

As the procession moved away with blaring horns, the street boys clinging to the gate posts waved to their ruler but he did not glance in their direction. The Agent bowed again, at his side Sarita curtsyed. Beggars ran along the pavement in pursuit of the royal cars. Then they were gone, and the Agent and the dark beautiful girl turned back into the garden where the empty glasses marked where their guests had stood. There was a terrible shambles in the kitchen.

Sarita said, 'Abdullah the Wicked is taking me to the pictures.' She seemed happy enough with that.

The stars gleamed. Fitfully the Agent wondered what damage had been done that evening, what small progress they had made towards the undoing of civilized life in the desert Emirate. He could not say, and very soon his mind wearied of the problem.

6

An hour before dawn on the day following the Agent's party, Colonel Masterman mounted an armoured car and entered the cramped interior through the turret hatch. He wished to see for himself what evidence there might be of incursions into Hassan from Ras Al Hadraif and to what extent the wells had been damaged. A British sergeant drove the vehicle and one of the few British private soldiers at Warboys operated the rear controls. It was dark when they passed through the barrier and took the desert road; the stars were still showing. The Colonel elevated the turret seat and sat with his head and shoulders outside the hatch. He felt the rush of warm air as the armoured car gained speed along the unsurfaced road, and he saw the shards of dust rising on either side of the vehicle and joining behind to form a low-hanging cloud that spread slowly into the desert. The headlights disclosed the long white road that had no feature but the advancing telegraph posts.

'A lovely morning!' the Colonel shouted through the hatch to Sergeant Brown at the wheel; but the sergeant could not hear him above the whine of the engine.

The Colonel was happy. For a few hours he was escaping from the trials of his command into the clean air of the desert. He knew the sensation of release known by a soldier when his command has shrunk to that which he can see—in this case a vehicle, two white soldiers, a gun, and small arms and rations for each man; it was a simple unit of force that would respond at once to his direction; it was compact and effective and capable of swift solutions. He would not bother now about Sloan or the Emir's directive that he should be released. He would not bother about Hassan. He sat with his back erect, his hands on either side of the turret hatch and drove happily into the desert—as if he were driving into nothingness, passing from the painful condition of life into the anonymity of death, from the light and colour of commitment into the dark of the void.

'This is the life!' he shouted to Sergeant Brown; and the sergeant nodded at the words he could not hear.

A white dawn enlarging above the Gulf showed him the road inclining into the hills which lay between Bir-el-Shama and the Hadraifi border. Here the soft rock was wind-formed, blown violently into strange shapes.

In the eighth century of the Hegira, a crazed and brutal harlot, Kabina the Wanton, and her son Ahmed, had laid waste these hills and founded the House of Al Farahid, or the Black Farahid as they were known, as the ruling dynasty in the region. It was said that Ahmed had ruled with ferocity for fifty years and left one hundred male children, these the fathers of the Black Farahid who had maintained the tyranny of the founder across the centuries, varying in their ability as rulers but displaying that perversity of judgement which was the true mark of Kabina. Today the earlier centuries were overhung with legend, but it was clear the battles for kingship had raged within the family. The sheikhs and emirs had come and gone in violence; there were many strange exits from power. The present difference between Hassan and Hadraif was simply a part of this family squabble which the Colonel could do nothing to compose.

He ordered the hatches secured. The driver closed and locked the forward port, and Masterman depressed his seat and lowered the turret lid; they were locked into the dark and jarring interior of the vehicle. Through the gunsight with its circular graticule he could see how the cliffs overhung the road and how the road itself narrowed into a defile where it might not be possible to turn the vehicle. Hadraifi tribesmen had been known to block the road and then to fire upon vehicles brought to a halt. The Colonel swung the turret with his shoulders and scanned the hills right and left. The growing light showed him only the empty rocks. To fire upon an armoured vehicle mounting two heavy machine-guns, even from good cover, would be madness; yet the bedouin was mad. Colonel Masterman, his problems reduced to an act of surveillance, felt the pleasure which came from an intelligent use of power against an unknown risk. He had considered the chance of the tribesmen bringing up a heavy weapon and piercing the vehicle and he had thought it unlikely they could either obtain one or use it properly if they did. They could have mined the road, but so far the Hadraifis had not used mines; and in any case this type of warfare was not the way of the bedouin. After an hour on the hill road the first sunlight was blazing on the white rocks outside and the Colonel's eyes were playing tricks with him—those tricks known to soldiers who have stared too long down a line of sight; he could see figures moving in the rocks, and strange buildings, each an illusion which he must make an effort to dispel. In fact there was nothing on the road but the play of the sunlight and the clouds of white dust disturbed by the vehicle; they had not seen a living creature. He was disappointed for the first time that morning.

'Never mind, chaps,' he said to the soldiers. 'We'll have a chance of action soon, I'll be bound.'

As it happened, both Sergeant Brown and the private soldier were hoping to escape action until their engagements ended some months later.

Three miles from a point where the rose-red Maledifah desert began, on level ground, a white oil drum and a derelict emplacement marked the Hassan-Hadraifi border. The colonel of Sappers who inscribed this frontier seventy years earlier had taken no account of the wells or of the tribal movements between them, and the frontier had only a geometrical validity. Colonel Masterman took care not to enter into Ras Al Hadraif even though there was not a living creature in sight; he did not want the Sheikh to complain of tyre tracks, plainly those of an armoured vehicle, passing the frontier, as this would be an embarrassment to the Emir. He turned instead on to a camel track which skirted the hills for a mile or more to the well at Bir D'lehj. Here an empty sheep pen, a tiny mosque and a rest house, both ruined, marked the position of the well, but the well itself was full of rocks and the water had gone. The Colonel got down from the vehicle and examined the ground beside the well. The tracks of a Land-Rover were distinguishable between the marks of animals and men.

So it was true; the Hadraifis had brought up dynamite and destroyed the well. The use of a Land-Rover suggested it had been state policy rather than an act of inter-tribal spite.

'Well I'm dashed,' said Masterman. 'What was the reason for it?'

No reason at all; not the smallest vestige of a reason could exist, even in the crazy mind of an Al Farahid. He was puzzled, dismayed; he did not like unanswerable questions.

The sun burned around him. The vast lifeless desert glowed red, purple, rose.

'It's beyond all belief,' the Colonel said angrily to Sergeant Brown. 'In a country devoid of water the destruction of wells is an act of suicide, an act of insanity. Even as an act of war between two states it is unacceptable. I don't suppose even the Sappers could make this well run again. The bedouin will die of thirst in this region, both Hassanite and Hadraifi.'

For the rest of that day Colonel Masterman was ill-tempered, and his anger deepened at the sight of a second well, that at Bir Telijja, similarly destroyed. He was distressed by waste, frightened by madness, alarmed at his own failure to understand the minds of the people who could do such things.

'Why did they do it?' he asked. 'Why?'

Darkness was spreading between the hills as they approached Warboys Camp. The Colonel fretted inside the hot and airless vehicle.

'I'll walk,' he said.

The vehicle stopped two miles short of the wire and he climbed down on to the road. The armoured car moved forward again and grew small in the dusk; he could hear the sound of the vehicle long after his eyes lost sight of it; then the noise, too, was gone, and the only sound was the breath upon his lips as he stood beside the road enjoying the cool dark and the silence of the desert. The lights of Warboys lay along the horizon. Walking in the desert was an indulgence he did not allow his troops; there were too many dangers in the low hills. For himself, he liked the small risk of a bullet spinning towards him in the darkness and he did not even take the precaution of mounting the higher ground to examine the path ahead of him.

His anger had passed now; his mind was empty with only a dull pain remaining from the sight of the ruined wells.

Colonel Masterman was not a reflective man but he could not deny, when he thought about it, that the task of the British soldiers in the distant parts of the world was nearly over. The old imperial attitudes could no longer be held; indeed, he was part of a litter left on the rim of the former empire and very soon he too would be withdrawn. They would never come back to the desert, neither would the warships enter these waters. In the end the foreign-based regiments would have no substance other than in memory; the soldier's world would be wrapped in the sadness of lost illusion. He walked down the desert road towards Warboys, enjoying the cooler air which now blew off the face of the desert.

He remembered the places he had seen in his long service, each bathed in the pleasant light of recollection. Most of them he would not see again; some had fallen to rival cultures, but many had simply gone their own way of change, litter growing where once the British tended flowers, the old cantonments falling into ruin. Now vultures perched on the flagpole yards, a baboon sat in the Colonel's chair. A pity, but it could not be helped. Power had passed from the soldier to the demagogue and the man of business. Japanese merchants controlled the parts of Asia where once the soldiers kept the peace. The effort was spent, the tradition closed, the job over. The long vigil was at an end because others less skilled, less disinterested had assumed the soldier's role; the old guard was standing down. Oh well, thought Masterman, it had to happen. Perhaps we did some good. I really believe we did.

He had walked half a mile down the desert road when a voice, speaking softly, accosted him.

'Great soldier....'

The words were in Arabic, spoken from somewhere close to him. He started, throwing open the flap of his pistol holster in a single instinctive movement.

'Who is it? What do you want?'

He was answered with laughter. He could not tell from where it came.

'If that is Hamid, you must report into camp,' the Colonel said abruptly. 'At once.'

'If that is Hamid,' the voice repeated.

'Do as I tell you. I will speak to you in the morning.'

'The great soldier will speak to the poor fellah in the morning.'

'Hamid, you need food and the doctor's help. Go now to the camp. I will warn them at the gate.'

'Love thyself,' the voice said.

'We shall find you, Hamid, and you will be punished.'

'Were the wells dry? Were the houses in ruin? Was every virgin violated? Tell me, my master.'

'I do not understand you.'

'He does not understand me.'

'Hamid, you must surrender! Come here to where I am standing.'

He heard a rifle bolt snapping in the breech and he moved quickly between the rocks beside the road. He called strongly, 'If you shoot at me, you will miss, and then My Lord the Emir will have you killed, as you know.'

'As I know.'

'It is true.'

'Even so, great soldier.'

A bullet whined over the Colonel's head at a great height.

'That was a foolish thing,' the Colonel said softly, but with furious emphasis. 'It is shameful to shoot at a fellow soldier.'

'The wells were empty, were they not? The bedouin is lying dead? The state is destroyed?'

The Colonel said nothing. Even in this extremity it was not his policy to discuss matters of this sort with private soldiers.

The voice said, 'Who would do this thing? Who would destroy wells in the desert?'

The Colonel did not reply.

'Who was it, master?'

'The Hadraifis,' Masterman said shortly.

'Aye, the Hadraifis.'

'Of course.'

'Live long, great soldier; live long in ignorance.' The man breathed heavily, as if in pain. 'You tell me it was the Hadraifis, master?'

'I do, Hamid. Who else? They are Hassanite wells.'

The man laughed in the darkness and moved to a greater distance from where his voice sounded less clearly. 'The soldier tells me so, therefore it must be true.'

Colonel Masterman made one more attempt to reach the wretched soldier who had been three days in the desert. 'Listen, Hamid. You must come into camp because your injuries will need attention. The assault upon you was cruel and I have arrested the officer responsible. He will pay the price of his offence, I assure you, and such things will not happen again while I am in charge of the Levy. I will not yield to pressure where Captain Sloan is concerned, no matter from where it comes. I will do what I can for you; I will listen to your story and take account of the punishment you have already received before passing sentence upon you. I will even forget the shot you have fired at me as I know the desert has done strange things to you. Now, stand up and let me see you!'

But Hamid hadn't listened; he had continued speaking while the Colonel made his appeal, to himself, to no one. He used the dialect of the Afarhid and the soft, homely phrases of the southern desert were interspaced with the language of the barrack room. 'The poor bedu must do as he is told. He must come into camp, where the sergeant will give him drill. He must clean the pots and pans....'

'Listen to me, Hamid——'

Colonel Masterman heard the soldier recharge his rifle and he concealed himself behind the rocks. Hamid spoke fiercely then.

'Away, great soldier; there is nothing for you here. Go back where you came from. Leave the Arab to his pains.'

He must then have left, because the Colonel did not hear him again, and soon afterwards a scout car from Warboys, alerted by the shot, came down the road from the camp. The Colonel ordered a search of the nearby desert but nothing was found.

'Poor devil,' he said. 'I don't suppose he'll ever come back.'

The Colonel was distressed by his encounter with Hamid. Madness frightened him, as did any break in formal order. His lack of ease would not let him rest and later in the night he walked the circumference of the camp inside the wire. Fears shadowed his mind, but he could not tie them to any particular cause unless it was the craziness of the bedouin. He wondered if they were insane beyond cure. Often they seemed to be. At night they entertained lunatic fancies; they believed the night shades of fable approached their tents and hung there just beyond sight; the phantoms cast their shadows, their webs of strange influence, over the sleeping or the barely awake; they terrified the dogs and penned animals; children cried in the darkness, the insane slipped into deeper madness.

Colonel Masterman, looking over the wire, saw a world without colour, without charity; the cold light seemed to stop even the movement of sympathy.

Somewhere across the desert a dog barked. He shivered and his fears multiplied. Hajji Kassim, of course, was as mad as the rest of them; but no matter what happened the Colonel would stick to his principles. He would not release Captain Sloan, who was justifiably under arrest. He would apply the laws of sanity in a country of the mad. He would follow his own star because he could do nothing else. Sloan would be tried and punished, and perhaps it would do some good.

The Colonel moved away from the wire, feeling no better. We've stayed too long, he said inwardly, and the others have all gone home. We're too few to make any difference. But I'll have to do it my way.

7

The soukh at Bir-el-Shama stretched for a distance along the harbour but, with contempt for the sea, the stalls were built to face inward. Across a narrow space a second row of stalls crowded the first. The path lying between them was shadowed and sometimes dark from the overhanging screens of reed and sacking, but the blinding light from the sea penetrated here and there in a swathe of gold. Further business was done in the narrow alleys leading off the soukh. The creek carried away the refuse of the market. In the harbour the dhows of the smugglers laboured against the light as they worked their way to the head of the inlet; here in the soukh, in the shadows, the business of the market, the endless small movement of sale and exchange, went on without interruption. There had been a market here since the time of Kabina the Whore; the converging of the camel tracks and the mile of deeper water had determined the place, and once established a market became the most immovable thing in Arabia.

In the middle hours of the morning you could meet almost anybody in the soukh.

Sarita stopped by the goldsmith to watch the engravers working patterns into sheet metal. They bent over their work with a concentration so complete they might have been members of a vocational order. Here in the filthy street there was an exquisite accomplishment. More than anything in the world, at that moment, she wanted a gold pendant of the sort displayed in the goldsmith's cabinet. Charles Peachy, ridiculous in shorts, fretted at her elbow, while from the corner of her eye she saw Abdullah the Wicked crossing the soukh towards them.

'My lady desires gold?' the Sheikh asked amiably.

'My lord has taken time off from the Department of

Sanitation?' asked Peachy, interposing his short body between them.

'Oh certainly. I have little to do there. We have no sanitation.'

'I *love* gold,' Sarita said.

She looked directly at Abdullah the Wicked and it seemed apt that this erect, charming and reprehensible person should offer her gold. His gaze was appreciative and deeply impertinent; his body inclined towards her in a gesture of inquiry. She recoiled from him in shocked enchantment. She wished her step-father would stop fidgeting, as his lack of grace tended to make them all ridiculous.

'I shall be pleased to make my lady a present of gold,' said Sheikh Abdullah, opening the goldsmith's cabinet and taking down a necklace of fine pendants tipped with lapis lazuli—a thing of sheer beauty. 'A poor thing, hardly worth the taking, but if my lady will——'

'I am sure she should not,' said Peachy.

'I'm sure I should not,' said Sarita, with less than total conviction.

But the Sheikh was already fastening the necklace round Sarita's throat, raising her hair with the lightest touch, blowing gently upon the nape of her neck; and she was rapt at the sight of the pendant rising and falling on her slim breast, untroubled by the touch of the Sheikh's long and wicked fingers in the hollows of her shoulders. Peachy heaved at his shorts in sharp discomfort. 'Really, Your Excellency does ʋs too great an honour. . . .'

Abdullah raised one hand to stem the objection. He glanced at the goldsmith, who bowed: the glance implied that the Sheikh would pay sometime or never as the mood took him because he was a member of the ruling house, and the goldsmith's bow acknowledged the rights of monarchy and begged that the Sheikh would save his life and the lives of his children in the next bloody holocaust.

'Isn't it beautiful?' Sarita said to her step-father. 'Isn't the Sheikh kind?'

Peachy, too full of words to say anything, simply nodded.

'I think my lady is pleased,' said Abdullah the Wicked; and in Arabic, 'She has a well-shaped bottom which pleases me, but her mind is unexceptional. Good day to you, Mr Peachy.'

The tall, elegant Sheikh folded himself into a tiny Lotus Elan and drove violently up the soukh scattering the donkey carts.

'Isn't it a lovely morning!' said Sarita as a shaft of sunlight falling through the shades caught the necklace and made it gleam.

She stepped into the soukh, picked her way through the sticky black filth that covered the path, and made her way along the stalls towards the mosque. Outside the abattoir a boy tugged a warm and bloody fleece through the dust; it still bore some resemblance to the animal that wore it though now it was fallen and empty in some terrible lapse from dignity. In the dark interior of the forge the Negro boys stood waist deep in sunken pits to work the bellows; the smiths were making nails, hammer heads and spades. Charles Peachy shuffled behind her, breathing heavily.

'Abdullah the Wicked is really quite nice,' Sarita said. 'He doesn't care for politics, only for beautiful things. This year he is going to India to find precious stones. Last year he went to Isfahan. I don't know why people speak badly of him.'

'He's politically stupid,' the Agent said despondently, 'and open to the influences of the bedroom. I don't like him much.'

'He has beautiful manners when he cares to use them.'

The hollows of her neck still bore the impress of Abdullah's fingers; she raised her shoulders to her ears in a flourish of satisfaction. Across the soukh the quilt-maker did not lift his head to look at her but continued his stitching cross-legged on the floor.

'A Sheikh is a Sheikh,' the Agent said, kicking things in the road. 'He's better than Saud the Fat, I suppose.'

Sarita could see the fat, amiable Sheikh standing outside the cloth merchant's, bowing copiously to them. It was part of the unfolding miracle of the morning.

'Father, it's Saud the Fat,' she said in wonder.

'So it is,' Peachy said gloomily. 'What rotten luck.'

Peachy had not enjoyed his morning in the soukh. At present he disliked all sheikhs and wished they'd go away and stop plaguing Arabia. He didn't want to speak to Saud.

'Admirable, admirable!' said the Sheikh, grasping their

hands. 'I had hoped to see you. You will take refreshment with me.'

'It is kind, but we should not bother Your Excellency,' Peachy said.

'It is kind,' said Sarita.

The Sheikh propelled them into a tiny booth where they were crushing ice and sugar cane, and bottles of fruit juice were kept in a refrigerator no longer working. With a diversity of aim common in the Gulf the proprietor also offered Persian enamels, flights of wild birds and carpet beaters.

Saud had kept Sarita's hand in his soft clasp. 'She is lovely,' he said to the Agent, 'lovely! How the gold suits her!'

No doubt the admiration pleased her. Peachy saw the breast lifting inside her shirt, while in their cages the Java sparrows beat their wings in a frenzy of alarm; but in fact Saud's tastes lay elsewhere, with the affections of boy harlots; he was simply being agreeable. They drank sweet citronade standing up.

The Agent inclined his head to inquire the motive for this courtesy. 'Your Excellency is passing the morning in the soukh?'

'Ah, yes; it is a place of great entertainment, I am never at a loss here. Why, do you know that the proprietor of this booth is engaged in smuggling small items of worth into southern Europe? He conceals rubies in the hinder parts of budgerigars. And the barber opposite—you can see his premises from here—for a few fils, while he works a seductive perfume into your scalp, he will show you his catalogues. Engaging if you are given to that sort of exercise; they display the most extraordinary contortions and ingenuities; but I understand that not all of them are available.'

Saud's face became grave, as if a cloud were crossing the sun: Abdullah the Wise, accompanied by falconers, was passing in the shadows outside.

'Such a diverting place, the market! So many strange purposes! My brother is again seeking what I can only describe as the Golden Whore. Needless to say, he has not found her yet, he finds only the slack embraces of a drab, but nothing destroys his romantic nature.'

'My Lord is amusing, as ever,' Peachy said.

The Sheikh did not alter the direction of his gaze and spoke with the same inconsequence. 'Yesterday the Colonel intruded into Ras Al Hadraif.'

The Agent said swiftly, 'I don't believe it; he's too punctilious, too sensible.'

'Of course. But the tracks of his vehicle continued half a mile over the frontier. They were plain to see.'

'An error, an oversight. The Colonel has the greatest diplomatic caution.'

'My dear Peachy, I am aware of it. Clearly the Hadraifis moved the frontier post half a mile back into Hassan.'

'Ah!'

'How very amusing,' Sarita said, and laughed.

'The Sheikh of Hadraif sees it as an armed incursion and has threatened the Emir with reprisals. The Emir is disquieted.'

The Agent said slowly, 'I trust someone of influence has told the Emir that the Colonel is innocent of indiscretion. He cannot believe that a soldier of Masterman's experience would enter Hadraif in an armoured vehicle at a time of tension between the two states.'

'The Ruler is disinclined to be reasonable.'

'But, for heaven's sake, the Colonel's so manifestly sensible——'

'If persuaded, the Emir would say that Masterman should have foreseen the Hadraifi rise.'

'That's absurd.'

'Not in the mind of My Lord the Emir, my dear Peachy.'

The Agent exhaled a long breath, deeply reflective. Then he said explosively, 'It doesn't make sense. What have the Hadraifis to gain from this manoeuvre?'

'It is recompense for the destruction of the wells.'

'Wells? What wells? The Colonel reported the wells at Bir D'lehj and Bir Telijja destroyed by Hadraifi agents. How can they recompense themselves for an action of their own? Yet . . . no, My Lord, I don't believe it!'

'Don't believe what?' Sarita asked, but she wasn't really listening.

'I suggest you give it thought.'

'The wells are used mainly by Hassanite tribesmen; only occasionally are they visited by Hadraifis.'

'So it is.'

The Agent said harshly, desperately, with failing conviction, 'No one would destroy his own wells. It would be madness. The tribesmen will die of thirst, ten Hassanite to every Hadraifi.'

Saud nodded.

'What Sheikh would sacrifice his own people to spite a neighbouring ruler?' Peachy continued loudly, for the sake of form, for the sake of some notion of right behaviour learned in the heartlands of Christendom. 'What Sheikh would destroy his own precious water because once in a while an adversary gains an advantage from it? It would be the mark of an insane, destructive intelligence, and one beyond all forgiveness.'

Saud smiled, and the Agent fell into a black silence, glaring at the glass of citronade. Sarita walked to the doorway where the sunlight struck the gold necklace, and she lifted the pendant beads to see how the light was reflected in the lapis lazuli.

The Agent continued weakly, 'The Colonel was convinced this was the work of Hadraifi agents using modern means of demolition. He's an experienced investigator, by no means given to hasty judgements.'

'Colonel Masterman no doubt spoke the truth as he saw it. His finding was the deduction of an honest mind; any other reasonable investigator would have come to the same conclusion. Even so——'

'——even so, even so,' Peachy shouted, losing his head, 'that was not what happened. To understand the workings of inter-state rivalry he would need to be a criminal lunatic. Even so, My Lord Saud! Let me tell you, the Colonel is too good a man for this pestilential place and it will cost him dear. What will happen, who can tell?—— But it may move even the callous heart of Hassan.' He paused; he had gone too far; but Saud the Fat merely raised his glass, his little finger projecting at an elegant angle, and finished his drink before speaking again.

'An abominable substance. I don't know why we drink it. Prohibition is the curse of Islam. My dear Peachy, the Colonel does not have to complete his secondment; he could leave us to our devilry.'

'He won't do that. It wouldn't occur to him to do so.'

'Then he must endure the situation as he finds it.'

'Yes, yes—ah, yes!' Peachy said. 'Tell me, Excellency—no, I mustn't ask you, you will not tell me, it doesn't matter.'

'If you mean, is the mind of My Lord the Emir in decay —is he entering the darkness of total insanity—I would say no, not yet. But it would be as well if he were not subjected to small frustrations. For instance, it would be of benefit if Colonel Masterman were to release the officer he is holding in close arrest, as the Emir has made his wishes known in the matter. He will regard it as provocative if Captain Sloan is brought to trial——'

'But the man is charged with a serious offence.'

'I beg your pardon? Whipping a native soldier, who was guilty of an attempt upon the life of his ruler?'

'The Colonel will regard it as a matter of unalterable principle that Captain Sloan should be arraigned before a military court. If you think he will overlook the need for justice in this matter, you misjudge him.'

The Sheikh said, without deep interest, 'The soldier assaulted by Sloan has gone back into the desert, where he is probably dying or dead; it hardly matters what happens now.'

'Colonel Masterman will not see it like that.'

'Come now, he's a man of reasonable intelligence; there's no great difficulty in the situation. Sloan was the instrument by which a guilty soldier was punished. That, at any rate, in the opinion of the Emir.'

Peachy spoke angrily, without caution—he spoke with the voice of a man who knew he could die only once for Arabia: 'That is the opinion of a ruler who would destroy his own wells, who would let his tribesmen die horribly of thirst, who is—by your leave—mad, mad!' The Java sparrows, alerted by this incaution, beat against the walls of their cages as the Agent put down his glass, bowed to the fat Sheikh and projected himself into the soukh, where his careless elbow brought down a pyramid of nectarines in the fruit stall next door.

Sarita said awkwardly, 'Thank you for the cold drink, Sheikh Saud.'

She and her step-father walked swiftly, without object, along the market place.

'What's the matter with you?' she asked crossly.

She disliked her step-father when he got in a rage. She didn't know why they were hurrying. The morning had gone out of shape.

She said, 'Stop, Father. I can't walk so fast.'

'In a thousand years there has not been the smallest advance in the direction of sanity,' the Agent said, 'not in Arabia. I don't believe in an Arabic culture. There is only weakness, falsehood and cruelty; there are only men like Hajji Kassim to degrade human kind with their foul politics and abominable devices. Of course the Colonel didn't understand!'

'I've broken my sandal. Why must you spoil things with your bad temper?'

They came to an untidy halt facing up the street.

The Agent said, 'My darling——'

'Shut up,' the girl said.

At the far end of the soukh, where the road emerged from shadow into the white light of the sea, as if to complete an underlying intention, stood the tall figure of Colonel Masterman. They stood looking at him as if at a statue.

'What shall I say to him?' Peachy asked. 'He must have seen us.'

'He doesn't see me,' Sarita said with sour conviction. 'He sees somebody that isn't me.'

'The wells were a terrible thing, not something he can understand. He mustn't lose faith, not yet——'

Sarita wished Colonel Masterman would go away. She waved to him weakly. She knew that when the Colonel looked at her he saw someone other than herself—his admiration was for a beauty not hers, his courtesy was addressed to a woman who stood behind her in time—and she was hurt, angered by his use of her. She felt a blade of outrage passing through her as he watched her now.

'Colonel, we don't often see you in the market,' the Agent said, approaching him on a zig-zag course.

'I wanted to see Saud. He takes coffee at the corn factor's.'

Sarita said nothing: she was in a blazing temper, conscious only of her broken sandal.

'The Sheikh has a headful of rumour,' Peachy said quickly;

'market gossip, unreliable stuff. I shouldn't concern yourself with Saud.'

'It was told to me—no, not exactly told; implied, perhaps—that the desert wells may not have been destroyed by Hadraifis. I imagined that Saud would deny it.'

'Who told you this thing, sir?'

'I cannot be sure. A man in the desert. It is necessary to contradict his story.'

'But what was his tribe, his interest, his political persuasion? What was his motive in speaking to you?'

'I really don't know.'

'Then forget it, sir. The truth is a lost dog. See, Sheikh Abdullah has given my daughter a necklace!'

Sarita displayed her treasure with a furious impatience and the Colonel said it was nice. They had nothing more to say at this time. They stood in the road while the people passed by. And meanwhile, in the shadows behind them, the business of the soukh continued—a business which had its origin in the life-giving endeavours of Kabina the Whore and which alone would survive the breaking of order and the departure of these pale figures.

8

When Colonel Masterman received the written evidence in the case of Captain Sloan he was puzzled by the lack of motive in his strange action. He had supposed the depositions would explain why an elderly officer with an instinct for obedience should take leave of his senses and cruelly punish a native soldier, but the statements added little to what he already knew: Captain Sloan had assaulted a man of the Levy, believed to be the soldier known as Hamid, at a time after midnight on a date in April. The depositions were handwritten in English, and they had been rendered into accepted usage by the interpreter; the words of the sentries and of the guard commander were in this way removed from the truth of the incident, whatever that might have been.

The Colonel read: '*No. 06427 Sergeant Ahmed Said, having made a solemn affirmation, states as follows: I am employed as a senior non-commissioned officer with the Hassan Levy at Warboys Camp. I am also known as Johnny Said, sometimes spelled Zaid, or as Mahomet Salumid....*' O Lord, the Colonel thought, we don't even know their names, nor that these are the right witnesses! Here in the sheikhdoms identities were not strongly marked and one man merged into another. '*At 0100 hours on 4th April I was on duty as guard commander at the main gate when I observed Captain Sloan, whom I recognized....*' So, the incident was seen by the guard commander. Well and good. He had watched the old officer mercilessly whip a private soldier, but he did not say why he had done so, nor what thoughts had coloured the officer's mind as he laid the whip again and again into the prostrate body. '*I observed Captain Sloan beating a private soldier I believed to be Hamid Mahomet, sometimes known as Hamad, Hamil or Hamet, but I could not be certain it was him....*' Nor can I, thought Colonel Masterman; I can't be certain of anything in this damnable business.

He laid the summary on the desk in front of him. It was a hot, still morning at Warboys Camp; distantly he could hear the sound of the men drilling on the parade ground, the shrill word of command followed by the fall of the soldier's feet, a sound that would have pleased him had it not been for his disquiet over Captain Sloan.

Confound Captain Sloan, he thought. The case was without precedent in his memory.

He called for Captain Lovelace, the Adjutant, because he wanted to speak to somebody, anybody, but there was no reply. A shadow lay across the veranda outside his door but the shy quiet movement showed it to be that of a native soldier and the Colonel gave him no attention.

He had read the short summary through to the end before Captain Lovelace came in from the adjoining office.

The Colonel said despondently, 'I don't like it, Tony. There's a total lack of white evidence, and I can't believe a court martial will be happy with the uncorroborated evidence of native soldiers. And there is a marked disparity between the evidence of one witness and another. Much depends upon what passed between Sloan and Hamid, if anything did. Sloan himself has declined to make a statement or to question any of the witnesses. The manner of the assault is not clear beyond the fact that a whip was used and the severity of the beating cannot be assessed because, of course, we haven't got the principal witness. However, I've no doubt there's a case to answer.'

Colonel Masterman didn't really want the Captain's opinion. Lovelace was a time-serving soldier at the limit of his promotion who would not give his mind to the problem. He had contrived the soldier's face and manner; his asinine voice, in which the northern accent was almost totally concealed, was a parody of a regimental voice. When faced with a problem outside his experience he would fall back upon a vague cynicism. He said now, 'It's a pity the incident was not seen by the orderly officer, or at any rate by one of the British other ranks.'

Indeed a pity. The Colonel nodded, displaying his patience.

He was aware that the senior company commander was standing in the doorway hoping the Colonel would invite him in. Major Tillotson always wished to take part in a discussion of policy, as if without his advice the Colonel would certainly reach an imperfect decision.

The Colonel waved to him absently. 'Come in, Arthur. Sit yourself down. Let's have the benefit of your advice.'

Tillotson would not need that invitation, of course, and the Colonel regretted his presence in the office. The senior company commander did not look like a soldier. He was one of a number of serving officers with a monkey's face, stiff cropped hair and an abrasive intelligence; he was built for employment on the staff and not in the field. His point of view was always different from the Colonel's, inflexibly held and expressed with cold patronage. The Colonel didn't like him and better understood Lovelace.

'As I see it,' Masterman said, tapping the summary, 'the written evidence gives a good example of the type of behaviour I most want to avoid now that the regular battalions have been withdrawn. It was a stupid act, of the sort committed by men in strange places when the normal framework of obedience is removed, leaving only the influences of native behaviour. There is always the risk of this sort of thing in hot climates and it can only be corrected—I am certain of this—by recourse to traditional discipline of the kind we all understand. Particularly Sloan,' he added, 'who is an old soldier.'

Tillotson at once hardened upon an opposite opinion. 'Perhaps I might suggest a medical solution. Let the whole thing get lost in psychiatric abstractions. It was, as you have said, irrational——'

'What? Bring in the medics?' The Colonel was startled; he had not thought of it. 'My dear Arthur, I don't want the Levy invaded by a lot of trick-cyclists. I've little faith in that sort of thing. Sloan has already been seen by the unit medical officer, naturally, and he has found nothing much the matter with him.'

'A purge,' said Lovelace, 'might be helpful.' He giggled; but the Colonel had not listened.

Major Graves and Major Kirkbride, who commanded the second and third companies, both young career soldiers, had followed Tillotson into the Colonel's office and now took seats by the window. The Colonel had not intended to call a conference of his senior officers and supposed the idea to be Tillotson's. He knew he had been manipulated against his will but nevertheless he waved a welcome to the two young officers who were, in any case, unlikely to hold strong opinions.

The Colonel spoke to the room at large. 'I am anxious about the discipline of the Levy as a whole. I cannot expect the native soldiers to have a proper regard for authority if I show weakness with a white officer. They certainly would not understand it if Sloan got out of this one on medical grounds. Besides, as far as I can tell, he's not insane, simply given to a loathsome form of sadism.' He paused, hoping for support for his opinion. In the ceiling of the small hot office the fan kept up a rhythmic commentary, like a third person.

Lovelace said, 'Of course he must take his punishment. He's a soldier; he knows what to expect. I'm not saying that Hamid didn't deserve what he got, but there are ways and means——'

'Of course,' said Masterman.

The simple solution, the soldier's solution; it had been effective from time immemorial. Graves and Kirkbride murmured agreement.

'I understand, from our party at the Agency the other evening, that the Ruler wishes Captain Sloan released.' Major Tillotson, with his habit of finding the bruise and then pressing exactly upon it, brought into the Colonel's mind the thought he most wanted to avoid.

'That's a political matter which must not affect my judgement,' he said crisply. 'I shall ignore pressures of that sort, Arthur—they are irrelevant to Sloan's innocence or guilt.'

'Of course; but in the circumstances——'

'You're not suggesting I should be influenced by the Emir in a matter of internal discipline, I hope.'

'No, but——'

'I should lose the respect of the entire Levy, if I did,' said Masterman, reinforcing his view, keeping himself within the limits of military certainty, guarding against the insanities of this place. 'The discipline of the Levy is my first concern. I have to consider not only the need to punish the individual but also of showing justice to the native soldiers as a body. Sloan has criminally assaulted one of their number; they are bound to wish the matter investigated. I cannot allow them to think we have a different standard of justice for white officers.' He smiled; he was happy to have reached a conclusion supported by the wisdom of the centuries.

Tillotson said slowly, concisely, 'This is a country of swift solutions, of rough justice. We are not at Aldershot now, Colonel. As the Ruler particularly wants it, and as we are here by his leave, might it not be as well if we adopted the medical excuse for not doing anything specific about Sloan? It's a time-honoured method of avoiding embarrassment, and Sloan is plainly some sort of lunatic, otherwise he would not have behaved in this stupid manner.'

Colonel Masterman was too polite to rebuke Tillotson for his obvious impertinence. He said quietly, 'I cannot agree with you, Arthur. There is a need to uphold our discipline if we are not to invite chaos. It's true that the Agent has been on the phone trying to persuade me to do something on the lines you suggest, but I have told him I cannot do so; it is not my way. Captain Sloan must be brought before a court martial here at Warboys. Besides, I have given my word——'

'Your word? To whom, Colonel?'

For once Tillotson showed surprise, which was not his manner: there could be no one entitled to ask for the Colonel's word in a matter of discipline, as his authority was absolute; it did not make sense. Even Lovelace raised his eyebrows.

The Colonel wished he had not spoken. 'I meant to Hamid,' he said. 'When I spoke to him in the desert I told him I would punish the officer responsible for his injuries. I don't know if he heard me, but I did give him that undertaking.'

The Adjutant's stupid face radiated amusement. 'But Hamid is quite probably dead,' he said, and laughed.

Graves and Kirkbride showed their discomfort in small, irritable movements.

'Quite,' said the Colonel quickly; 'I did not mean that it was a matter of much importance. However—no matter that he may be dead—I still feel some obligation towards him.'

Tillotson had said nothing, perhaps not wishing to enter into a matter so absurd. He said now, with scant courtesy, 'I don't think we should do anything to lose the good opinion of the Ruler.'

'I agree, Arthur,' the Colonel said, 'but not at the expense of regimental discipline. You must let me worry about this one. My primary concern is to show the men that I respect their rights.'

Tillotson said swiftly, with a lack of emphasis that displayed his complete self-confidence, 'Plainly you must do as you think, Colonel. But I think the Ruler will bring in mercenaries if he loses faith in the Levy.'

Colonel Masterman sat up abruptly. He disliked the suggestion. Mercenaries were a tribe of stateless criminals whose loyalty could be purchased for a fee; they were one of the obscenities of the Third World. 'I think it most unlikely,' he said tersely, showing his anger, as if a sharp denial made the idea impossible. 'There would be no purpose in such a thing.'

'It has happened elsewhere in the Middle East.'

'Not where there has been a decent force led by seconded regulars. I must ask you, Major Tillotson, to leave regimental policy to me. I have made up my mind that Captain Sloan must face a court martial for the good of the unit as a whole. I will remand the case this afternoon. I'm certain it's the best thing.'

The officers went away soon afterwards and he heard their voices as they crossed the sun-smothered courtyard below. He had asked the Adjutant to prepare a commanding officer's orderly room for three-thirty; it would be necessary for him formally to read the charge against Sloan and to invite his statement before remanding the case for trial by general court martial. He felt the better for his decision to try Sloan before a military court as this would meet his need for a tidy, just solution; and, wretch though he might be, Sloan must be given the chance to disprove the charge against him, or of bringing to light any mitigating evidence. The Colonel was cheered; the old solutions were always best.

The shadow of the native soldier still lay along the veranda outside his office door, and now that his mind was disengaged it beckoned his attention. 'Who is it?' he called in Arabic. 'What do you want?'

The shadow did not move.

'If you wish to see me, the door is open. Do not feel afraid.'

The soldier came slowly to the door, where he stopped and saluted with regimental vigour. It was Sergeant Major Ramadi, the senior native soldier, and he was ash-white with fear.

The Colonel greeted him boisterously. 'Come in, come in, Sergeant Major! I am wholly at your service.'

Ramadi would not take a chair; instead he stood to attention in front of the Colonel's desk, bound by the discipline that created him, too frightened to say a word. The Colonel was accustomed to this reflex of the native soldier and he spoke softly, warmly in the soldier's tongue. 'What is it, my comrade? What can the Colonel do for the Sergeant Major?'

At the limit of fear, Ramadi said, 'It is Captain Sloan...'

'Oh, you don't have to worry about that, Sergeant Major! I realize there has been concern in the Levy over this unfortunate case. I can assure you Captain Sloan will be brought to account in the usual way.' Masterman smiled; he was glad to put Ramadi's mind at rest, thankful for a chance to spread word of his decision among the locally enlisted personnel. 'You may, of course, make this known to the men.'

Perhaps the Sergeant Major had not heard him; he simply repeated his words. 'It is Captain Sloan. The men are angered.'

'Quite so; I'm sure they are. But they will be satisfied by what I've told you.'

'They wish him set free.'

The Colonel thought, Dear God, what *now*?

'I beg your pardon,' he said firmly. 'I am sure you are mistaken. The Captain committed a serious offence against a local soldier.'

'The men desire that Captain Sloan should be set free.'

Colonel Masterman was so astonished he overlooked Ramadi's insubordination. Clearly the Sergeant Major was in fear of punishment, and the Colonel could only suppose that some intimidator had obliged him to oppose his Colonel's will. It was an unique, disturbing situation.

He said calmly, 'Look, Ramadi—I know there are many in the state who would use any threat, any inducement to get what they want. I know you are frightened and don't mean what you are saying. I want you to tell me who it is that has threatened you, and I promise you that, when you do, I will protect you and your family and if necessary send you outside Hassan.'

'You will do what I ask, master? You will set the Captain free?'

'No, I will not. He will be tried, and punished if necessary.'

The skin was taut over Ramadi's cheek-bones, his hands were in constant small movement. He said then, so quietly the Colonel barely caught his words, 'There will be trouble in the Levy. The soldiers cannot rest.'

Plainly the Emir's agents had been at work in the Levy. A chill of dismay at the loss of authority, which the Colonel feared more than anything else, broke inside his body as he sat at his desk facing the Sergeant Major. He allowed none of this to affect his voice. He said clearly, without rancour, 'You must tell me all you can. I will protect you, as I have said.'

'I do not understand the Colonel. I do not need protection.'

'It is clear to me that you have been used by others to make me change my mind about Captain Sloan.'

Ramadi did not reply. Then he said uncertainly, 'No one has spoken to the soldiers. It is their own wish, my master.'

The Colonel's mind wandered into confusion, and for the first time he wondered if he was wrong. He was at once vulnerable, aware of his ignorance, deeply humbled. 'Why is it, Ramadi? Why should the soldiers want the Captain free? He cruelly whipped one of your own people.'

'He did so with affection.'

'I do not understand you. Hamid was nearly killed.'

'Even so, master.'

'It does not make sense. You must be wrong.' He was lost, utterly, with no idea upon which to build. He knew the fault to be his own and that the terrified man before him was his only guide. He said quietly, using the homely phrases of kitchen Arabic, 'Fellow soldier, tell me what you mean.'

'Captain Sloan revered the bedouin.'

'But in the stores he swore at you, he used his fists, he called you wogs and cattle.'

'Yes.'

'And he visited the worst places in Bir-el-Shama. Unclean, vicious places——'

'So it was.'

'Then I do not see what you mean, Ramadi.'

Ramadi's next words the Colonel found difficult to translate as he was using the vocabulary of the southern desert, but they seemed to mean 'He loved us with the force of his heart'—something like that, something at the limit of the Colonel's comprehension.

'I do not follow you. He was cruel to the Arabs. Hamid may die in the desert, or he may already be dead.'

'The soldier was guilty. He attacked the father of the state. It was an act of impiety.'

The Colonel spoke incautiously, forgetting the rank of the man before him. 'A man of depravity, a man of unkindness——'

'He is King, no less.'

'But without heart, Ramadi.'

'Perhaps. It does not matter.'

In this quiet office, where the sun played on the blinds and the fan thrashed in the ceiling, where the only sounds other than their voices were the cries of the water carriers in the road outside and the distant howling of a dog—here the seconds passed slowly, the passage of time was almost stopped as the Colonel stared at his knuckles, admitting himself the pupil of Ramadi, knowing the soldier had risked punishment to guide him. So, it is not as I supposed, he thought. It is different. Always it is different. And yet a commander must follow his conscience or he is lost.

'Even so, old friend, I must do things as I see fit,' he said now, rising from his desk and placing his hand on Ramadi's shoulder. 'An officer may not inflict an illegal punishment—he may not use a whip against a soldier.'

'It is your will, master, that Captain Sloan shall be punished?'

'It is, Ramadi.'

A decision had been upheld. A decison had the force of law behind it; it was final, absolute and comforting.

'If it is the Colonel's will, it is my will,' said Ramadi.

Colonel Masterman had served long enough with the Arab

levies to know that, despite his admirable drill, the bedouin soldier could always break from discipline when his heart was touched; his generosity could not be suppressed by the military habit; and it did not surprise him that Ramadi, having heard his decision, should none the less grasp his Colonel's hand and press his lips into the palm.

'I thank you, soldier,' said the Colonel, who was moved.

'I shall do it my way,' he said to himself, as he waited for Captain Sloan to be brought before him. 'Only the commander can perceive the widest consequences.'

When marched in by the Adjutant, Captain Sloan looked old, tired and shapeless. His heavy face was grey and without expression, and to Colonel Masterman he looked to be what he was, an elderly NCO mistakenly commissioned late in life and uncomfortable in his officer's uniform. He paid little attention to the proceedings as the Colonel read the charge and told him of his decision to apply for trial; he did not make a statement, he did not deny the charge of assault. When the Colonel finished, Sloan simply nodded, saying nothing.

'Well, there it is,' Masterman said when they had gone. 'I've done what I can. We'll simply have to see what happens.'

9

Charles Peachy had no further ambitions in the diplomatic service and in any case he was unlikely to receive advancement. After thirty years of effort he found himself in a tiny sheikhdom with an unfamiliar name and with no prospect of a better appointment. He didn't really care. If he thought about it at all, he accepted that his colleagues had a better right to promotion; they had approached their work in a sensible order of priority; he had wasted his time in the pursuit of small, lost causes. And they looked so much better in uniform! Certainly, he had a better knowledge of the Arab temper than any other official, but he knew nothing of the issues that dominated the larger embassies, the terrible demands of security and profit, because he had always been a partisan of the trivial. He loved the desert and the desert people. To him, the Rub al Khali was not just a wilderness of sand without point; it was filled with strange motives. The cruelty of the desert kings he disregarded and the sufferings of the people he put down to the brutality of the sunlight. He saw the desert as a place of sublime exaggeration, where the hero became more heroic, the lover more entranced, the villain more irredeemably wicked. He did not want to go back to the pale countries of northern Europe where there were only dull days. He was quite happy here. He accepted each day as it came. Were it possible, he would like to die in Arabia.

After the death of his wife many years earlier, he had found himself the guardian of a step-child whose precocities had tried him severely; but later she had filled the whole of his life. She was the child of his wife's early and brave encounter with India. From the first days Sarita had treated him with the exasperation of love and he had become more patient and enthralled. He thanked God she was not of Europe; she belonged to the Asia to which he had given his effort and affection; she responded with the same alterations of mood he had known in the audience chambers of Allahabad and Bir-el-Shama: but more than anything else she was part of the desperate entanglement with Asia that overcame British officials of the second rank when they lost their discipline, drank too much, and realized they could never go home.

This evening Charles Peachy had certainly been drinking. There was no chance he would be quite sober before morning. He laughed at his predicament and abused those nearest to him. He shambled along the upper veranda of the Agency towards the servants' quarters, kicking a rattan chair ahead of him; Sarita had gone to bed, disgusted with his drinking, and he needed the company of other voices, other tempers, before he sought oblivion by one of the means open to the corrupt in a desert sheikhdom.

He seated himself above the small courtyard, where the servants' quarters opened: he could hear their voices below, he could hear the squeal of complaint that filled every courtyard east of the Mediterranean, but he could not see them. He threw an empty bottle down on to the cobbles, where it shattered. 'Leave your lechery, leave your abuses, and listen to me!' he called in their language. 'Come, children!'

They came slowly, laughing; they were used to his weakness. The children threw pellets of earth at the balcony. 'Drunkard!' they shouted. 'Womanless drunkard!'

Peachy enjoyed his commanding position above them. 'Was it worth it?' he asked. 'Was it worth the sweat and the foul breath? For what, my children? For disgust, for remorse, for satiety——'

'Shut up, old man, fat man!' they said.

'It's too hot for such things. Arabia is not made for love, only for abuses.'

'You do not know love. You cannot love a daughter.'

'Love is the gift of the educated,' he said stoutly. 'You are poor, unschooled, ignorant peasants. The bedouin does not care for love; he abuses sheep. Love comes with the separation of the mind from the body and *that*, little ones, is something you cannot know, being without educated intelligence.'

He beamed at them, and they shouted obscenities. 'Come

down, Christian! Leave your virtues; come down from your balcony. We will show you blessings unknown to you. Come, fat Christian!'

'Never, never, never!' he cried. 'I sit here with my virtues, with my enlightenment. I do not desire the oiled bodies of the bedouin.'

He wanted to do mischief. From among the faces below, which were those of the Agency servants, their families, their families' friends and others he had not seen before, one face was missing—the timid, scholarly countenance of Zamil the clerk. Now more than anything he wanted to annoy Zamil; he wanted to pour scorn upon his faulty intelligence, his poor opinions, his degree in accountancy; and he knew no sport would be more popular with his companions who regarded education as a deformity of the spirit. Zamil lived alone in a small apartment facing the courtyard which had once been a garage, and his status as a man of education was made known by the plate he had fixed to the door: *V. K. Zamil, BA, Clerk to the Government.*

The moonlight played in the courtyard.

'One is absent,' Peachy said wickedly.

'No,' they replied, 'we are all here.'

'Shame on you, when you do not know your betters!'

'Oh, it is Mr Zamil you mean. He is hiding; he is engaged in solitary satisfactions.'

'On the contrary, my children, he is reading books you would not understand; he is employing his luminous intelligence; behind that door there is a great light that would dazzle you were you to open it.'

'We do not believe it. We saw him just now and he was wearing his under-garment.'

'You will perish in dirt and ignorance because you do not recognize—you have no means to recognize—the irradiation of the personality that comes from a study of accountancy. You should give a proper respect to Mr Zamil, who has his name written on his door.'

'It is true, master. Mr Zamil is a man of wisdom, whom we should revere despite his practices.' They were laughing, trying the door handle, calling his name.

'Certainly,' said Peachy complacently. 'Ali Kadir, make an

obeisance before the doorway. Who is that scoundrel with you? Abu Behkr, is it?—proud name for a miserable wretch; make certain he too prostrates himself before the doorway of Mr Zamil, no matter what that gentleman's present occupation may be.'

'Zamil!' they cried. 'Learned one! Leave your consolations and come out into the courtyard with the poor bedouin.'

'O Zamil, do not hide the splendour of your intelligence behind a closed door,' Peachy supplemented strongly. 'Come out, display the glories of your mind, show these poor people how to make a double entry and a trial balance; do not hoard such wisdom within your bachelor establishment.'

'Learned one,' the people said, 'show us the trial balance!'

'Zamil,' said Peachy.

'Zamil, Zamil!'

As Peachy had foreseen, Zamil was too simple-minded to ignore the clamour outside his door; he emerged now into the moonlight wearing a long shirt; and he was proudly upright, his scholarship showing in his pale brow and fallen cheek and in the pens and pencils stuffed into his pocket. He stood upon the door-step, eighteen inches above the level of the courtyard, looking with imperfect hauteur upon the people outside.

'Great master,' they said, 'we thank you for leaving your books and your spirited diversions and for attending to the needs of the ignorant.'

Though bewildered, Zamil recognized his duty to defend the good name of the instructed no matter that his voice was hampered and his hands could only make womanish gestures of derision. It would have been better had he remained silent. The servants put their hands over their ears and shrank away from him, as if he spoke unknowable things.

'They do not understand, my friend,' said Peachy from the balcony; 'these cattle, with the muck of the pen upon them, whose instinct is for the spawning of children, whose hands are always raised in violence—they do not understand a mind set free from the tyranny of the loins.'

'No, we are ignorant, we do not understand,' the servants said.

With a poor attempt at irony, Zamil said, 'My thanks to you all—and to you, my master—for your insinuations. It will make no difference in the end; you will be overtaken by the workings of history.'

'Those are dangerous books,' Peachy said; 'too dangerous for an empty head. You had better read poetry, my lonely scholar.'

'I research into history, master.'

'Then remember that for every opinion there is a contrary argument of equal strength.'

'The story is plain.'

'Not to me, grave historian, nor to these brethren. You had better let these maidens rob you of your undershirt than cloud your brain with an interpretation of history. They will teach you the past, the present, the future because there is nothing in them but the anarchy of the bedchamber—nothing but savage responses to immemorial temptations.' Peachy, risen from his chair, was leaning over the railing, warm with his subject.

'You will fall!' the people said, in sudden alarm.

'I will not,' Peachy said proudly. 'It is not in the nature of a government servant to fall off a balcony; they take to the stairway, as is fitting. Tell me, scholar—is history made plain, is the world set free from superstition——?'

'So I believe.'

'Then every donkey-boy beware the bloodbath that must follow! I do not trust you, rational man, nor your scheme of history, nor anybody else's; I am one with the Great Whore and the chamber pot. Let me tell you, scholar—let me tell you now and for ever—there are no ordained solutions because it is not the humour of the stars.'

Having delivered himself of this truth, Peachy collapsed into his chair.

Zamil was angry; his head swung in denial and his hands made movements of dissent; and when it came his voice contained a proper venom. 'You do not know, you cannot say. You are not trying to remake, only to maintain. You love only a half-caste girl, who cares only for jewels.'

At another time Peachy would have been angered at this description of his life's purpose, but at the moment it seemed altogether apt.

'Aye, so, Zamil,' he said happily. 'And so much the better

for the safety of these poor children.'

He left the chair to represent him at the edge of the balcony and stumbled through the warm dark to the outside stair. He did not know where he was going, but he was happy —he was nearly drunk, distinguishing no small scruples but only the lunatic truths. He got down the stair without mishap and walked in the moonlit garden. Nothing there but shadow and the hum of insects. He bellowed verses in English and Arabic. He stood by the gate in parody of a sentry until he lost his balance and fell into the vines. Later—it might have been an hour; the moon had changed its position; he had drunk again from the decanter—he stood outside the little pavilion under the Agency wall. He did not know how or why he came there. The following minutes—perhaps two, or five—were lost, withdrawn from his memory. His next impression was of the small neat interior with the air just shifting the curtains and the girl lying where the moonlight fell. She was beautiful beyond astonishment. He did not know if she was awake or asleep.

'Filthy drunk,' she said without great heat.

'My daughter——'

'You look terrible. Your shorts are coming down. I don't like men who drink, who shout at the servants, who are sick in the flower beds.'

'——my daughter, whom I love——'

'——oh, go away!'

She struck him softly, absent-mindedly, with contempt and boredom. 'Pull your trousers up,' she said; and Peachy pulled them into his armpits.

Having made her point, Sarita giggled and drew the sheet up to her chin. 'What was that you said to Zamil?' she asked, amused.

'He's a forlorn peasant who reads books by the cold-minded.'

'Your face is bleeding. You fell into the vines.'

'I was attending to the security of the Agency.'

'I will help you.'

She raised herself to his level, folded her arms round his neck and licked the sore place. She said, speaking now in Hindi, her voice so close it filled the whole of his mind, 'Sometimes I am of Asia. It is my duty to help my father.'

'I am not your father.'

'No.'

'Then it is obscene.'

'I am nothing, belonging nowhere. You are my father.'

'You know that I am given to you.'

'It is my safety.' Then in English, in boredom, 'You'd better get some sticking plaster from the kitchen. You're going to look terrible in the morning. I don't know why you do such things. No, I'll do it.'

She rose from the bed and, taking his arm, propelled him into the garden. They crossed the lawn like ghosts.

'I love you, Sarita,' Peachy said.

'I know, I know!'

In the light of the kitchen there was a merciless reality. She was brisk, competent, pressing down the plaster with strong fingers.

'You'd better not go out,' she said.

'I want to.'

'Then take one of the servants with you.'

'I'll go alone.'

'It isn't safe, as you know. You're such a fool with these people.'

'It doesn't matter.'

She kissed him briefly, coldly, the kiss destroyed by the electric light, and left him.

Outside the Agency gate, in the dark road between the gardens, the fool's purpose was resumed. It was the purpose of Arabia. He moved from shadow to shadow laughing, falling, addressing the cats in French and Arabic. The vagrants sat under the walls covered in rags and he searched his pockets for money. 'Old woman, old woman—how is it with you? Does it pain you, this idleness? Where is your home, your children?' They said nothing; they never did; they only stretched out their hands to take the money given; they did not ask why a white man should be walking the gutters in the darkness. 'Why do you cry, fledgling? Has your sister gone?' The children stared with impassive faces, hard faces; with their unblinking gaze they seemed to look upon poverty as others looked upon the ocean. Farther into the town, where the stalls began, there were lights showing: here by tiny flames the engraver, the scribe, the herbalist worked steadily through the night, each offering a private challenge to the universal disorder.

Peachy hammered on the doors, spoke through the shutters; he wanted the town to hear him.

In an unmarked house at the back of the soukh they were still awake. Peachy greeted the old Armenian woman with affection, raising his hand to her cheek. 'Mother, tell me how it is,' he said. In this tired house, where the act of imperfect love added nothing to the sum of bitterness, there was a sort of charity. Peachy talked to the women for an hour, as associates, as friends, forgetting what he came for; then she reminded him gently, reluctantly, and Peachy bowed to her, brushing the tips of her fingers with his lips.

'Madam, I am weary.'

She did not press him to stay. He had drunk too much; he was old, tired, wanting only to talk. In this country of Kabina there was room for all sorts of affection.

He stuffed money into her hands and went out into the night again, where the moon was falling into the hills.

10

The court martial at Warboys Camp was held under the presidency of an officer flown in from Europe. The four members were appointed from units outside the area and a Judge Advocate was sent from England. A large office on the ground floor of the headquarters, cleared of furniture, served as the court-room. A table covered with a green baize cloth, with chairs along one side, and set with a Bible, place markers, a water bottle and glasses, pencils and paper, accommodated the court. The prosecution and defence had small tables on either flank and the court orderly had a seat beside the door. Colonel Masterman paid a visit to the court-room to make certain the furniture was in proper order; he asked for more ventilation as the temperature was high.

In a private room of the officers' mess he greeted Colonel Trafford, the president, whom he knew slightly. 'Sorry to coop you up in here,' he said. 'As you'll agree, it will be better if you and your members don't mix socially with the Levy until the case is decided; in a closed community like this the officers are, naturally, bursting with their own opinions, and you'll want to keep an open mind. The servants will bring you anything you require.'

He paused; he did not know how to go on without seeming to prejudice the accused officer. He said, 'I felt it necessary to apply for court martial for the sake of regimental discipline. You will understand what I mean. There was political pressure upon me to release Sloan which, inevitably, I had to ignore. However, while I don't wish to do anything to prejudice a fair hearing, I hope the case can be dealt with quickly and Sloan removed from Hassan without delay. If he is guilty, of course,' he added. 'I did not mean to anticipate your finding.'

Colonel Trafford was a regular of robust appearance and long service, and he had only limited scruples. He looked amused. 'I shouldn't worry,' he said. 'I'll have it sewn up for you in a brace of shakes—half a day, I should think, from the papers. I gather the fellow is likely to plead guilty, which will save us trouble.'

'I had heard that he might,' said Masterman, disliking this discussion of the case. 'He may of course offer evidence of his innocence, if he wishes.'

Trafford exploded in laughter. 'I doubt that he will. I doubt that he will!'

'I expect not,' Masterman said, and left.

He went up to his office, where he could be among familiar things; he walked the threadbare carpet between the two windows, now and again lifting the wicker shades to glance into the yard where the court-room door was in view; he hoped to see that the trial had opened; he wanted the case disposed of and Sloan committed to serve his sentence elsewhere.

He heard footsteps in the yard below as Sloan was conducted to the court-room under escort. From the window Colonel Masterman watched the uniformed figures passing through the sunlight, and he saw the guard at the door come to attention and salute as the small party entered the court-room. He felt a fleeting satisfaction: the court had opened, he had done what he could.

He took comfort in the small, poorly furnished office, in the routine orders pinned to the notice board, in the wicker shades rising and falling as the air blew in through the open windows, in the glare of the white buildings outside—these were the things he knew, the trappings of good order, of common sense, of the law from which there could be no departure.

In the pillared hall of the Ruler's palace, where the parrots and monkeys were chained upon high perches, where leopards guarded the door, the Emir sat upon a golden cushion. When the cushion irked him he replaced it with a folded grain sack; when the monkeys chattered he threw walnuts at them until they were silent. His mind was not full. He was concerned, dully and without form, with a sense of impropriety. He did not bring it to the front of his mind but now and again it troubled him—an unease, an insecurity, a lack of comfort which in time might vanish or develop the force of shuttered anger.

Although it was no longer remembered, Hajji Kassim once had a harlot strangled when she displeased him; another more gifted he had rewarded by setting diamonds into her navel. When his courtiers bored him, he had been known to take a favourite horse into the council chamber and there to confide secrets to him while the household waited in ante-rooms elsewhere. His Highness the Emir did not rage; he issued his instructions from a cold heart. He had killed no one with his own hands, and likewise those hands had never conveyed love, healing or forgiveness. The magistrate knew the Emir's mind so well there was seldom room for complaint: he severed the hand of the pick-pocket, cut out the slanderer's tongue, removed the eyes of those who looked with insolence upon the person of his Ruler. In Hassan, truth was the impulse of the moment. The desert gave no quarter, extended no mercy, made no allowance for ignorance. When the sun gave a harsh judgement, why should the sheikh be merciful? In the desert there was nothing to blur the edge of guilt, to urge a gentle response; there was only the hard light and the black shadows of the Rub al Khali. The Emir did not show concern when his tribesmen died of thirst in the Maledifah desert because the wells no longer gave water, nor did his heart fall when the children of the shopkeepers, ruined by the military withdrawal, grew thin and died. And he did not regret, or particularly recall, a girl of pleasure who fled from the palace into the sands, there dying in the sun. It was not the way of the Black Farahid to be much concerned with the lives of other people.

Hajji Kassim sat on the floor and called for coffee. He said nothing and ignored the voices of his courtiers, which he did not separate from the chattering of the monkeys. Everyone talked at the Emir's court, and the hooded falcons screamed and beat their wings. Now the Emir was frightened but he did not put a shape to his fear. He had a sense of wrong, of motives within the state which were not his own; some part of the sheikhdom had taken separate life and he saw no difference between separateness and hostility: it was a contradiction of his will, a danger to his person; it was the beginning of pain and death and the extinction of the dynasty.

When the Chamberlain asked if he could share the coffee, Hajji Kassim poured it down his neck. The bodyguard laughed, the falcons stretched their wings and stood upon tip-toe, the monkeys rattled their chains. In the rumpus that followed the Emir forgot, for a while, his fear; instead he rolled upon the floor, laughing strangely.

In the court-room at Warboys, Colonel Trafford heard Sloan's plea of guilty, but he did not write it down in the proceedings. The room was hot despite the fans. On either side of him the members of the court in best khaki drill waited in silence for him to speak. They were quiet, nervous, frightened of error. The fans kept up a downward draught which they could feel on the backs of their hands and which made the green table-cloth move slightly at the corners. Colonel Trafford had decided he would hear the witnesses rather than a summary of the evidence; the difficulties of interpretation, and the slack minds of the native witnesses, had left him in doubt as to the appropriateness of a plea of guilty. He wanted to hear the voices of the Arab soldiers, to ask them questions. Accordingly he told the court that there were aspects of the case he found difficult and he would, at his own discretion, enter a plea of not guilty at this stage.

Sloan sat heavily in the chair beside the defending officer. His face was grey, dull and disengaged. He paid little attention to the court, and Trafford wondered if he was asleep.

When he had finished writing, the Colonel blotted the entry and asked the prosecution to give evidence of the offence. He sat back in his chair, feeling the heat. Captain Barrie, who appeared as prosecutor, called Sergeant Ahmed Said, the guard commander on the night in question and the principal witness, and with the help of the interpreter he put together Said's account of the incident outside the wire. The Colonel listened closely.

It was moonlight; Said did not know the time. He had been inside the guard hut when he heard the voices of the sentries along the wire. On inspection he had seen a figure, whom he believed to be the soldier Hamid, approaching the gate from the desert. The soldier had called abuse at the sentries but Said could not remember what he had said. Hamid then sat down outside the gate. After a time, the length of which the witness could not remember, Captain Sloan had come down to the gate carrying a whip. He did not speak to Hamid, and Hamid said nothing to him. Captain Sloan then used his whip against Hamid. . . .

The fans kept up their rhythmic attention. Trafford rammed his thumb into the underside of his jaw, far from satisfied. It might mean anything. The incident was becoming lost in the differences of language and custom. He interrupted the prosecutor.

'Can the witness say for how long the accused officer beat the soldier Hamid?'

The interpreter engaged in a hectoring dialogue with the witness.

'He says he cannot remember.'

'How many strokes, then?'

'He is not certain. Perhaps ten, perhaps twenty.'

'Can't he be more exact?'

'Twenty, then. He says twenty.'

And if I said fifty, he would agree, Trafford thought, as it is not wise or courteous to disagree with authority. Damn and blast all subservient native soldiers! He continued, 'I want the witness to pay particular attention to the next question. With what severity did Captain Sloan use his whip?'

The interpreter did not understand the question himself. He was silent. The sweat ran down his neck.

'How hard were the lashes?'

'He does not know. He could hear them from where he was standing, and he could hear the breath escaping each time from Hamid's body.'

Now we're getting somewhere, Trafford thought.

'Was Hamid standing up or lying down?'

'He was lying down.'

Trafford knew that his next question would be beyond the powers of the interpreter and the intelligence of the witness; it belonged in the world of legal definition, where the nuance of a single phrase could make the difference between guilt or innocence; but none the less he had to ask it. 'Is it the opinion of the witness that the soldier Hamid, either by word or gesture, could have given Captain Sloan the impression that he co-operated in, or at least failed to offer evidence of his objection to, the whipping he received?'

The interpreter stared, saying nothing. As I supposed, Trafford thought. How does one conduct a trial in a place like this? He rephrased the question, and in doing so lost half the point.

'Did Hamid try to prevent Captain Sloan from whipping him?'

'He did not.'

'Can the witness give any reason, within his observations, why he should not have done so?'

'He cannot.'

'Did anyone else attempt to stop Captain Sloan from whipping Hamid?'

Said had nothing to say despite the barking of the interpreter.

'The witness does not understand the question. They were native soldiers; Captain Sloan was a white officer.'

'Oh, I see.'

Colonel Trafford felt uneasy. A factor was undisclosed, a question had not been answered, and now it was slipping from his mind. He wanted to question Hamid. He wanted to ask him why he lay in the sand and allowed Sloan to use his whip against him. He decided on another line of inquiry.

'Can the witness tell me this, then. In his opinion, did Hamid represent, either then or at any time, a danger to himself or to the guards or to the security of the camp?'

It was gone now; it had escaped his mind; perhaps it didn't matter.

'He does not know.'

'Could the shouting of the sentries and the abuse called by Hamid have been interpreted by Captain Sloan as a danger to the camp?'

'He does not know, he cannot say....'

Of course he can't, Trafford thought; he doesn't begin to understand what happened. Sloan was a filthy bugger who whipped a native soldier for kicks.

Captain Barrie, who came from a fashionable regiment and whose concentration was often faulty, concluded Sergeant Said's evidence and let him go. He then called the two sentries who had been nearest to the gate and who offered corroboration of the evidence given by Said. In taking them through their statements, Barrie confused one soldier with the other when referring to the original depositions, which Trafford noted privately, but as their stories were the same the Colonel did not correct the error. Both were named Mahomet, in any case.

We'd better get on with it, he thought.

When the case against Sloan had been presented, the President addressed himself to Captain Barrie. 'Is it your intention, Captain, to call the soldier Hamid?'

'I cannot, sir. He is absent without leave.'

'Has an attempt been made to find him?'

'It has, without result.'

'I assume that, in approving the charge, the convening authority has been unable to take into account the injuries sustained by Hamid, should there have been any.'

'Quite so, Colonel.'

'Is there any chance that Hamid will be recovered, shall we say, within a reasonable period?'

Barrie smiled remotely. 'The desert is a large place....'

'I am aware of it, Captain. However, in the absence of Hamid or of evidence as to his injuries it is obviously not possible to sustain charges of bodily harm.'

Trafford scowled. He didn't like the case. Should Hamid be wounded or dead, the charge against Sloan would be more serious than the one upon which they had arraigned him, but plainly they were unlikely to find Hamid.

'Go on,' he said testily. He had to proceed.

In his closing speech, Captain Barrie did no more than summarize the evidence and suggest the charge of common assault was proved. Colonel Trafford had no doubt that it was. Addressing the court, he announced his readiness to accept Sloan's plea of guilty on the evidence he had heard. He thanked Barrie for his presentation of the case and closed the court while he and the members considered their verdict.

It did not take them long. Captain Sloan had taken a whip to the soldier Hamid and used it against his prostrate body observed by the guards—as indeed, by his original plea of guilty, Sloan had admitted. 'I've no doubt the charge has been properly proved,' Trafford said cheerfully. 'We are not asked to say *why* Sloan assaulted Hamid, only that he did so; and despite the poor quality of the native evidence there can be no doubt that the incident took place as described in the charge sheet. For myself, I'm happy to forget the question of motive, which was plainly a sordid compulsion difficult for a normal man to understand. In the circumstances, I think we are bound to find him guilty of common assault.'

Guilty, then: he wrote the finding down before asking the orderly to reassemble the court.

'And turn up the fans, sergeant, for heaven's sake; it's like an oven in here,' he added.

Colonel Trafford then announced the finding in open court. Sloan dropped his head an inch, it seemed in submission to the authority of the court, but perhaps it was just from weariness at the length and formality of the trial. He didn't seem dismayed.

The defending officer, a junior captain with more enthusiasm than experience, then read a plea in mitigation of sentence. He dealt with Sloan's length of service, which was more than thirty-five years—with his accumulation of most of the campaign medals, with his commendations for meritorious service and good conduct; and he made the point that Sloan had volunteered for secondment to the Levy from a comfortable job in the United Kingdom. He offered no explanation of Sloan's strange conduct (Trafford could tell that, despite the eagerness of the defence to present an effective plea, Sloan had not been helpful to him); he simply pointed to the strain of service in a hot climate, to the anxieties of his appointment as Quartermaster, and to the loss recently of his widowed mother—circumstances which had combined to place him under stress and to account for his departure from rational behaviour. The plea ended with the usual apology for the offence and with the request for leniency.

Pretty thin stuff, Trafford thought, as he thanked the

defence for his plea and closed the court for consideration of sentence.

Charles Peachy waited in his office at the Agency for the sentence to be announced. He was disturbed by reports of unrest in the Levy as a result of the court martial and, like Colonel Masterman, he wanted the matter disposed of as quickly as possible. He had already made a request through diplomatic channels for the sentence to be confirmed with all speed, so that Sloan might be removed from Hassan and things returned to what passed for normal in the Emirate. His own attitude to punishment was subjective and unlikely to find support in Hassan, and certainly Colonel Masterman would not agree with it: in his opinion there had been sufficient pain already in the affair of the soldier Hamid to satisfy any scheme of punishment, and precisely who bore the pain did not matter; it fell upon human nerves, that was enough.

Zamil came in then to tell him Saud the Fat was outside, waiting to see him.

'Let him in,' said Peachy, in weariness. 'I might have known it.'

Saud was breathless, amiable, heaving with small courtesies. 'Such a hot day, my dear Peachy. Such a dreadful place to be in summer. When the globe was quartered the Arab nation was unfortunate, was it not, in the place allotted to them? It has always been my impression that as a people we drew the short straw. However, it was not my purpose to bother you with these reflections.'

Peachy wondered what the Sheikh's subject might be: his purpose, the Agent felt sure, he would not reveal.

'You will have heard, Mr Peachy, that My Lord the Emir has scalded the Chamberlain with boiling coffee. A distressing affair—not important in itself, except perhaps to the Chamberlain, who is greatly put about and in hospital care—but disturbing in what it tells us of My Lord. Clearly the Emir has a need to divert his mind from his anxieties. A practical joke is always a symptom of his concern. I recall, during the first Hadraifi invasion, that His Highness once laced the morning fruit juice with a purgative, causing some stir in a later meeting of the Council of State—a stir, I may say, made the more remarkable because My Lord had locked the doors of all the retiring rooms.'

From the folds of his robe the Sheikh brought out a small bottle of smelling salts which he sniffed with an air of critical attention. He avoided Peachy's eye. His thick fingers replaced the stopper delicately; he nodded with approval. 'So far, I understand, there is no sentence?' Then, without waiting for an answer, he said, 'Of course not; these formalities take so long to complete. You will realize the Emir is concerned that Sloan should have been tried with this offence and regards the court martial as provocative.'

'It had not escaped me,' Peachy said.

'To his mind—to the Arab mind—there was a magnificent fitness in Sloan's punishment of Hamid.'

'So I can understand.'

'And coupled with the Colonel's incursion into Hadraif——'

'——an Hadraifi fabrication, My Lord; as transparent as glass——'

'——coupled with that incident as it appears to His Highness the Emir,' Saud said firmly, 'a severe sentence, one seeming to damage the life or reputation of Sloan, would be difficult for the Emir to understand. He would regard it, shall we say, as an offence against his person and dignity—even, perhaps, against the security of his office.'

With infinite care, Peachy said, 'Excellency, I must ask you to use your influence with the Emir, and your knowledge of European thought and justice, to assure him that such thoughts are groundless. Sloan's offence was real, in total contradiction of an officer's responsibility, and any English commander, no matter what his background or intellectual capability, would have applied for court martial when faced with that evidence. To suggest that the trial undermines the Emir's authority—or that the Colonel intended that it should—is, to put it plainly, absurd.'

'No doubt, no doubt,' said Saud lightly. 'However, we are not dealing with a rational intelligence—we are dealing with a mind deeply suspicious of the motives of other people, particularly those commanding great physical power. Like every other monarch in this region, the Emir is mindful of conspiracy; everywhere he sees dark shadows, base intentions, the bloody hand of the regicide. You will recall that every palace revolution in recent years has been effected by the military or with their connivance.'

'But, my dear Sheikh, we are talking of a British officer, a man of unimpeachable integrity!'

'Quite so; it's a black fantasy; nothing more.'

'Then surely——'

'——surely, what? Nothing in this country is sure, Mr Peachy. You are as familiar with the Ruler as I am. You are not innocent enough to suppose, as I suspect the Colonel does, that the North European habit of rational behaviour is shared by the Arab people. Though he has not yet brought it to the front of his mind, the Emir is plainly discountenanced by Colonel Masterman and inclined to look elsewhere for his security.'

Peachy whispered, 'I know, I know!' The terrible possibilities of a failure of trust multiplied in his mind.

'In that case,' Saud continued, 'and taking into account the dangers of any duplication of military responsibility, I suggest that you use your connections with the British administration to make sure that the sentence upon Sloan, which I assume will be severe, is not confirmed by the military authorities. This would be seen as a rebuff to Colonel Masterman and to his design in punishing Sloan, and it is possible the Emir would then see him in a more favourable light.'

Peach said swiftly, absently, 'I can't do it. We don't work like that. The administration would never intercede in the workings of a military court.'

'Come, now! A minor court martial, in an out-of-the-way place like Hassan——'

'A properly constituted court, sir—fairly conducted, a part of the judicial system of the country.'

'But, in the circumstances——'

'No, My Lord; that is not possible. I should meet with an absolute refusal to intercede.'

Saud the Fat worked up a small bolt of wind from the depths of his stomach where it seemed to be troubling him. He said, with no change in his composure, 'Mr Peachy, I am wondering if you realize the dangers of our situation. My brother is a man of sudden changes of heart, of loyalty. His disaffection can be a very terrible thing. In our present dispute with Hadraif, and more particularly in the wretched affair of the desert wells, he is vacillating, sensitive and liable to extremes of temper. It is unlikely that Colonel Masterman violated Hadraifi territory; certainly he says that he did not; but while the Emir is angry at the treatment of Sloan he would sooner blame Masterman for an incursion into a neighbouring state than he would blame the Sheikh of Hadraif for changing the position of the frontier post. You understand me: it is of more satisfaction to his mind to find fault with an upright man than with one of unquestionable villainy. That, at least, is my opinion.'

It was Peachy's too; but he could not divine Saud's motive in speaking the apparent truth—at least, not yet, though the outline of an idea was forming in his mind—for the Sheikh would not utter truths from habit or for the sake of a quiet conscience.

'Excellency, I cannot intervene where the court martial is concerned beyond asking for the confirmation of sentence to be given as quickly as possible, which I have already done. British courts are not open to political influence.'

The Sheikh nodded; he did not seem offended. 'I accept the point; it is plainly impossible for you to act. That being so, will you please consider this alternative. You must persuade Colonel Masterman to make a full and unqualified apology to the Emir for his intrusion into Hadraif.'

The Agent did not reply at once. Then he said, 'My Lord, I will accept that you are serious, and I will tell you that I would be reluctant to persuade anyone to apologize for an error of which he was innocent. In his heart, the Ruler must know that the Colonel did not enter Hadraif and cannot require an apology.'

Saud raised his eyebrows, as if surprised by the Agent's naïvety. 'The question of his innocence is hardly the point; the Emir is unlikely to trouble his mind in that respect. He is at present gravely at issue with the Colonel and an apology, were it sufficiently elaborate and inclusive, would be taken as an affirmation of loyalty.'

Peachy hung his head, feeling at once very tired and at odds with the entire Arab nation. 'It would be meaningless, absurd; the abasement of a distinguished officer without cause——'

'Without cause? It would re-establish the Colonel in the Ruler's favour. Surely that is cause enough?'

'I'd rather die than ask him,' the Agent said weakly, hopelessly, seeing the force of Saud's argument. And he was troubled, because as yet he could not see why the Sheikh wanted to repair the rift between the Colonel and the Ruler. What was the advantage for Sheikh Saud? He was suddenly angry, ready to sacrifice the entire Emirate for one assertion of the truth. 'Lord Saud, I won't do it! Such an action would involve us all, not only the Colonel, in an absurd dishonesty.'

Saud pulled a thread from his robe and spoke with the same assurance as before. 'Then I must tell you what will happen, Mr Peachy. The Emir will consider setting up an independent and alternative force within the Emirate.'

Peachy felt sick. It was possible; it was likely; it had the impact of hideous truth.

'You take my point: His Highness will find it necessary to have a mercenary force, perhaps not a large one, to balance the power at the disposal of the British Colonel. His staff has aready been in touch with an agency in Brussels.'

'I can imagine nothing worse for the ultimate safety and improvement of the state.'

'Even so, Mr Peachy.'

'These are terrible people, Excellency—without loyalty, without conscience, without remorse—who will take any side, support any cause for payments in cash. They can always be bought off for a higher price. They are the odious product, the rank obscenity of the Third World.' He was speaking his mind aloud, for no one's sake but his own; he was giving a moral definition in a country that did not care for such things.

Saud was barely listening; he was cleaning his nails with a little pointed blade. 'It is true, as you say, they seldom think correctly.'

The Agent, for no reason he could think of, felt a further cold dismay; he was moved by a deep unconscious instinct he did not examine.

'My Lord, what is correct thought?'

He spoke softly, fearfully, reluctant to draw the sickening conclusion.

What, indeed. Saud did not answer; he had said too much, giving too little attention to the form of his words. Peachy had it now. Behind the petty stratagems of Saud the Fat lay the great blind orthodoxy whose argument was composed of stale platitudes. Correct thought! What could that be but tyranny; and what could follow from it but cruelty and death? What poor hope for humour, mystery and love when the world thought correctly? What would the drunks and whores do then? He's a lousy Marxist, Peachy thought. Why didn't I think of that before?

'I cannot believe, Mr Peachy, that either you or the Colonel would wish to see the introduction of mercenaries into Hassan,' the Sheikh said. 'Nor, of course, would I.'

No, sir, I'm sure you would not, Peachy thought. Now at last he understood Saud's mind and his desire to re-establish the authority of Colonel Masterman. The men of revolution much preferred to deal with the conservative mind, whose workings they could predict, whose reaction to challenge had been described—with the man who was the closely observed opponent of their designs—than to have dealings with the men of shifting loyalty. The mercenaries did not fit into the scheme of revolution; they were a complication, a factor which upset the equation and destroyed the symmetry of the problem. No wonder Saud was dismayed at the thought of a mercenary army in Hassan.

'Sheikh Saud,' said Peachy, too dispirited now to speak other than his exact thought, 'I cannot agree that any slight gain that might come from a dishonest apology could possibly do lasting good. It's as bad to fabricate guilt as it is to fabricate innocence—somewhere, sometime there would be a recompense; and I will not persuade Colonel Masterman to take part in a deceit of that sort. What would it be but a little black farce, without point? I will however tell him of the Emir's displeasure and of your concern. Beyond that I won't go, not even for peace in Hassan.'

He was being reckless and stupid, and it would come to the

same thing in the end, but at least he had not gone along with the foul politics of Saud the Fat.

The Colonel, waiting in his office, hoped they would bring him news of the sentence before luncheon. He listened for the sound of Sloan and his escort crossing the yard to the court-room which would tell him the court had reassembled for sentence. Two sparrows played in the sun-drenched yard below, but there was no other movement. The Colonel felt sorry for Sloan, though he could not condone his offence; it was wretched that a long career—longer than the Colonel's own—should end in shame and indignity; for certainly the court would cashier Sloan, divesting him of his commission and decorations, as a part of their punishment.

A door was opened in the yard below; footsteps in unison crossed the paving stones; the screen door of the court-room opened against the spring and slammed closed after Sloan and the escort passed inside to receive sentence. A minute; another. The Colonel watched from the window. The sparrows in the dust below flew up to the edge of the roof and there shook their feathers into shape. The building creaked in the midday sunlight. The door opened again and Sloan came out, escorted and without his cap. He was marched back to his quarters, his shoulders rounded, his step drifting, his uniform stained with sweat; he seemed no more concerned than he had been earlier in the day; and to Colonel Masterman he looked what he was—an elderly officer, shapeless, dull, discredited. So the court had imprisoned him; it could hardly have done otherwise. It was a very ordinary scene.

A donkey coughed in the animal lines. A fly crawled across the Colonel's desk. There was not the smallest change in the manner of life at Warboys Camp following the trial of Captain Sloan.

Colonel Trafford came up the outside staircase two steps at a time. He was in a robust good humour.

'That's it,' he said. 'Cashiered, six months. No complications. I'm sure the authorities at home will take him off your hands in a day or two; so I should relax, old chap, and forget it.'

'I am grateful,' Masterman said. He could not find his next

words very well. 'It pleases me—if I may say so—that you didn't award the maximum sentence. I wouldn't have wished to see that.'

Trafford was stripping off his medals and loosening his collar. 'He's crazy, of course. Too long in the sun; something like that. He'll get maximum remission, I've no doubt, and a compassionate award of pension in view of his long service. I shouldn't fret about him if I were you.'

'No,' said Masterman. Then, 'An odd fellow. I didn't understand him precisely.'

'Dirty old man,' said Trafford.

'I suppose so,' Colonel Masterman said.

Along the shore six miles from Bir-el-Shama the shells lay on the sands in clouds of white, yellow and rose. No other part of the Arabian coast had such shells; only in the creeks and indentations of the Horn, where the tide carried them from the off-shore beds, did they lie in such profusion of shape and colour. The sea, here in constant small movement, was breaking in a narrow inscription of white, the waves blue, the undersides emerald. Except for a lateen at the horizon, a white triangle resting on its point, the sea was empty. A mosque and minaret, some square white houses, all derelict, and a broken path connected with no other road, made up the whole of the scene.

To put things right in the sheikhdom, to return to decent relationships, the English community had arranged a beach party below the Jelubi Mosque which it was hoped the ruling family would attend. A picnic was preferred to an apology. Lorries from Warboys had brought out tents and coloured sunshades; the Agent had procured a basket of crayfish from the coast of Muscat and cartons of Danish lager from the Agency cold store. As a safeguard, and with a discretion superfluous in an Arab kingdom, Colonel Masterman had placed armed soldiers beyond the dunes and a general purpose machine-gun behind the balustrade of the minaret. The tents and sunshades announced a civilized purpose; a picnic was something which surely the bedouin would enjoy; and in mutual satisfaction the rift over last week's trial would possibly disappear.

Meanwhile, at Warboys, Captain Sloan remained in his quarters awaiting confirmation of sentence.

'I do not care for picnics,' said Mrs Masterman. 'There is so much discomfort. I do not find it possible—neither, I'm sure, do you, Mr Peachy—to squat in the manner of the bedouin, which seems to be necessary at these gatherings.'

'I am sure you will be comfortable in one of these deck-chairs,' said the Agent. 'The servants will adjust the shades.'

At their backs the dunes dissolved into mirage.

'Sand,' said Mrs Masterman. 'Why could not Clive find a place without sand? Never mind, Mr Peachy; you need pay no attention to me.'

'I want to swim,' said Sarita. 'I have my costume on underneath.'

'Not until the Sheikhs have gone, needless to say,' Peachy said.

'I don't see why not.'

'It isn't their way; they might be offended.'

Some distance from the shore the cormorants were feeding. At a shout from the beach they rose into the air, a revolving black cloud, descending on to the shoal again as it drifted further away.

'I think the guards are adequate,' the Colonel said. 'Lovelace, you'd better see that the British Other Ranks have sandwiches. Are those figures our guests? They are a great way off.'

'A mounted hunting party,' said Peachy. 'You can see the falcons rising. I don't think they are coming to the picnic.'

'A disagreeable sport, which I do not care for,' said Mrs Masterman. 'There should be a Society.'

'There may be twenty guests, perhaps more,' the Colonel continued. 'I do not know how far the disaffection has spread. Of course, we will show absolute courtesy and avoid discussion of our recent difficulties.'

'That seems to me the best plan,' said the Agent.

Mrs Masterman said, ignoring her husband's plea for nicety, 'In India there was invariably a handbook describing how such things should be done. It is the type of thing that would be issued by the British government if they had not forgotten our existence here.'

'I expect so,' said the Colonel.

The Sheikhs came on horseback, crossing the horizon at a distance of a mile, descending the apron of a dune in plumes of dust. The horses were magnificent, with necks and tails arched in aristocratic display; they were white and grey and chestnut. The Sheikhs rode bare-backed, their huge sandalled feet hanging close to the ground.

'The Emir is unable to come,' said Abdullah the Wise. 'A disappointment to him; but another engagement has kept him at the palace. He has sent his motor car.'

It was there, at the head of the dune, the splendid white Rolls with the red and gold pennant—not exactly the Emir but his representative, keeping them company; an obligation to the beach party had been accepted, the rebuke was not absolute.

'I have brought a kite,' said Abdullah the Wicked. 'I wish the Agent's young lady to hold it while I run with the string.'

Colonel Masterman bent over his guests, intent upon their comfort. The other officers inclined their shoulders in close attention. 'Lovelace, we'd better offer lemonade to the Emir's driver, and to any of the bodyguard that may be present,' the Colonel said. 'Please see to it. A pity the Emir could not come.'

'He is there,' said Mrs Masterman. 'He is there with the falconers.'

'I really cannot believe it. In that case he could as easily have come to the party.'

'They are too distant to be certain,' said Peachy.

'Look, look, look at Sheikh Abdullah's kite!' Sarita said.

In the first hour the party was filled with haphazard movement. Then the servants spread the tables with crayfish tails in mayonnaise, green salad and charcuterie, but these pleased only Saud the Fat, who alone among the sheikhs had enjoyed a European education. 'You have Chablis?' he asked. 'Ah, in this small tent, where one may fill one's glass concealed from the critical gaze of Allah. Very thoughtful of you, my dear Colonel.'

They laughed, sitting under the sunshades at the edge of the sea.

'Afterwards we have races,' said Abdullah the Wicked.

Abdullah the Wise had the long sad face of profound scholarship and the reputation for ignorance. His face gave the impression he would at any minute utter an unmistakable truth; in fact he was usually wrong. The Emir employed him on minor errands because, so they said, he was too stupid to be dangerous, and as his mind could not hold more than one idea at a time he was unlikely to be engaged in double purposes. The pursuit of harlots was his recreation and his only known weakness. He said now, gravely, 'His Highness joined a hunting party soon after daybreak, but he has returned to the palace for his engagement.'

Mrs Masterman said, 'He is riding with the falconers. He is still in the desert.'

'I quite understand,' said the Colonel. 'A pity he was unable to be here.'

The silver and glass made darts of light which played on the insides of the sunshades. It became very hot. It was not really a nice place for a pinic. Behind them, where the falconers rode, the sun struck the desert with a terrible impact.

In a little while, in the watery mirage, they could see strange loose-limbed creatures moving towards them. At first they seemed to be ragged old men of great height who shambled with a sailor's gait across the sands; they were a crazy satire upon living creatures, conceived in sarcasm, finished in disgust, set down as the only proper inhabitants of a continent without grace. They moved at a constant pace towards the party, piercing the mirage, taking firm shape.

'Ah, the camels,' said Abdullah the Wicked. 'I had them sent from the royal stables. They will run races after lunch for our enjoyment.'

'Sheikh Abdullah is a wonderful person to have at a party,' said Sarita.

Peachy nodded. Abdullah was the most truly amiable of the Sheikhs, and without political ambition. The camels came to an untidy halt and a groom held them in a fan formation while the guests finished their lunch.

'I make a book,' said Abdullah the Wicked. 'I have very much money in bags.'

'I do not think that is a very nice idea,' said Mrs Masterman, 'not at a picnic.'

'We make bets. No one shall lose. I have enough money for everyone to win.'

Yes, Abdullah was moved by his goodness of heart, not by a desire to take the edge off the Ruler's disfavour. Even so, the Agent did not like to see him taking such risks. The money, in Gladstone bags, was lifted on to a table by a court servant.

Half an hour later the riders took the camels to a starting-point a mile down the shore, where in the mirage they walked upon long legs.

'Excellency, please tell me in which direction the camels are racing,' Mrs Masterman said.

'Why, in this direction, my lady.'

'Where then is the finishing point?'

'Here by your chair,' said the Sheikh delightedly.

'Are they coming? I cannot see them.'

'I think they are coming,' the Colonel said.

'It is disquieting. Mr Peachy, I hope you will tell me which of the camels is leading the race,' Mrs Masterman said earnestly.

'I ride in the next race. We have races until nightfall,' Abdullah said. 'Look, they have started, you can see the dust rising!'

'I think the party is successful,' Colonel Masterman said quietly to the Agent. 'It was a pleasant thought, and con-ciliatory, for Sheikh Abdullah to have arranged camel racing, even though it does not appear to be well managed. Can you see what is happening? I do not have my binoculars.'

'One camel has run into the sea, I think; the others are concealed by the dunes.'

'I cannot believe they will complete the course; but it was a friendly gesture, which I appreciate. Ah, Captain Lovelace is offering our guests coffee while they are waiting; a sensible idea.'

The stewards took coffee between the tables, and the sun caught the silver and gleamed in the white porcelain.

'These are very pretty cups,' said Mrs Masterman. 'I think the pattern derives from Limoges, but I cannot be sure. The service is the one thing of value introduced into the Mess by my predecessor; otherwise her taste was hardly to be admired.'

'Sheikh Saud will take brandy,' the Colonel said.

'I do not think the camels will be here for a long time yet,' said Abdullah the Wise reflectively.

'I am sure they will not,' said the Colonel. 'Well....'

Mrs Masterman said, 'Mr Peachy, if that camel is coming

in this direction, kindly stop it.'

'I do not see how I can, Mrs Masterman.'

'You can wave your arms, or something similar.'

'Why does it run so oddly,' Sarita asked, 'from side to side?'

'Mr Peachy, I rely on you to do something,' Mrs Masterman said.

'I remember similar races in the north of India,' said the Colonel. 'It was always the most ungainly animal that had the greatest speed.'

'Mr Peachy, at *once.*'

'A tremendous race!' cried Abdullah, as the camel vanished behind them. Nothing could undo his good humour, not even a social disaster of a unique kind. 'Everybody has won! There are fifty dinars for each lady, twenty-five for each gentleman.'

'An unfortunate finish,' said the Colonel. 'I will help you, my dear.'

'I regret that I was unable to do anything,' said Peachy stupidly.

Towards evening, when the sun weakened, they walked for a time along the beach until the minaret of the Jelubi Mosque was as thin as a pencil and the sunshades a patch of absurd vermilion against the sand—picking up shells, competing in colour, size and complexity, saying nothing about Sloan. Mrs Masterman accompanied them in a Land-Rover.

'I do not know why we pick up shells,' said Abdullah the Wicked moodily. 'I do not care for shells. Look, a lemonade bottle, clouded by the sea! It is more beautiful than the shells.'

'The beach is unique for its shells,' said Peachy.

'Sand, Mr Peachy, and more sand. Arabs have no liking for sand.'

'The falconers are still riding,' said the Colonel, 'over there towards the sunset.'

'A foolish occupation, which I do not care for,' said Abdullah. 'The peregrines have a disagreeable temperament.'

'My brother the Emir is a keen falconer,' said Abdullah the Wise objectively; 'that is to say, when he has no other engagements to keep him at the palace.'

'They have been riding all day, since early morning,' said

the Colonel. 'Falconry is a sport I do not understand, although I believe it to have an ancient fascination for the royalty of the Middle East. I cannot think what game they can have found in that part of the desert.'

'Rats,' said Abdullah the Wicked; 'sometimes foxes.'

'They have never gone away. I have seen them there against the white rock and in the neighbouring dunes.'

'A ludicrous pursuit, meaning nothing.'

At the end of the beach, where the sands were intersected by an inlet, they turned and gathered round the Land-Rover. The sunset suffused the sky with amber, the sands turned to coral. Sarita and the Sheikhs wandered down to the edge of the water to throw stones.

'I am certain the party will have done some good,' Colonel Masterman said reflectively, 'although there were things I would have wished otherwise. I cannot say if the Emir's engagement was a diplomatic one. At any rate, it is a pity he was not here.'

'He was here—he was here in the sands,' said Mrs Masterman with bleak certainty.

'I do not think so; I cannot be sure.'

'That was the royal hunting party, and they were watching us. It was his humour.'

Peachy said, 'Certainly the minor Sheikhs had a good time, and their goodwill is important to us. Just look at them throwing stones into the sea!'

Sheikh Saud and the two Abdullahs were playing ducks and drakes with Sarita at the edge of the water. They looked very happy. Their cries of pleasure carried a fair distance along the shore and back into the desert. At the site of the beach party, a mile away, the orderlies were taking down the tents and sunshades and loading them into three-ton lorries. Clearly nothing had been lost by the picnic, and if the gain was slight, and lasted only so long as their voices continued, none the less it was an achievement of a kind.

12

The routine inspection, conducted by officers of every service and in every unit overseas, followed a familiar pattern. The inspecting officer, carrying his cane under one arm, folding his hands behind his back, keeping his eye alert and his pace brisk, was ushered by the senior non-commissioned officer through the guardroom, the detention cell, the armoury and fire section—through the soldiers' lines, their ablutions, kitchen and dining hall: it was a long hard walk during which he must keep his mind awake, answer each question, complaint or excuse, allow his instinct to tell him which cupboard they hoped he wouldn't open, which locker top was thick in dust, which lavatory was without tissue. The experienced officer could expose any disorder. Asia would never submit to discipline; these blankets, however, could be properly folded. Outside, on every hand, the world was in disarray, indisciplines raged like violent seas, but within these white walls, within this investing wire, they had washed the paintwork and stood the beds in line.

Colonel Clive Masterman, DSO, formerly of a good county regiment, was one of the last British officers to conduct routine inspections in the theatre east of Suez. He was not an ideal inspecting officer. He did not like to disturb people too deeply, and therefore he did not probe into corners with the thoroughness shown by some of his subordinates. The NCOs preferred to be inspected by the Colonel than by the company commanders. This morning at eight o'clock precisely the inspecting party left Headquarters and crossed the road towards the guardroom and armoury. The squat buildings, the acacia and palm trees lining the road, the vehicles and donkey carts, were hung with a thin brown dust which blew off the desert and gave Warboys its pervasive colour. The camp did not look smart; the drab hand of Arabia had undone every attempt at formal discipline; the paintwork was blistered, the woodwork was bleached and bent by the sun.

The Colonel was accompanied by the Adjutant and by the senior British and native NCOs; the other officers would be standing by at their places of responsibility, waiting to receive him. The Colonel passed from the glare of the sun into the cool interior of the guardroom. He was received by the guard commander. He glanced into the fire buckets. The water was not clean; he directed that it should be changed. His eyes made a quick traverse of the windows and walls and he noticed—without giving it close attention—that the glass was cloudy and the whitewash wearing thin. He gave orders that the windows should be cleaned and the walls repainted. He walked quickly into the sunlight and covered the twenty yards to the armoury while the rest of the inspecting party, who could not match his pace, trailed in poor formation behind him.

The job bored him: he kept a sharp pace to complete his inspection in the shortest time.

In the armoury, behind the barred and shuttered windows, the small arms were neatly racked. He took up a rifle and opened the bolt: clean enough. He complimented the armourers and went back into the sunlight. He was beginning to sweat.

The white kerbstones, the sign boards, the flagstaff—his eye flowed over them critically. Nothing on earth would make Warboys other than a dowdy camp. He crossed the square to the native lines and approached a hut in the centre of the row, and the soldiers sitting under the veranda roof rose stiffly to attention. As it happened, Colonel Masterman always entered the same hut when he made his random choice and the other huts he never inspected. He was not himself aware of it; but the soldiers knew.

The ablutions, which smelled of stale soap; the kitchen, where the steam had mildewed the walls; the Asian latrines. . . .

'Not too bad,' the Colonel said to Lovelace. He never said anything else. 'Please pay more attention to the fire appliances. The rest was satisfactory.'

He paused before dismissing the party; his inspection was not complete.

'I shall visit the prisoner by myself,' he said. 'You may fall out.'

The others saluted and went away, and the Colonel walked slowly across to the officers' quarters. This was not a duty he cared for. He had never liked Sloan, he had felt only awkward in his presence; and now that Sloan was under sentence and awaiting removal to prison the Colonel's awkwardness had turned to embarrassment. However, he could not avoid the duty, and accordingly he entered the officers' quarters, climbed the stairway to the balcony and knocked upon Sloan's door.

He waited for Sloan to reply. Hearing no answer, he knocked again, but still there was no sound from inside the room. His instinct told him to go away, leaving Sloan to whatever peace he had found, but he remembered he was making a routine inspection and that a word with the prisoner was expected of him.

He opened the door and went into the narrow bedroom. He smelt the stale smells of bachelorhood. Sloan was asleep in the chair, his head on his chest, his hands brushing the floor; his trousers were unbuttoned and his stomach protruded into the fly; his face was grey, the lips parted and quivering with each short breath, the cheeks and eyelids sagging and in the ugly movements of sleep. The Colonel was nonplussed at this sight of the man he had ruined and he felt as if some violence of his own had brought Sloan to this end. The room contained no picture or memento which might have affirmed a friendship or marked some part of his long service. Sloan was done for, and now there seemed to be as little in his past as there was likely to be in his future.

The Colonel cleared his throat. 'Sloan, are you all right?'

The former captain opened his eyes and gazed at his commanding officer without seeing him.

'Is there anything you want? Anything I can do to help you?'

Sloan's mind, never alert, had been slowed by his confinement, and he did not understand the question. Then he scrambled to his feet and stood at attention, holding his trousers. 'I beg your pardon, sir. I did not hear you come in.'

He seemed glad to welcome to his quarters the man who had ordered his trial, and Masterman was discomforted and uncertain what to say. 'You are comfortable, old chap? I trust your bearer is continuing to wait on you.'

'Oh yes; it's all right; I'm quite happy.'

This might have been true, as he did not seem distressed.

'You have books?'

'No, sir. I don't read books.'

'Anything to pass the time?'

'It isn't necessary.'

The Colonel said guardedly, 'I imagine the confirmation of your sentence will be received in a few days' time, and that you will be away from here soon after that. It shouldn't be too long.'

'I understand.'

'In the meantime, in view of the hot weather, you may ask your servant to bring you beer if you wish. I am happy to relax the regulations in that respect.'

'Thank you, sir.' He might have been grateful; certainly he smiled remotely.

'The duty officer will call upon you. We have not, of course, a chaplain, but if it would be any consolation I will ask the clergyman at Faleh-la to come across and see you. I don't know his denomination, I'm afraid.'

'It doesn't matter. I don't want to see him.'

'You cannot be sure, Captain. It might be of help.'

'I don't need help.'

Masterman tended to believe him; for a man who lived without books or ornament, and who wanted no one, must be self-sufficient to an unusual degree.

'I see—well, it's for you to decide. There's nothing, then, that I can do?'

Sloan turned to the window and it was a moment before he spoke. 'The man Hamid. He has returned to barracks?'

'He has not.'

'I had thought he would return. I am sorry.'

'Why did you suppose he would come back, Captain?'

Sloan did not answer and the Colonel felt unable to repeat the question.

Sloan said, 'When you spoke to him in the desert, did he say he would come back?'

'He did not.'

'I don't understand it. He's a good soldier.'

Masterman tried not to show his anger. 'In the circumstances, I do not expect Hamid to rejoin the unit.'

The prisoner glanced at his commanding officer as if he had expressed a strange opinion. 'I think he will come back. It would be unlike him to desert the Levy. It would only be excusable if he were dead.'

The Colonel did not intend to be drawn into a discussion of Hamid's disappearance or its consequences, but he was moved to say, 'Captain, I don't pretend to know what drove you to punish Hamid and to bring so much trouble on the unit. It is beyond my comprehension. But I do assure you Hamid will not return, and that even if he did his long absence, and his other actions, would make it impossible for me to retain him in the Levy.'

'Of course,' Sloan said. 'That isn't the point.'

'I must confess, Captain, that I find the point hard to distinguish.' He felt a need to understand what had happened. 'If there is something you wish to tell me—something I don't know—then I am prepared to listen; but naturally I should find it hard to accept any argument opposed to fundamental discipline, in which I believe. Well... ?'

He thought Sloan might be persuaded to speak; he seemed to be putting words together in his head, and he was smiling, as if his ideas were compelling and likely to find acceptance; but then, when the words would not come, his face clouded and he shook his head. 'It was necessary; that was all.'

'I would like to understand, Sloan. At present I do not understand.'

The former captain smiled; it might have been in patronage, but he made no attempt to explain. At length he said, 'I expect you will find it difficult to understand, sir.'

'But it has meaning for you, as you have sacrificed your career for this purpose.'

Sloan shrugged. 'My career? It was not an important thing. I was a captain of the Ordnance.'

'No one wishes the indignity of court martial and imprisonment.'

'No.'

'Then why, man, did you leave yourself open to these consequences? You were familiar with service discipline. No commanding officer could have overlooked what you did.'

Sloan looked up sharply, it might have been in apology. 'I accept what you did, sir. You couldn't have done anything else.'

The reflex of the long-serving soldier, which obliged him to agree with his commanding officer, was still strong in the former Captain Sloan; but Masterman had the impression that nevertheless the prisoner bore him no ill-will; and he was reminded of the bond of fellowship, almost of affection, which so often joined the defaulter with the officer who punished him. However, the Colonel could not discuss his own actions with a discredited officer and he did not continue that line of thought.

They were still standing in the centre of the room, Sloan holding his trousers. The Colonel could not sit down while he was conducting his inspection of the unit.

The Colonel was surprised when Sloan spoke sharply.

'It doesn't matter, you know. What happens to me doesn't *matter.*'

'Of course it does; there are your friends, your family.'

The former soldier raised his head an inch, it might have been in proud denial of such relationships.

'And if nothing else there is the good name of the Levy to be considered.'

At that, Sloan was disconcerted, and he seemed to be thinking of the possibility for the first time. 'Do you think so, sir? Do you think I can have done harm to the soldiers?' He looked at the Colonel anxiously, seeking a better opinion than his own.

'I must believe your action has done the unit some harm.'

'I see. I'm sorry.'

Masterman concealed his surprise that Sloan should apologize for something that should have been obvious to him; and he was aware, again, that Sloan's mind followed a course different from his own, one hidden from him, and he blamed himself for his failure to understand an officer under his command. He said, 'Frankly, I am at a loss. We are both regular soldiers. Each of us has spent a lifetime in the service. We have conformed to the same disciplines. Therefore it is strange to me that we should be so far apart in our conceptions of duty. It's this place, isn't it? It's Hassan that has affected you?'

He knew Sloan wanted to say something. He waited patiently as the prisoner's lip tried sentences without speaking them. He needed an answer, and he knew he must learn the truth now or lose it for ever. Sloan was trying to tell him, to put the matter before his commanding officer, but his ideas were strange compulsions that words would not describe.

He said finally, 'It's different here.'

'I am aware of it, Sloan.'

The former captain had made his best effort; he had tried to explain himself as his duty required, and he had failed. The Colonel had remained attentive, but now he raised his shoulders in helplessness, regretting his inability to find common ground with Sloan.

'I'm sorry, but I cannot understand you.' Then, for Sloan's comfort and to conclude the interview, 'I don't think you'll be detained too long at Warboys. You'll be away soon.'

Sloan did not seem to care one way or the other. He had fallen back into the lethargy of imprisonment. 'Don't worry about me, sir. There's no point now.'

Masterman paused, looking at his feet, wondering if there was any meaning in the last remark.

He took his leave of Sloan, who came roughly to attention without releasing his grip upon his trousers.

Strange fellow, the Colonel thought, as he went down the stairs outside. I'll never know the truth of it.

He walked slowly back to his headquarters, his inspection completed.

If there was unrest in the Levy at the imprisonment of Captain Sloan, the Colonel did not notice it. Certainly the men had disliked the trial and had said so to their NCOs, but Masterman was convinced the needs of discipline had been served and that in time the soldiers would benefit. He wanted to see the last of Sloan; now he belonged properly to a prison in England with the nameless people who had fallen from grace. He called Peachy, reporting the calmness of the Levy and his belief that the affair would pass over without difficulty. The soldiers' dissatisfaction had not taken tangible form, he said: there had been some untidiness on parade that morning, some show of impatience which the officers could not correct, but the long-term effect would be beneficial, he felt sure.

The Levy continued its normal life. The guard changed; the evening muster and roll took place without incident.

At dusk the Colonel took a gin and tonic on to the roof of his quarter where he might enjoy the cooler air. The outlines of the camp dissolved in nightfall; the face of the desert shone with an amber glow as if it kept some part of the day's fierce heat.

Masterman and his wife seated themselves at the edge of the roof where they could overlook the camp and the desert. The Colonel was happier than he had been for some time. Things were better than he had hoped. He recalled earlier years in the theatre east of Suez where he had always been most happy. 'Dorothy, my love, it's strange in the East, and it's a terrible place in many ways, but it grows on you in time. Look at the desert in the evening light! Have you seen such a thing elsewhere? I have not; I cannot like Europe; I have been too long in the East to have eyes for anything else. I do not want to leave here yet.'

He left it at that, and Mrs Masterman had nothing to add. He kept his eyes on the receding desert while his ear remained alert to the sounds inside the camp: he heard the crash of mess tins in the Asian kitchen, the patter of a donkey drawing a refuse cart, the swell of vulgar music from the other ranks' canteen: this was the stuff of overseas service, and he wanted no more than to sit here with the night-scented air blowing off the desert, with the glass between his fingers, with nothing between himself and the vast, featureless landscape.

Down at the main gate the guard was being checked; the sentries returned the call from every corner of the wire.

Like many serving officers Colonel Masterman was frightened of retirement. He couldn't think what he would do in England; there, in the rains, in the dull society of English people, he would decay. It was only in the beautiful and maddening countries of Asia that he felt alive. He knew that his manner of life could not continue. With the withdrawal of the regiments from Arabia, he was the last senior officer in the region, and this style of service would not be repeated. His own job would be over very soon.

He might have slept for a moment. His wife was speaking now, breaking into his mind.

'Of course, Clive, we shall have to leave here soon. You must be prepared for it. All this is over, as anyone can tell.'

He was irritated; he couldn't say why, because he shared the opinion. 'I do not see how you can know that. There are difficulties, of course, but we shall overcome them. I don't see why we can't stay here indefinitely.'

'You are avoiding the truth. There is nothing left for us here.'

It might be so, but for the moment the desert was still there; he could smell it and feel its warmth; his service continued through the long minutes. 'We have still a job to do,' he said. He did not know if he was pleading with her or affirming his own belief.

'We are already in the past,' said Mrs Masterman. 'The matter is not in doubt.'

'How can you be sure?'

Her lips were held firmly together; she had given her opinion and did not seem to care if he accepted it or not.

'This is my life. I do not know another one,' the Colonel said.

He rested his chin in his hands, and a night bird called from the acacia tree. A second passed; another.

A step upon the outside stair, and the duty officer, Captain Barrie, came on to the roof.

'Colonel, you must come with me, at once!'

'I see,' said Masterman. 'It is bad news, is it not? It is the prisoner?'

He did not know why he said that; he had no reason to suppose things were amiss with Sloan.

Barrie nodded. 'I have sent for the medical officer. It can only have been a few minutes ago. I had called on him, as you directed.'

Colonel Masterman was a professional officer who never allowed his composure to slip. He rose from his chair, begged his wife's leave, and went with Captain Barrie down the staircase and towards the officers' quarters. He wasted no time in questioning the duty officer. His mind was empty but for the job in hand; he must inform himself of what had happened and issue his instructions. He was calm, swift and effective. He ran up the staircase to the balcony and went straight to Sloan's door.

Inside the room the scene was as his mind had built it. Sloan lay in his chair, much as he had lain that morning when the Colonel made his inspection, but now his chest was sticky with blood and his head inclined at an absurd angle. His throat hung open where the blade had passed. The flies which entered at the window were already settling on the wound.

'Poor devil,' the Colonel said. 'I hadn't thought it likely. He seemed quite happy earlier in the day.'

The former Captain Sloan, with the same decisiveness in punishment he had shown in his treatment of Hamid, had not waited for the confirmation of his sentence but had devised his own penalty—the traditional penalty for error.

'I wonder why he did it?' the Colonel asked softly. 'It wasn't necessary, was it? I suspect it was just this place.'

He could do nothing but tidy up. The decision had been made by another mind than his and it was firm enough. The terrible imperatives of Arabia were not amenable to his command but were rebel forces, clothed in violent colours, given to fierce loyalties and unalterable punishments. He could not think what would happen next.

13

The full moon, riding above the Gulf, inscribing in outline the town of Bir-el-Shama but giving it no depth, cast a multitude of fine shadows which moved slowly as the face crossed from the water to the sand. At some moment in this traverse of the moon, Captain Sloan had died, the blade falling from his hand. In the dunes the shadows were soft and merged one into another. The desert had lost its size; it had become small and intimate and without terror. Nocturnal animals, the mouse, the bat, the jerboa, passed noiselessly between features they alone recognized. There was a remission, a reconciliation, a blurring of intention. The meaning of each small movement was lost as soon as it was made. Things that happened seconds ago were as remote as pre-history.

Colonel Masterman, firm in disorder, silenced the frightened voices and went to his headquarters to signal news of the incident to his administrative formation in the United Kingdom. He did not let himself think of the consequences that might follow from Sloan's action; for the time being he was simply a soldier reporting a casualty, and he forbade his officers to discuss the matter with the men. But in the native lines they had already heard of the death of Sloan, and though the news travelled slowly at first, inhibited by the darkness, it was not long before it reached the guards on the inside of the wire.

At a wadi where they had hoped to find water but which in fact was dry, where the moon lightly sketched the palms and sea almonds, Charles Peachy and his step-daughter lay on the still warm rocks in ignorance of what had happened. There being no water, they were, as Peachy put it, 'moon bathing'.

They had not spoken for a time. They were happy, wanting only what they had, adrift from the problems of Hassan, enjoying the silence of the desert which magnified each breath.

Peachy said then, 'You ought to go from here.'

'I won't.'

'It isn't safe. It's coming to pieces, and the Colonel won't hold things together.'

'I won't leave you. I don't care about the rest.'

She was wise by night; only in the daylight was she perverse. The rocks they lay on were swimming in space.

'The Colonel admires you, I think,' Peachy said.

'It isn't me. It's somebody like me.'

'He won't do anything about it.'

'He doesn't even know it.'

'I suppose not. It's a pity he cashiered Sloan.'

They lapsed into silence, forgetting about Sloan.

Across the fringe of the desert, on the other side of Bir-el-Shama, Saud the Fat took brandy in his elegant white house. Though his ear was the most alert in the sheikhdom, he had not yet heard that Sloan lay dead. He rolled the brandy in the glass and held it to his nostrils. His visitor, whom he did not care for, teetered from one foot to the other—a dull, parsonical, cringing fellow, a member of the Orthodoxy he was obliged to cultivate.

'For heaven's sake sit down, Zamil, or stop fidgeting. What is it you want? Books? Well, there are plenty of those.'

For all his mastery of the doctrine, Zamil could not yet sit down in the presence of a member of the royal house. 'I have enlarged my understanding of the first principles,' he said, making an obeisance. 'I am instructed in the fundamental equalities.'

'Oh—quite,' said the Sheikh, who didn't really believe in them. 'Take any books you require.'

He cupped his hands to the brandy glass, ignoring Zamil. The imprisonment of Sloan, and the political disadvantages that might accrue from his martyrdom, had almost slipped from his mind.

'The Agent and his daughter have gone bathing in a wadi,' Zamil reported, as if any intelligence were better than none. For good measure, he added, 'It is dry, I am told.'

But Saud the Fat paid no attention. Instead he wondered what the Colonel was doing.

So far no messenger had crossed the moonlit desert outside his house.

At the palace, though courtesans and informers passed in and out—and each was skilled in intelligence as a matter of professional obligation—they had not yet heard that Sloan lay dead in his chair. On the roof Abdullah the Wicked shot at the bats as they dodged between the minarets. He caught the star and crescent surmounting the Emir's private mosque with a resounding bull's-eye. Once, when no better target appeared, he discharged his weapon at the face of the moon. In a chamber below Abdullah the Wise considered, with all the force of a nature deeply engaged, which of the available harlots was likely to prove the most comfortable and obliging in the moonlit hours, a subject that could not be treated lightly. He paid no attention when a riddled bat fell upon the window-sill outside.

The Emir walked through the corridors unable to sleep, and the men of the bodyguard, forbidden rest, kept pace from shadow to shadow. The banging on the roof they had already identified. The Emir was in a mood of despondency edged with fear which had always been his temper when his rule was ignored. The imprisonment of Sloan meant nothing to him—any more than did the scourging of Hamid—but the cashiering of a soldier, the stripping from him of his warrior's clothing, was something he understood. It was the supreme insult, the final indignity, and he could not understand why Colonel Masterman should have ordered such a punishment. He was puzzled, dismayed, ready to use the small devices of a sheikh's displeasure but withholding as yet the cold rage to which his nature was given when his eye made out an unmistakable enemy.

At Warboys Camp, a little before midnight, a sentry whispered the news across the wire. Captain Sloan lay dead in his chair, and his throat was cut.

The rocks by the dry wadi were cooler now; the moon hung centrally in the sky. Sarita rested upon her arm, gazing at her father. The moon spread an innocence around them in which it didn't matter what she did.

'You should go,' he said, 'while there is still just time.'

'There is still time.'

'Time still,' he said.

On the far side of the wadi a figure grew between the rocks. They could see the white skull cap and the robe but not the face.

'Who is it?' asked the Agent, alarmed.

'It is I, master.'

'What do you want, Ali Kadir?'

'To make known to you the death of Captain Sloan, by his own hand, an hour ago.'

'It is true?'

'Aye, master.'

Sloan dead: the dangers multiplied at a stroke: his fear, his love had now a savage emphasis.

'I can't think of it now,' he said, pressing his cheek against the back of the girl's hand. 'Not now.'

The messengers ran bare-footed in the desert, throwing short, hectic shadows on the moonlit sand.

'What?' said Saud the Fat, his glass now dry. 'Dead, you say? Dear me, that puts an altogether different shape upon it!'

'Captain Sloan dead?' Zamil could only repeat the words while his mind slowly adapted to the new idea. 'Dead?'

'Yes, *dead*,' said Saud irritably; 'at the hands of Colonel Masterman, of course.'

'But——'

'But, nothing! That is the way it will appear to His Highness the Emir. It is very inconvenient.'

'I had not considered the possibility.'

'Oh, shut up!'

At the palace they were making ready for bed at last. To conclude his practice, Abdullah the Wicked fired his shot-gun into a tank of tropical fish, and the guppies leapt on the brushed silk carpet. In a distant corridor Abdullah the Wise led by the hand a Sudanese princess with long slim legs and a brow of polished ebony. Word spread through the palace from the kitchen that Captain Sloan had taken a blade to his throat. When he heard the news, Abdullah the Wicked broke the gun and removed the spent cartridges reflectively; he drew his mouth into a little circle, considering the matter; then he whistled. Abdullah the Wise was informed at his bedroom door, but the matter had not strength enough to cut through his present train of thought and he waved the messenger aside.

The Chamberlain told the Emir: Sloan lay dead in a widening circle of blood at Warboys Camp. The Emir paused in his perambulation, his mind becoming still, fixed on a single notion: at last he was relieved from doubt, with a clear picture of his enemy. He continued his walk without speaking, and the bodyguard resumed their surveillance of him, moving from one shadow to the next.

Peachy stared at the livid moon, knowing that each second was an indulgence that would soon be withdrawn. The girl was quiet, waiting for him to speak, to tell her they must go.

'Not yet,' he said. 'We won't go yet.'

But she rose beside him, silently, offering her hand; and he clambered upright and went with her away from the wadi, where only the thin trees marked where they had lain, and towards the Land-Rover, slipping in the sand.

'Wait. . . .'

The voice, speaking Arabic, was distant but clear in the soundless desert. Peachy stopped dead in his tracks. A voice in the desert was no strange thing but nonetheless he was frightened.

'What is it?' he asked.

'Had the stream no water?'

'None. Who are you?'

'A soldier.'

'Then you should be in barracks.'

They heard his laughter and an obscenity used in the soldiers' lines.

'Tell me, my master, where is Captain Sloan?'

'At Warboys.'

'Aye, so—at Warboys. Is his eye alert, is his tongue keen? Does his breath play upon his lips?'

Peachy said strongly, 'Hamid, come here to me! The desert will kill you. The Colonel will be lenient, I am sure.'

'Yours is not the voice to tell me such things, Lord Agent.'

'The Colonel has already ordered you home.'

'Nor his.'

'Whose, then?'

The soldier laughed again and said something that Peachy did not catch.

'What was that?'

'A matter of no account.'

'Yet of concern to me.'

'Tell Captain Sloan I will come when he commands me.'

'I cannot do that, Hamid.'

'Nor *can* you, master. He would not hear.'

As a last appeal would be useless, Peachy said nothing more.

The voice said, 'Love thyself. Love thy daughter. I will not come in.'

They stood in the sand waiting but the soldier did not speak again. After a while they moved on, slowly, towards where the Land-Rover made a patch of white in the desert.

By this time there was hardly a soul in Bir-el-Shama and the investing desert who did not know that Captain Sloan was dead.

'What does it mean?' Sarita asked.

'It depends on the Emir,' said Peachy.

14

Colonel Masterman called a conference of his officers at ten o'clock next morning. Of the four companies of native soldiers, one had not attended the first working parade, another was under strength, the third had not carried arms. The fourth company was at normal strength but restless and inattentive. The soldiers had not tried to conceal the absences; they had simply left a blank file wherever a man was missing. The officers and NCOs of the absent company took up their positions on the parade ground as if the company were behind them. During the parade the Colonel paid no attention to the astonishing indiscipline, and when he made his inspection he simply walked past the vacant files as if nothing was wrong.

When the officers were seated in his office, he said, 'Gentlemen, I will not hide my concern from you. There are no supporting British troops; the nearest reinforcements—even supposing political permission for their use was given—are in the United Kingdom, and I understand it will not be possible for a frigate to reach us for at least five days. Neither can I be certain of the support I may receive from the Ruler in re-establishing order within the Levy. Not a happy position, you will agree. However, to count our advantages, I am glad to note that all the native NCOs and more than half the Levy are loyal, or partially loyal, and when you consider the degree of intimidation that must have taken place it says much for their determination. I also understand from my conversation with the Political Agent this morning that there are forces within the Emirate, distinct from those influenced by the Ruler, that hope to see my authority restored.'

He paused. He knew the anxiety, greater than any other, that a commander feels when defied by his own soldiers. When soldiers disregarded their commander they must be moved by a rival affection of greater strength, and his fear was increased because he could not understand why this should be. What had there been in Sloan but the dull features of a long-serving captain of the Ordnance?

He cleared his throat. 'Of course, there may be motives—political motives, the origin of which is unknown to us—behind the present unrest. Certainly the soldiers had an affection for Sloan, though I find it hard to guess why; but there must be another, a more positive reason for their disaffection with me and those who serve me, and we must try to discover what this is.'

Major Tillotson, who had been restive during the Colonel's introduction, said now with a candour that was barely civil, 'I think it was just Sloan. I don't think there was anything else.'

'I cannot agree, Arthur. That wouldn't make sense.'

'Not to us, Colonel, perhaps; but to the soldiers it might.'

'Well, I have given my opinion and I will stick to it until somebody shows me it is wrong. My purpose in calling this conference is of course to decide our next action.'

In the last hours he had given much thought to this problem, drawing on his long experience of locally enlisted forces. His instinct told him to arrest the rebellious soldiers and to lock them away until their cases could be heard, but he knew it would not be possible. Where would he detain, say, two hundred soldiers, and how could they be guarded? His mind returned to the idea that devious forces were trying to destroy his command. Tired of waiting for his judgement, the officers were beginning to talk between themselves, so he continued at once, 'Clearly—if this is possible—we must identify and arrest the ringleaders.'

'Of course,' said Lovelace, his stupid face coming suddenly to life.

'Are there any?' Tillotson asked. 'It was a demonstration of sympathy for Sloan, not an organized rebellion.'

'——as I was saying, we must catch the principal culprits. (Two opinions are possible here, Arthur: I cannot believe that an entire company can miss a parade unless someone has used powerful persuasion.) In this matter I propose to use the native NCOs as sources of information and then a small force of loyal troops to effect the arrests. Once we have the ringleaders inside—I can't believe there are more than a dozen of them—I think the rest will fall into line.'

A simple solution, a soldier's solution, based on the notion that there was always a power whose aim was opposed to one's own: find the enemy, isolate him, destroy him. The Colonel waited for the approval of his officers.

Tillotson said, without force but with complete self-confidence, 'It will be effective only if there are enemies to arrest; not otherwise.'

'They are there, Arthur. I know they are there!'

'Then what is their aim?'

'Who can say, in a place like this?' Their motives belonged in the world of ugly politics—a place understood by others, not by him. 'There are forces, of course, that would welcome our ineffectiveness—alien, evilly-minded people, controlled from abroad—and it's likely they have picked upon Sloan's unhappy end as a means of breaking down our discipline.'

'But who are they, Colonel? What do they wish as an alternative to the present system?'

'It is not for me to judge. This part of the world is riddled with interests contrary to our own. There are Maoists, Trotskyists, Pan-Arabian Leftists—any number of them, all intent upon removing Western influence as quickly as possible, leaving the field clear for their own operations.'

'We have always known there were agents within the Levy,' said Lovelace. 'It would be surprising if there weren't.'

Masterman said, 'And I know very well that the Leftist element in the state and elsewhere would like nothing better than to see my authority destroyed. They do not like the presence of an effective, disciplined force in the Emirate; they would much prefer it if we were dispersed.'

Major Graves and Major Kirkbride, the junior company commanders, nodded their agreement; but neither would have dared to contradict his commanding officer in any case.

'Well, it's for you to say, Colonel,' Tillotson said, in the manner of the man who has issued his last warning. 'But I don't think we should overlook the possibility that the present indiscipline arises only from native sentiment. These people are crazy; they swing this way and that, like birds on the wing, without motive or final direction. We should not look for hard-line opportunists in a situation which is emotional in origin. The main danger—so it seems to me—is that, through our difficulties with the men, we will lose still further the confidence of the Ruler, and that he may be inclined to import professional gunmen as an extra safeguard.'

The Colonel said firmly, 'I suggest that you are looking too far ahead, and too speculatively. As soldiers we should confine ourselves to verifiable fact. I propose to act in the way I have described; and I will accordingly be grateful if the company commanders will now speak to their NCOs with a view to identifying the trouble-makers. We will then arrange their arrest. After that, I will call a parade of the entire Levy and speak to the men myself.'

It seemed a workable plan. The officers murmured their agreement and went out.

The Colonel had decided personally to interview Sergeant Major Ramadi, the senior native NCO, and he sent for him as soon as the officers had gone. In the present crisis the Colonel was at his most alert, and his ear recorded the sounds from outside—the voices, the footfalls—as he listened for the evidence of trouble. When Ramadi came, he was dressed with his accustomed care and his salute was given with the usual flourish.

'At ease, at ease, Ramadi,' the Colonel said.

Ramadi could not stand at ease; he was as stiff as a plank, his feet together, his thumbs at the trouser seams, a picture of discipline in a unit where discipline was failing. The Colonel spoke in homely Arabic.

'A sad day, Ramadi, when the soldiers will not obey their officers. I had not expected this, not in an Arab Levy.'

The Sergeant Major did not relax his stance, nor did he speak, but his eyes filled with tears.

'Why is it, Ramadi? Who has been speaking to the soldiers? What makes them remain in their barracks with the doors closed? I expect you to tell me, old comrade.'

The Sergeant Major raised his head in proud loyalty, but he had nothing to say.

'These people—those that have been speaking to the soldiers

—they are cruel, ambitious folk, without heart or charity. They may have plans to destroy all that you and I and the soldiers most value. You must tell me what they have said to you. You must tell me which of the soldiers have been spreading their message.'

His ear, still alert, could detect no unusual movements in the camp, nothing to suggest the soldiers were in mutiny.

Still rigidly at attention, the Sergeant Major spoke over the Colonel's head, towards a point high up on the back wall of the office. 'There are no cruel people, master. There is no message.'

'Come now, soldier; it would be a strange thing in this part of the world if there were no enemies inside the camp. I know for certain that several of the soldiers have been instructed in politics outside the country.'

'So it is, master, but they are quiet.'

'How can you be sure?'

'I am sure.'

The Colonel's experience over the years had taught him to mistrust the simple solution; he knew that usually an action sprang from a diversity of aims; and he was therefore unable to accept that the soldiers were moved only by their sympathy for Sloan. 'You must tell me what happened,' he said now, abruptly, to the Sergeant Major, the subahdar, the person most likely to know the answer.

'The soldiers are dismayed.'

'But why? They have not been injured.'

'An injury was done to Captain Sloan.'

The Colonel said quietly, 'By his own hand, was it not? Captain Sloan turned the blade upon himself.'

Plainly the Sergeant Major did not like to contradict his commanding officer, whose rank invested his words with authority, with a kind of truth, but his loyalty required him to speak frankly.

'The soldiers believe that Captain Sloan was killed by the Colonel.'

Colonel Masterman felt a deep wound. He had wandered into an ugly region where he no longer knew the landmarks. He knew there were truths, imperatives hidden from him, and he was frightened by their looming shapes; they belonged in a new, strange, dangerous world that was not his own.

'The soldiers say that? They believe that I killed Sloan?'

These were pointless questions; the Sergeant Major had given his message, and elaboration would not make it easier to understand or to bear. The Colonel exhaled a long breath.

'So, then, it was I who killed Sloan. I might have known it.'

He threw his paper-knife across the blotter; then he fell to a close consideration of his finger-tips. He did not know how long elapsed before his soldier's ear, which had continued to listen for any sounds of disorder outside, heard voices raised in anger, the sound of wood splitting under enforcing tools, and the cries of savage accomplishment that followed. He hurried to the window but could see nothing. Sergeant Major Ramadi had remained at attention, too proud to take notice of this further evidence of poor order.

'What is it? What is it, Ramadi?'

The Sergeant Major shook his head, as if the truth was too painful for the Colonel to hear.

'You must tell me. At once.'

'They have taken Captain Sloan.'

'Taken him? What do you mean?'

Again the question was without point: his professional mind had at once related the sounds to the forcing of the mortuary door and the escape of the perpetrators with Sloan's body. He felt shocked, as if Arabia could do nothing worse than this; it was a vulgarity so great his mind had difficulty in believing that soldiers under his command could be guilty of such a thing. Captain Lovelace, the Adjutant, ran in from the veranda to tell him what had happened, but the Colonel, his soldier's instinct working independently of his inner mind, was already on the phone to the guard commander.

'They must be stopped at the main gate. The body is to be recovered. You may use what force is necessary, but not your fire-arms. If they get into the desert, they are to be pursued.' He rang off. 'Yes, Lovelace; I know what has happened....'

Lovelace was smothering idiotic laughter.

'I can see nothing in this for amusement, Captain. It is a grave indignity to the body of an officer; I am deeply concerned.'

The guard commander rang then to report that the guards had stood fast, averting their eyes, while the party ran into the desert dragging the body of Captain Sloan. The Colonel felt sick.

'What will they do with him, Ramadi?' he asked weakly.

'They will bury him, master. Somewhere in the desert.'

'I see. I am grieved by this. I had planned to give him military honours no matter that, by right, he was no longer eligible. After all, he died in uniform.'

'He will be buried with reverence,' Ramadi said.

'What? You think so?' The Colonel barely heard him; he was thinking of the funeral that might have been arranged. Then he asked sharply, 'What reverence did they show when they snatched his body from where it lay, when they dragged it through the dust? What sort of affection was that?'

If Ramadi answered, the Colonel did not hear him.

'I don't know,' Masterman said later, tired to the point of exhaustion. 'Perhaps they meant it sincerely. It's this place. I don't understand it fully.'

The company commanders reported little result from their interviews with the NCOs; the men had acted in sympathy with Captain Sloan, and it seemed unlikely they had been encouraged by agents from outside. Masterman was not satisfied; he felt certain some force whose aim was the breaking of order had taken part in the affair, using the restlessness of the soldiers for their own harsh ends. He sent a party of British NCOs into the desert to try to catch the rebels and recover the body of Sloan, but he knew the chance of finding them in that vast area was small.

At eleven o'clock, by appointment, the Political Agent called at the Colonel's headquarters to discuss the situation. He brought with him the two Sheikhs best informed of the state's affairs, Abdullah the Wise and Saud the Fat. Abdullah wore his look of scholarly hauteur which for many disguised his stupidity; Saud was as gracious and urbane as ever.

The Colonel said affably, 'Come in, come in, gentlemen. The steward will bring coffee. I hope those seats are comfortable. An unfortunate morning, but I think we will get things back to normal shortly.' He was calm and effective—a regular officer facing danger with the required cheerfulness.

Peachy said, 'Quite so. I'm sure the disturbance is temporary.'

'I would expect so,' said Saud.

'I must tell you the Emir is dismayed,' said Abdullah, who had no feeling for the opening courtesy.

'I do not think there is need,' said Masterman. 'Plainly the men were in sympathy with Captain Sloan and have been distressed by his sad end. I confess their reaction has surprised me, because I had not supposed they would feel so strongly about an officer who was, perhaps—how shall I put it?—dull and undistinguished: however, it was so, and I have learnt something of the soldiers' romantic spirit as a result. I must also believe there has been some manipulation of the soldiers' fantasies by those who do not wish us well. But I am convinced we can restore order by dealing sharply with cases of real insubordination, and by a firm persuasion of the majority. That, at least, is my intention.'

Speaking with a precision which suggested much fore-thought, Peachy said, 'I feel certain, gentlemen, that we can rely on the Colonel and his officers to restore order within the Levy. This is a military matter in which the civil element should not interfere. Inevitably the Ruler is concerned at any weakening of authority within his armed service at a time when he is in dispute with a neighbouring state, but I am sure that he will be satisfied provided it can be shown that authority has been re-established quickly and effectively.'

The Colonel was surprised: he had not supposed there was a likelihood of the matter being placed in other hands; but he had respect for Peachy's intelligence and honesty of purpose, and he knew he would not have spoken so without reason.

Saud gave a series of little coughs to clear the phlegm from his throat, his hand placed delicately across his lips. 'Of course —there is no question—discipline must be left to the military authorities. In any case, the civil courts have no jurisdiction in this field.'

On the telephone that morning, Peachy had told him he had friends in the state who hoped to see his authority renewed. He knew Saud to be a man of devious ambition, but plainly, at this moment, the Sheikh's aims coincided with his own.

'I hope, gentlemen, that this may be agreed,' the Colonel said. Like all soldiers, he was alarmed at the prospect of civil interference in a military problem and could think of nothing he would welcome less.

Sheikh Abdullah, whom the Colonel knew to speak usually for the Emir, sat bolt upright to deliver the Ruler's message. He spoke in the toneless voice of a civil servant giving judgements from a brief. 'The Ruler is concerned at the soldiers' indiscipline and wishes the culprits handed over to the magistrate for punishment.'

'Excellency, I could not do such a thing——'

'It is the Ruler's wish.'

'It would be contrary to the warrant I hold—which, as you know, was negotiated with the Ruler's representatives in London.'

Abdullah said nothing more: the finer points of the law were not his obsession.

The Colonel thought rapidly. Were he to punish the guilty soldiers, he would give them detention in cells, with duties in the kitchens and latrines as an additional hardship; the magistrate, moved by the Ruler's indignation, would put them to death.

Abdullah said, 'Then I may tell His Highness that you will release the guilty soldiers into civil custody?'

The Colonel knew that Peachy was shaking his head and that he himself must stand firm on a point of principle. 'Sheikh Abdullah, I am the Ruler's servant and he has my undivided loyalty. But I cannot ignore the terms of the agreement negotiated by the London agency and under which I command the Emir's army. I give you my word I shall do everything I can to restore order and to punish the guilty as soon as I can, and I shall use my full powers of punishment. Beyond that I cannot go, nor I think would any professional soldier in a similar appointment. I'm sorry, but that is my decision.'

Peachy smiled at him, confirming his agreement, and Masterman felt relief at having spoken his exact mind no matter what the result might be.

'I believe the Colonel has made the only possible decision,'

Peachy said. 'I will speak to the Emir in the same sense.'

'So, for what it's worth, will I,' said Saud, 'though I do not have my brother's total confidence.'

The visitors rose to go, and the Colonel escorted them on to the veranda with polite attention. Taking his hand, with the outline of a smile on his face, Sheikh Saud said, 'If my opinion has any value for you, Colonel Masterman, I do not think any outside interest has played a part in the soldiers' discontent.'

The Colonel nodded at this news, but he did not know if he could take it seriously. From the veranda rail he watched the palace car move towards the gate, and he wondered what message Abdullah would give to the Emir. Peachy, at his side, was strangely excited.

'Colonel—my dear Colonel—you were splendid! I entirely agree with what you said: there's no point, even in this extremity, in compromising on a matter of principle.'

'It wasn't possible to say anything else, of course.'

'Well, some might have temporized; it was better to make plain the point beyond which you will not be forced. A wonderful thing!'

Masterman raised his eyebrows. 'My dear chap, as a result of my stand, we may go to the wall—both of us.'

'Then,' said Peachy happily, '—then, God bless you, we go with a semblance of pride.'

Despite his anxiety, the Colonel smiled, but at once his mind clouded. He said, 'I can't imagine what the Emir will think of me now.'

'A dark, strange mind; there's no point in predicting which way it will turn.'

'I think I know, I think I can guess——'

He led Peachy back into the office as if his next words were a blasphemy that should not be overheard. He said, 'It's a terrible thought, but following a failure of confidence, I'm afraid he will be inclined to engage mercenary forces.'

Peachy's good humour vanished in a trice. 'It is true, it is true! Oh my God, it is true! Certainly there is that chance.' He brightened then, and took the Colonel's arm. 'Listen. If you can reassert your authority quickly, and punish the offenders, then I think you may regain the Ruler's confidence.

It's a chancy business, but we would be foolish to expect other than long odds in a place like Hassan. I'm sure you'll do what you can.'

'Of course,' said Colonel Masterman.

Peachy turned to go but the Colonel called him back. His mind was confused.

'Tell me, Peachy—tell me this. I have to know the answer. Sloan was a dour old officer without charm or intelligence. He behaved inexcusably towards Hamid; he showed a brutality beyond anything I have seen in thirty years of service. And yet the soldiers cared for him. His death has moved them to indiscipline. They honour his memory. Why? Tell me why? What can they possibly have seen in Sloan?'

'He was an Arabist, I think.'

'But he had no education, no culture.'

'It might not matter. An Arabist is no one in particular. It's a state of mind, of the heart.'

'There was no one else, then? It was only Sloan?'

'I must believe so,' Peachy said.

The Colonel nodded. He would not argue with the Agent on a matter of this kind; it was not his way. It hurt him to have understood the soldiers no better.

A final point troubled him, upon which he must settle his mind. 'Sheikh Saud has shown me much kindness. He does not wish to see me discredited. Why should he care?'

Peachy spoke carefully, as if he were giving a lesson in first principles. 'An interesting point. Saud is a Marxist who doesn't wish to see his enemy destroyed. He——'

'That doesn't make sense, Mr Peachy.'

'Not to you, sir; but it will do to Saud.'

'Everyone hopes to see his enemy destroyed.' The Colonel was irritated by paradox, by the strange movements of politics.

'The purity of the problem was in danger, of course. Saud does not want the picture confused with mercenaries. He sees you as his traditional opponent, one for whom he has an affection, and over whom he is bound to triumph in the end. He does not want to see you destroyed by the wrong forces. Still less does he want to see you destroyed by Sloan, who fits nowhere into the picture. He wants to put an end to you himself. The prophecy must be fulfilled exactly. I'm sure you follow me.'

The Colonel smiled then. 'Not with any ease, Mr Peachy, if I am honest. However, you will know best in matters of this sort. I'm not very good at politics.'

'Your task, sir, is to re-establish order within the Levy.'

'I know,' the Colonel said. 'I will do my best.'

He ordered the soldiers to parade and the NCOs went shouting through the lines. Lovelace reported a stiffening of the soldiers' anger; some had locked themselves into their huts, others more inventive in disobedience had taken down their routine orders and burnt them on the edge of the parade ground. Those who had escaped with Sloan's body had not returned, neither had they been seen by the search party. The Colonel turned to the problem of getting the men on to the parade ground, finding relief in action; he ordered the NCOs to pass through the barrack huts three abreast carrying truncheons and basketwork shields, to divide the groups, to clear the soldiers into the open where the officers directed them into company order. Those who would not parade were left where they sat to be arrested and transferred to the cells.

The Colonel knew he must act swiftly; he had to re-impose the restraint of discipline, to get the soldiers back into their ranks where the reflex of obedience would control their limbs. He told the officers to double the men on to the parade ground and to keep them marching on the spot so that the rhythmic fall of the feet would mesmerize them into a sense of order. As a safeguard, he had stationed men of the headquarters company, whom he knew to be trustworthy, on the roofs surrounding the parade ground; they were armed with rifles and twenty rounds each, and they stood where they were visible to the assembling Levy as a curb to violence and for another purpose which the Colonel had explained privately to Sergeant Major Ramadi. Within twenty minutes, the officers reported most of the men on parade; the hard core of malcontents, of whom there were eleven, had been marched to the guardroom and there interrogated. But there was nothing to be learned from them; they seemed to be in a dream.

Colonel Masterman took the centre of the square and faced the Levy. The dressing of the ranks was poor in a force whose drill standard was high. Automatically he put the parade at ease, called them back to attention, and ordered 'right dress'. It was badly done; the stamp of the feet lacked all precision; the ranks swayed forward and back in a parody of their usual performance; but the Levy had responded to his command. He stood the men 'easy'.

He had not planned what he would say. He knew that only with a spontaneous address in the men's own language, one aimed at the heart and not at the mind, could he hope to recover the affection of Arab soldiers. He looked at the ragged companies standing without pride on the dun-coloured square —he looked at them for more than a minute in silence, turning his head to observe the armed men on the surrounding roofs, letting the companies see the direction of his eyes. Then he said strongly:

'Soldiers, this is a day of shame! I had not thought I would live to see the day when an English colonel must defend himself from the bedouin. Look, look where the guards are standing! Their rifles are charged, their bandoliers are full; they are there to protect the life of your colonel because he can no longer trust his soldiers not to turn their arms against him. You are rogues and cattle.'

He paused. There was movement in the ranks, which swayed like grasses under the first breath of wind—a movement of shame; but it was small. He let his voice drop lower.

'Listen. I know that you had love for Captain Sloan. I know that his death has distressed each one of you. Why he had your love and I did not is hidden from me, but I accept that it was so. There are those whom the bedouin loves and no one but the bedouin can say why. But hear me in this! Captain Sloan was found guilty by a court of soldiers of an offence against a bedouin; he cruelly whipped the man Hamid, whipped him nearly to the point of death, and he was obliged to accept his penalty. Sloan was unjust, cruel, mad.'

The soldiers were angered at this. The ranks stiffened; a mutter of dissent moved back and forth across the parade. But the Colonel knew he must speak the truth of his mind because, better than any others, Arab troops knew when an officer spoke dishonestly. 'Aye, it was so!' he continued, raising his voice. 'He was wrong and he was punished. But—listen to me, soldiers!—Captain Sloan made the final choice himself, and it was a brave and terrible choice he made. It was not the court's doing; it was not my doing. Captain Sloan took the blade in his own hand and drew it across his throat because that was his choice. I do not know why he spilled his blood. You who loved him can tell me. But you cannot tell me it was your colonel who raised the knife, your colonel who killed Sloan, because that is not true.'

A soldier in the first company whom the Colonel could not identify shouted an obscenity which was repeated by others. 'Foul yourself, master!' they said. 'The Colonel killed Captain Sloan.'

'Is that the opinion of the soldiers?'

Some shouted assent; but others were quiet, shamed into silence by the Colonel's anger.

'It is a foul lie spoken by a foul people. There is treachery here; there are men with cruel hearts who would turn their tongues against a fellow soldier, who will not listen to the truth because they do not wish to hear it. They are offal and refuse and I will not let their shadows touch me.'

The dissenting voices were louder now. One or two soldiers broke rank and moved into the open the better to shout their abuse.

'Murderer,' they shouted.

'Pig offal,' the Colonel jeered.

He knew the Arab temper; he knew that only a simple and daring gesture would move the soldiers into obedience. And he wanted them angry, because he knew their anger to be followed closely by their affection.

'Now let us judge the strength of the bedouin's word,' he said, allowing contempt to show in his voice.

He ordered the officers to fall out. They saluted and left the parade ground.

'Sergeant Major Ramadi, withdraw the guard,' the Colonel said.

He heard the order repeated round the square and he saw the guards disappearing from the flat roofs. He was alone with his soldiers. The sun blazed upon them; the white buildings dazzled his eyes. The soldiers in their poor formation were still bound by their instinct for obedience, but it was at the point of breaking; they had reached the moment when they must either mutiny or resume their discipline.

He withdrew his pistol from the holster and threw it away from him: he threw it with disdain for the soldiers' opinion, for the Levy, for Hassan, for Arabia. He stood facing them unarmed, in silent contempt, as the seconds passed and the last restraints of discipline held them in check.

'I say that the soldiers lie. I say that Captain Sloan was guilty. I say that Captain Sloan took his own life. I say that the soldiers are rogues and pig offal and a disgrace to their tribes and their rulers because they do not want to know the truth.' He looked along the broken ranks in a cold fury. 'The soldier who says that the Colonel lies, that he is not speaking the truth of his heart, may leave the ranks and face me.'

They were quietened by this challenge. The ranks did not dissolve further, but there was movement within the formations, one, two, three soldiers moving forward, only to be restrained by their companions; harsh words were spoken between them. Then he heard a murmur of approval and shouts in his favour. The soldiers were no longer of a single mind. The Levy was broken between mutiny and obedience.

'Listen, soldiers!' the Colonel continued, using a softer voice and the simplest Arabic he could find. 'You loved Sloan. You took his body away and you buried it. You spoke over the grave. The soldier you loved now lies in the desert covered by the sand because that was your wish. I do not know why you did this, and I shall punish those who carried away his body when they return, but I know you acted in faith with Captain Sloan and in the manner of the bedouin.'

The ranks quivered, a ghost of discipline returned. The soldiers were shy, embarrassed, whispering; they resumed their dressing one after another; they shuffled out of mutiny and into regimental order while the Colonel waited in silence. He dared not call them to attention yet because he could not rely upon their obedience: instead he let them fall back into their places, habit dictating their movements. Then he heard the parade becoming silent, as if waiting for him to speak again— as if they acknowledged his right to command them from his position at the front of the regiment.

Now he must risk an order which they might or might not obey because he had to re-establish the authority of his voice beyond all doubt. He chose a moment when there was no sound whatever, when they were still, silent and ashamed.

'Now listen to your Colonel,' he said softly. Then he raised his voice to ceremonial pitch and gave the unequivocal order known to all soldiers. 'Parade—atten-*tion*.'

They did it weakly, with no sort of polish, and instinctively he put them at ease again.

At the second command the men responded with something like their regimental snap.

Better leave it there, he thought.

'Sergeant Major Ramadi,' he called. 'Dismiss the parade and order the men to clean barracks.'

He left the square and walked swiftly back to his office. He would keep them cleaning all day, putting a shine upon the camp, wiping away the stains of mutiny. He felt wretched that such measures should be necessary.

Peachy had watched the parade from an upper window. 'Colonel, you were wonderful,' he said, taking his hand.

'Oh?' Masterman was surprised by this warmth. 'My dear chap, I shouldn't have reached the point where it was necessary. I dislike these expedients.'

Minutes later Lovelace reported that the soldiers had returned to barracks and had taken up cleaning materials.

'A pity the soldiers lost their discipline,' the Colonel said. 'It shouldn't have gone like that. Somewhere I have been wrong. And now, of course, I will have lost the Emir's trust.'

15

At the foundation of the state, now so long ago no one recalled with certainty the year or even the century in which it took place, Kabina the Whore had asked for a garden to be planted by the sea. This lapse into sentiment was at odds with the manner of her life, which had been given to intrigue and to the elimination of her enemies by excruciating means; but some of the time, at least, she was entitled to be a woman, to take pleasure in the scent of roses, and legend told how the beach gardens to the south-west of Bir-el-Shama had been designed by her as a place of rest and delight. The Kabina Gardens, to this day, was the name by which they were usually known. A later tradition made it plain the gardens had been relaid in the last century by a Persian lady of wealth and discernment who had sown with some regard for the violence of the climate and the indolence of the gardeners. Like every garden in Arabia, it was beautiful not so much for the luxury of its growth but for the contrast it made with the desert; and it was true that the trees were hung with dust and the ground strewn with litter. Still, it was a garden; the sunlight hereabouts was broken by leaf shadow, and you could hear the birds moving in the branches, the creak of the bamboos, the splash of fish rising in the tanks.

Many stories were told of the Kabina Gardens. In the earliest years a lady of degree had here embraced a Sheikh with such totality of passion that she had loved, conceived and borne him a prince, all in the space of an hour. Nowhere was this story recorded; it was none the less believed. Another tale was sometimes told by the credulous. Once every hundred years, they said, the gardens were filled with nightingales singing in perfect harmony, and those who were lucky enough to hear their song lived for ever in contentment; but as no one could say when the last occasion took place, whether it was a year or nearly a century back, it was not possible for the believer to place himself between the trees and profit from the phenomenon. Today only the dates, the figs and the flame trees had survived the departure of the British overseer; they had sunk their roots into the moisture far beneath the sand. The oleanders, the poinsettias, had died.

Some days after the Warboys mutiny, an agent of the Emir brought his equipment into the gardens and surveyed the paths and open spaces with an experienced eye. He was a silent, dedicated member of a small group of specialists who worked internationally, whose fees were high but whose skills were prized. In this field of work, daily increasing in complexity, the amateur could no longer employ his hand; but in the new world of infant states, where each was marked by a savage innocence, and even in parts of the old world, there was a growing need for professionals in this role. These men were quick, efficient, restrained; the job was done with as much decorum as the proposition allowed. The executive who came to the gardens was a fair-haired Swede, no longer young, with a face so handsome and symmetrical it seemed devoid of human impulse; his manner was so polite it rendered him nearly invisible. His suit was tastefully chosen and cut. He did not like the present task because the order had been imprecise and relayed through too many intermediaries; he much preferred to be briefed by the principal. But he knew that in these states the principal seldom gave his instructions personally: he simply made known his wish, or perhaps only his distaste, allowing his servants to decide how the job should be done, and then of course there was misunderstanding when his wish was put into effect. The executive changed now into his working dress, the beret and camouflaged overalls which had become the uniform of the New Left, the merciless, and the soldiers without loyalty; and he waited.

Sarita was bored. At the Agency that morning nothing pleased her. An hour before her father and the Colonel had left for the palace, to congratulate the Emir on his birthday, and no one remained for her to talk to except Zamil, whom she despised. The Agency was dead; even the cats had deserted the walls, and the sparrows, which sometimes bathed in the dust under her window, had disappeared into the shrubbery. The scene outside her window—the grass through which the earth showed in patches, the few thin shrubs, the stairway to the balcony—looked so familiar she wanted to make some violent alteration there, one that would satisfy her need for change. Perhaps the Agency might fall down. She cleaned and shaped her finger nails and painted them carefully. Then, that moment gone, and adrift in the timeless morning, she put her chin into her hands and stared into the garden. Let something happen, she asked. The silence sang in her ears and slowed her mind until it nearly stopped. She was fixed in boredom. Even the flies on the wall didn't move.

At first she did not see Abdullah the Wicked, although he was squarely in her sight; her mind did not respond to the robed figure standing with magnificent presence in the middle of the lawn. He said, and she did not hear him, 'Lady, where are you?' Her eyes had lost the power to distinguish images; she was looking at the blank face of boredom.

'Lady, I bring you pearls!'

She woke slowly, her eyes cleared. She filled with expectancy and her breast rose. She touched her hair into obedience, pulled her dress straight, and went into the garden.

'Ah!' said the Sheikh, with something like a bow.

'Good morning, Sheikh Abdullah,' said Sarita.

His attention was fixed wholly upon her; no preoccupation of any other sort disturbed his mind. With a gesture of the hand disclaiming any credit for himself, he passed her a black case in which lay a three-string necklet of pearls with a diamond fastening. 'You may wear it in your hair, should you prefer, or at your ankle. Give it to your servant if it does not please you.'

It pleased Sarita to the point of vertigo. Her words stopped at her lips. Custom forbade her to thank a Sheikh for his gift, no matter how munificent it might be; but she raised her eyes to his face and smiled at him, revealing the whole of her pleasure, and he discarded her thanks with a curt shake of the head, as if a fly had alighted on his nose.

'You are lovely, Miss Peachy,' he said from a distance.

'You are kind, My Lord.'

'Where there is wealth there is no kindness.'

'There is, of course. You do not have to give me pearls.'

'I do so because it pleases me.'

'But you do it, none the less.'

They were detached from the humdrum, in a place of exceptional possibility. Then the Sheikh said, returning to the commonplace with reluctance, 'Ah yes, the matter of my call. I had hoped to see the Colonel before he left the palace, but I missed him there. I have been to Warboys; he is not there——'

'He will probably return here with my father. You have a message for him, Excellency?'

'A message? Yes, a message. One of importance.'

'I will pass it, if you wish.'

His practical eye came back to her face, where it dissolved in admiration. 'Miss Peachy, I will take your hand to my lips, if you will permit me.'

'Well, if you wish,' Sarita said.

'It smells of roses.'

'It is nice of you to notice.'

He retained her hand for a minute, working his lips along the knuckle; then he dropped it with an exhalation of delight. 'You say the Colonel has not returned, Miss Peachy? He should be here by now, surely? My message is of the utmost urgency. I came with all speed, wasting no time.'

'Then he cannot be far behind you.'

'Well, of course, I went first to the jewellers, as I could not come with empty hands. And, it is true, I examined three cases before I was satisfied. So, lady, he should be here!' He presented this logic with a show of triumph.

'I expect, My Lord, that he has stopped on the way.'

'Stopped? You say he may have stopped? Where would he have stopped?'

'At the gardens, perhaps.'

'The gardens? Oh!'

'I know the Colonel makes a habit of walking in the gardens when he passes there.'

Sheikh Abdullah paused to consider this news. 'I see. Then perhaps my message loses its importance.'

He brightened fractionally and guided her towards the

flower beds so that he might admire the poor showing of stocks and delphiniums. 'Flowers and more flowers,' he said. 'Miss Peachy, I may support your elbow?'

Sarita asked cautiously, 'What was it you wished to tell the Colonel, Excellency?'

'It is of diminished interest; the point becomes lost with the passage of time.'

'I do not see how that can be.'

'Lady, you are more beautiful than these flowers.'

'Is there something we should do?'

The Sheikh looked grave, as if the exercise of thought, to which his mind was unaccustomed, used the whole of his energies; then he smiled with decision and purpose. 'We will go to the gardens, madam. We will look for the Colonel there!'

Sheikh Abdullah was too big for the tiny white Lotus which was his favourite vehicle and he closed the door with difficulty. His large sandalled feet could barely distinguish the brake from the accelerator and they made a fitful progress out of the Agency garden. Sarita had a sense of urgency, although she did not know the point of Abdullah's message; plainly it mattered, otherwise he would not have come in search of the Colonel. Something was wrong; danger threatened, and she must help. She knew the Colonel saw someone else in her, someone lost, and she disliked this use of her; but she was partly that person, she had the face or the voice, perhaps only in a tiny degree but none the less the image of something he had loved, and it was therefore necessary for her to go to him with the warning of danger. She pressed Abdullah to hurry as they passed through the traffic of the market.

'Is it bad, Excellency? I don't want anything to happen to the Colonel.'

'It is bad,' said Abdullah, 'very bad.'

A donkey cart blocked the narrow street, and to increase their speed the Sheikh drove into the rear of the cart and propelled it forward at a dizzy pace. Sarita closed her eyes as they completed the length of the street and came out at the beginning of the desert road.

'We go across the sands,' said the Sheikh, turning the car from the road and into the stony desert. 'We save much time.'

'Be quick,' Sarita said.

With no feature in view but the distant rim of trees where the gardens began, Abdullah depressed the accelerator to the fullest extent. He could distinguish only two speeds, slow and fast; the rest was a sophistication to trouble other minds than his. The car swayed and leapt across the uneven surface.

'We travel through the air, like birds,' said Sheikh Abdullah. The car began a wide circle in the desert as the Sheikh, intoxicated with movement, chased their own tail. 'See, Miss Peachy, we come back where we started!'

'Please, Excellency, be quick,' said Sarita.

She had to find Colonel Masterman. She had to warn him of danger.

They reached the gardens three minutes later; and a flight of parakeets, disturbed by the noise, rose chattering from the palms. Sarita walked quickly between the trees where the sunlight lay softly on the path and the noise of the sea just reached her. The sweet scent of the dates was everywhere under the palms. It did not seem a place of special danger. She hurried on, Abdullah behind her, until she reached the sea, where the light was reflected on the undersides of the palm fronds and the beach was a blaze of white. She could not see the Colonel; her mind filled with shapeless fears.

She called, using her full voice, 'Colonel, Colonel!'

The garden gave back nothing but a heat-deadened echo. He was not here, then; he was gone.

She said, with less strength than before, less conviction that he would hear her, 'Colonel, we must speak to you. It is Sheikh Abdullah and I.'

He did not reply. But her voice was heard by other ears, trained ears that responded at once to the smallest stimulus. The Swede went casually to a distance. In the emotionless craft to which he was given there were margins of risk beyond which he might not venture.

Sarita searched the shore until she came to the formal part of the gardens where she turned into the main walk and started back towards the desert. Abdullah, bored with searching, lagged behind her.

'It is useless, without point; there is no one here,' he said.

She didn't speak, in case she should cry. She ran forward to get out of his sight. In a moment she was lost in the shadows, one tree looking like the next, and she stood still in fear. She hadn't the strength to call again. She didn't know why she was here, what she was doing. The gardens were full of dangers she did not understand.

'Colonel Masterman,' she said silently, and cried.

She could not move from the spot. Her name, called twice, did not release her from this imprisonment.

She needed a soldier's help, but the Colonel himself was in danger, and were he to be lost there would be nothing left but herself in the threatening shadows. No one else had the strength to save her; the rest were pale phantoms who stood with gaping mouths, their hands to their ears, waiting for the soldier's aid.

It was a minute before she heard him properly.

'My dear, you were looking for me? Your father and I had stopped to walk in the gardens.'

The Colonel walked towards her along the line of the palm trees with a firm infantryman's step. She shook her head to free herself from strangeness.

'Yes,' she said, angry now. 'Sheikh Abdullah has a message.'

'He has given it to me.'

'Then we can go from here? At once?'

He was concerned for her comfort. He raised his hand to the point of her elbow, but she turned away from him, in anger, in spite. She walked three paces towards the sea. The Colonel, filled with solicitude, followed her and put an arm along her shoulder, and she swung back to him and buried her face in his shirt.

'It isn't me,' she said through shuddering lips. 'Not me.'

'I beg your pardon?'

He didn't understand. He didn't know what she was talking about.

'It was somebody like me, wasn't it?'

He held her firmly, gently, without intrusion. 'I had not thought of it particularly. If I have distressed you in any way, I am sorry.'

She knew she had touched him where he was weakest, but she was lost, fearful, ready to hurt. 'It makes me angry, that's all. You weren't looking at me. You were looking at somebody else. It's something in my face, isn't it, that reminds you of her?'

The Colonel was moved, but he did not release her. He looked towards the sea, as if into the past, and he said nothing for a time. He paid no attention to whatever dangers there might be in the gardens. Then he said, 'I don't talk about it. I don't even think about it. But, as you have asked me, I think it is your eyes.'

'They are the same?'

'Yes.'

Sarita said, 'I can't like her very much, even though she looked like me.'

The Colonel guided her back towards the path where her father waited for them. She remembered, then, there were other people in the gardens besides themselves.

'Where is Sheikh Abdullah?' she asked, in sudden alarm.

'At the base of this tree,' said the Sheikh, 'exhausted with searching.'

'I think we had better leave the gardens as soon as possible,' the Colonel said. 'Sheikh Abdullah, I am deeply grateful to you. I suggest Miss Peachy rides with her father and me in the Agency car; we will take the most direct route back into Bir-el-Shama and I will give my instructions over the Agency telephone.'

They walked through the mottled shade to where the car was waiting. Sarita gave up trying to understand what had happened; she simply placed her trust in Colonel Masterman and sat by his side as they drove down the hot road towards Bir-el-Shama.

'I find it hard to believe such a thing possible,' said Colonel Masterman in the seclusion of the Agent's study. 'We have only the word of Sheikh Abdullah, and he is unreliable, at best—a charming fellow, of course, with a generous heart, but hardly one to make rational judgements. The whole story has the flavour of romantic invention and I decline to take it seriously.'

In the depths of gloom, Peachy peered at the whisky in the

bottom of his glass and reached, for the third or fourth time, for the decanter. 'Quite. It was romantic invention,' he said.

'It must have been.'

'I don't know.'

'Mr Peachy, I have served a long time in a great many places and I am accustomed to the perversity of native rulers. I was aware I had lost the affection of the Emir over my prosecution of Captain Sloan and that soldier's unhappy end, but it doesn't follow, not even allowing for the extremes of Arab temper, that the Ruler should now wish to remove me from the scene. It doesn't begin to look likely.'

'Of course not,' Peachy said, his eyes closed, seeing visions; 'that isn't the point.'

'He would need to be a man of insane suspicion and inhuman malice if we are to believe this of him.'

'He would.'

'And, on top of that, it would be stupid to polish off the commanding officer at a time when we have just re-established discipline in the army.'

'Certainly; as you say.'

'So what are we left with?'

Peachy opened his eyes abruptly, disliking his ugly visions. 'We are left, dear Colonel, with an insanely suspicious and malignant human being who is also a military idiot.'

'You don't believe that.'

'I am bound to consider it possible.' He was drunk, his mind was absurdly darkened, otherwise he would never have made his next urgent point; but it sprang from him before he had time to consider its fitness. 'Get out, Colonel. Don't stay here. Don't lose your life in this rank desert where it can't make the smallest difference in the end if the army stands still or runs away. There's nothing here worth the price they're asking.'

The Colonel laughed generously. 'You make it sound tempting, Mr Peachy. Unfortunately my engagement requires me to stay here.'

'I will ask the British government to replace you.'

'I wouldn't thank you for doing so, old friend. In the first place, my secondment has not expired; in the second, I could not pass on to another officer the present shambles without a severe attack of conscience. At a later time, when things are normal, I will think about relinquishing my appointment, I promise you.' He placed his arms on the Agent's desk and leaned forward earnestly. 'Listen, Peachy—we must see this thing in a reasonable light. Hajji Kassim is unstable and without much heart but there are things in his favour. He once attended a British military establishment and it's possible something rubbed off on him there. Not much perhaps, but a little. He has also had the benefit of much European advice since oil was discovered in Hassan. And—a point to remember —he has enough money to satisfy any whim, any physical desire or perversity he may have; and you can't tell me he doesn't indulge himself in these ways in the seclusion of the palace. All this doesn't add up to a man who would be likely to put an end to his army commander.'

'The Al Farahid suffer from congenital insanity. Anyone will tell you.'

'Not in every generation.'

'They've got whore's blood, the lot of them. Hajji Kassim more than most.'

'There's no point in exaggerating our situation.'

Sarita came in to show them Abdullah's pearls, which she had arranged in her hair. She held her head this way and that. 'My darling, they're beautiful!' said Peachy, with sudden joy.

When she had gone, the Colonel said, 'I must go. I must not keep you talking.'

'Take care,' the Agent said with rapt concern.

He showed the Colonel to the car, and after it had gone he stood looking at the place where it had vanished. His mind was empty but for his distress. After a time—how long he couldn't say—a car came into his sight at the point where his eyes still rested and he supposed it was the Colonel coming back. His heart lifted: he was drunk enough to suppose that Masterman had returned to say he was going away, returning to England, quitting the Levy, the desert, the whole combination of dark impulses that was Arabia. But the car had a different shape and carried a different passenger. Saud the Fat alighted backwards.

'A vexing morning, full of tiresome expedients,' he said to Peachy in the drive. 'No, my dear Agent, we will not go inside: at a time of turbulent politics to withdraw into an inner room is to be suspected of conspiracy, as you know. We will walk in the garden. What gorgeous blooms you have!'

They crossed the poor turf, here adulterated with camel grass, and looked with close attention at some withered marigolds.

The Sheikh said, 'I cannot go to Warboys; that would be considered as treachery only a little less culpable than the Colonel's. However, I have done what I can to mend the situation.' He paced the length of the Agency wall before speaking again. 'My Lord the Emir is not a man who welcomes discussion of his problems. He is hardly what the British would call a good committee man. He prefers to rule with a series of decisions formulated in the darkest parts of his mind and made known only to those whose job it is to carry them out. The dismissal of an officer, for instance, which you might expect to be discussed in an administrative sub-committee, becomes in my brother's style of government an exercise in medieval cunning and brutality.'

'Then it was true,' Peachy said, his mind swimming with grief. 'I had thought it must be true.'

'He had cause for dissatisfaction, of course. I must believe the Colonel acted without political deftness in his dealings with Hadraif and more particularly in the affair of Captain Sloan——'

The Agent let that pass.

'——and in failing to hand over the mutineers for civil punishment——'

Say not a word! the Agent thought.

'——but the form chosen for his dismissal from service can hardly be considered appropriate in a modern state.'

Peachy took a deep breath. 'Lord Saud, am I to believe that the Emir employed a gunman to shoot down a loyal servant in the fullness of his life because of disagreements of policy?'

'Frankly, Mr Peachy, you were supposed to believe nothing of the sort. It would have been made to look as if Hadraifi agents had effected the shooting.'

They paused at the end of the lawn. Standing with them was the sour spirit of Hajji Kassim, a dull, ugly shade, scowling with morbid suspicion.

'But the Emir would have killed him, none the less,' Peachy insisted.

Saud had the delicacy not to give his opinion. 'I have already said that I abhor these methods. As it turned out, the girl's voice alarmed the gunman so that he withdrew. My admirable younger brother, admittedly with some departures from the main course of action, had brought her to the garden in time for her to intervene.'

So that was how it happened: the executioner was raising his weapon, giving effect to the Emir's will, working for cash, when a girl's voice cut through the trees.

Peachy said, 'Excellency, how did Abdullah know what was planned; how did you know——'

'A palace informer, who came to me after he had seen Abdullah.'

They retraced their steps towards the gate, the sparrows jumping ahead of their feet.

'I have done what I can to prevent a repetition of this absurd strategem,' the Sheikh said. 'It cannot do other than harm the long-term interests of the state. I have told the Ruler I will feel obliged to reveal the truth if he resorts to these methods in the future. They are fanciful, archaic, and in the event often inefficient. Svenson has already crossed the state boundary.' The Sheikh exhaled a draught of wind as if to rid himself of the taste of Hassan. 'You may tell the Colonel as much of this as you think fit.'

'He doesn't believe it true. He thinks it was an invention of Abdullah's.'

'Then perhaps he should be left in ignorance, with still some loyalty to the Ruler.'

'I don't think it would affect his actions one way or the other.'

Saud started back towards his car, to be halted by the Agent's sudden voice. 'Tell me, My Lord—is the Emir mad? Will he destroy the state?' These were dangerous questions to ask in Arabia but Peachy was drunk and no longer cared.

Saud the Fat was not disturbed. He continued his leisurely progress after a moment's hesitation. 'You must find your own answers, Mr Peachy. There are remedies, of course, for all conditions.'

He drove away through the gate and Peachy kicked the gravel left and right in the drive. On the lawn behind him Sarita danced with her shadow, the pearls now at her ankle. His mind was stretched to the point where he felt his skull would break and spill his miseries on the ground. O Hajji Kassim, Hajji Kassim, he thought, that was a cruel thing, and I would have killed you myself if you had succeeded. But like so much else in Arabia, the plan had failed in action when the unexpected happened—when a girl's voice intervened.

16

The mercenary soldiers dispatched by an agency in Brussels arrived in Hassan at the end of the following week. They were Swedes, Germans, expatriate Poles, white and Negro Americans, Australian drop-outs, and some Irishmen. A scum in anyone's opinion. Their commander was an Irish-American styling himself Major Kennedy. These soldiers had served variously in Africa, Southern Arabia, in parts of the East Indies and in the lawless savannahs of Latin America; they were deeply tanned, as it seemed the temperate regions had less need of their services, and their mood was extrovert. Their lingua franca was the English of the American criminal minority, and their weapons were drawn from various sources, but largely from the French market where such things could be had. They lodged in the old Arabian Hotel, reopened for the purpose, and they littered the floor with cigar butts and damaged the paint and plaster. The Agent reported their presence to London; but London was not much concerned. Though brought in at great cost, the mercenaries were not welcomed by the ordinary Hassanites, who could not understand how a man could fight without passion; in a country of fierce loyalties the paid soldier did not fit into an accepted tradition; and the mercenaries were seen to be beyond engagement, in some heartless limbo of their own. They took their liquor in the hotel bar, doing violence to the fittings and sending out for hired company; their asymmetric faces were reflected brightly in the mirrors which lined the walls. Their job had not been defined. They were to take their orders, should there be any, from the Captain of the Emir's bodyguard, himself a stateless malcontent formerly of the Yemen and wanted there by both the royalists and the revolutionaries on charges of corruption.

A fortnight after their arrival, telling no one of their intentions, a company of the mercenaries left the Arabian Hotel and disappeared eastward. Even in the vastness of the desert it was not possible for a party of foreign soldiers to pass unreported and within hours the Agent had been told of their presence on the Hadraifi frontier. It was likely enough: the agreement under which the Levy was raised and led disallowed its use in other than defence, and the Emir, whose suspicion of Hadraif had deepened, could well have decided to use his new force in an offensive role. A day later a report reached Charles Peachy of the killing of two tribesmen, presumably Hadraifi, at Bir-el-T'jef.

Two dead men: it didn't mean much in Arabia. But Peachy raged through the Agency, and when night fell he drank himself into a mindless stupor. In the dawn light, when the Gulf waters were misty and still, he crawled to the balcony rail and looked down the shore to where Bir-el-Shama, which was nothing more than an eruption in the mud, a cluster of flat roofs the same colour as the coast, lay round a small bay at the edge of the water: age-old, unchangeable, on the dark side of the world. His head was splitting, in a minute he would be sick; he hung over the rail like a discarded pillow and jabbered in Arabic; he berated the town and the desert with obscenities which now and again turned into senseless invective: 'O murderous, merciless, uncharitable Hassan....' It did him no good; he felt sick in the mind and stomach.

'I will resign and leave this place.' He said it out loud to the chattering sparrows, knowing he wouldn't do it, knowing the dull shapes and colours of England were more than he could bear—knowing moreover that he was part of Arabia, sharing in the corruption, savouring the foul taste, for as long as he should live. 'It isn't fair,' he said, with much weakened invective; 'it simply isn't fair that I should get stuck with Arabia.'

His mind spun with words, ideas, blasphemies which he needed to speak; what was more, he needed to speak them to Hassan itself. He wanted to tell the state how depraved it was, how total the penalty would be. Of course it would make no difference in the end. The state was moving into wickedness as surely as the stars moved. Charles Peachy, although without a deity, was close enough to the spirit of Allah, the One True God, the Inscrutable, to accept the fatalism of the desert, to admit the predestination of evil, to know that nothing he could do would alter by so much as a hair's breadth the collapse into darkness in which the Hassanite people were engaged. But, even so, it would be fun to speak the fullness of his mind, striking a blow for Free Will, that naked waif, in the heart of Islam—laughing in the face of every blind fakir who sat in a pool of shade contemplating the process of evil: he would scold them in the language of triumphant reason, serving no purpose but his own need for action.

He rubbed his forehead where the pain was greatest and knew he was not yet sober. The sun shone in a watery sky. He knew then, without any doubt at all, that he was going to abuse Hajji Kassim, and that following this necessary action he would probably sail into the middle of the Gulf and drown himself in the muddy water. The aim was correct, the design perfect; he couldn't imagine why he hadn't thought of it before. He dressed himself in clean khaki drill and combed his hair, for abuse was a serious matter which should not be attempted casually. He rang for the Agency car and set out for the palace in a mood of clear decision.

Quite possibly I'll murder him as well, the Agent thought, his mind warm with the possibility; we'll have to wait and see.

As he drove through the market, where the laden camels were kneeling in the dust, his mind dulled and he began to feel sick again.

What is the point? he asked.

There was no point. Evil would prosper. This was Arabia. Long ago the camels had withdrawn from the conflict into a silent disdain for the country and its people.

The car continued along the desert road towards the palace. He was now quite sober, his senses alive to the increasing heat and the bitter smell of the desert at early morning. He could foresee the shape of his conversation with Hajji Kassim: he would express his regret at the deaths of the Hadraifi tribesmen (as if it troubled the heart of the Emir); he would point out, in reasonable terms, that the employment of mercenaries

on tasks of this kind did harm to the name of the Emirate (as
if that damaged name could be worsened); he would ask for
the mercenaries to be withdrawn from the Hadraifi border,
where they were likely to provoke an invasion (as if the Emir
were interested in preventing war): he would say nothing of
his rage and drunkenness, nothing of his fears for the Ruler's
sanity, nothing of his alarm as the sum of disgrace was increased hour by hour.

The palace with its white colonnade and façade came into
his sight just then. Here and there the early sun was catching
the domes and minarets and making them gleam.

He left the car at the first court, which was filled with
askaris of the palace guard, mounted and on foot, with brightly
robed visitors from the southern sheikhdoms, with petitioners,
prisoners and vagrants—the riff-raff of an Arabian court,
crouching under the walls where there was a line of shade,
moving behind a veil of dust at the far end of the enclosure,
waiting a day or a week for an audience, a punishment, a hand-
ful of charity. Their faces were set in the lines of patient
endurance; they did not question the workings of kingship
which might require their hands cut off or filled with silver
dollars. They paid no attention to the European in his khaki
suit who stood looking at them, it might have been with
affection or disgust; like themselves, he responded to the
archaic will of the court, he had some design, some fear, some
blinding hope that brought him to the Ruler.

Charles Peachy passed the dividing screen into the second
court, a roofed and pillared hall, where the Chamberlain and
the palace servants welcomed him and gave him coffee, sweets
and jellies. In the corners of the hall, the leopards with their
slave attendants lay in beds of straw. The servants knew him;
they brought him a chair because they knew he couldn't squat
on his hams—a gift lost centuries ago by the Europeans but
retained by the bulk of mankind—and they smiled at him,
showing happy nubian faces—faces that would have disturbed the Societies of Europe and America which con-
demned the institution of slavery. He did not decline the
Emir's hospitality, as that would be a churlish thing to do in

Arabia; he took the chair and chatted with the slaves while they filled his cup from a long-spouted coffee pot; and he enjoyed the refreshment, the cooler airs of the hall, the outrage against civilized values that surrounded him.

When he had finished his coffee, he bowed to the Chamberlain and went into the hall where the Emir was holding his majlis, or audience, assisted by his brother Abdullah the Wise. Peachy could not at first tell which of the robed figures squatting on the floor was the Emir; he could not trace the sound of whispered counsel, which was endlessly continued, to any particular person; then he noticed a small, unremarkable figure, whose robe was as stained and worn as any other, waddling from one group to the next, returning the nod of recognition, listening to the spoken petition, arguing, cajoling, issuing the edict in the same intimate whisper—at which the petitioner bowed in acknowledgement of authority, whether he had received a reward beyond his dreams or a sentence of death—and then moving on to another voice, another problem, another answer: it was the Emir, the khalifa, the sheikh of sheikhs. The Agent had not chosen to present his argument at the Emir's majlis, and in doing so he would be departing from diplomatic practice, but he realized he would be approaching his ruler when his mind was most open to persuasion, when the habit of listening to the needs of the people might make him amenable to reason, and in this hope the Agent waited with the same patience as the other petitioners, sitting on the floor with his back against the wall.

They waited in silence; they were beggars, merchants, criminals and Sheikhs—and one professional diplomat with a mission to prevent war.

The fans in the ceiling counted away the hours. At midday he had not yet whispered into the ear of Hajji Kassim. Now slaves brought in mutton curry and orange juice, and the Emir took his meal where he squatted on the floor. With his own fingers, and from a common dish, he served the murderer and his two sons whose testimony he had been hearing.

An hour later the Emir had reached the place by the wall where the Agent sat. Hajji Kassim did not seem surprised that Peachy should attend the majlis; he simply turned an ear towards him and waited for him to speak.

147

'Charles Edward Milner Peachy, of Wimbledon and Bir-el-Shama, Political Adviser to the Emir.'

He spoke in Arabic, the language of the majlis, but Hajjim Kassim beckoned an interpreter, it might have been for the Agent's comfort or perhaps to interpose a barrier between them.

'His Highness recognizes Mr Peachy,' the interpreter said, 'and trusts he is enjoying good health.'

Plainly the Emir wished them to speak in their own languages for reasons of his own; the Agent therefore continued in English. 'His Highness has done me the honour of listening to my advice in the past.'

'His Highness has gained much from the inestimable advice of Mr Peachy.'

'And we have often found a basis for agreement in matters affecting the well-being of the state.'

'There has been, as Mr Peachy says, a perfect accord.'

The Agent's heart sank; his appeal would be lost in Arabian courtesies unless he could find a means of reaching the Ruler's inner mind. Hajji Kassim, squatting beside him, kept his sharp eyes on the floor.

He decided upon a direct approach which might move the heart of an Arab in an audience such as this. He said, with warmth, but with little hope of carrying his point, 'Your Highness, there has been trust and friendship between Arab and Englishman for two hundred years. We have admired the same things—the power of God, the utter right of the individual to reach his own ends, the solitude of the desert: both are warrior nations, both disregard the opinions of others, both are proud, strong in adversity, and undefeated. Each recognized the other as his equal in the earliest times. Each can laugh at the absurdity of the world, and neither is given to the dogmas which have disfigured this century with their cruelty.'

This was too much for the skill of the interpreter. Peachy waited as he struggled with an Arabic rendering of these hyperboles—which Peachy himself could have made better— and he saw the Emir nod his head, perhaps in agreement, perhaps only in acknowledgement of the Agent's lunacy.

Hajji Kassim, will you just *listen*, Peachy said inwardly; keep the venom out of your soul, recall that you are King and that kings must be merciful.

The interpreter finished; Peachy continued. 'The Colonel and his soldiers are distressed at the introduction of mercenaries into Hassan. They are a symbol of the Ruler's mistrust of his loyal soldiers. The mercenaries have no love for Arabia; they are mean and squalid and shameful, their presence on the border will provoke war with Ras Al Hadraif, and their loyalty can be purchased at a higher price by Your Highness's enemies.'

The Agent paused and the Emir waited patiently for him to continue. 'The murder of the two bedouin was a shame. They were poor men searching for water. They were shot down by mercenary bullets because the mercenaries must earn their wage in the only way they know. I beg Your Highness to withdraw Major Kennedy and his soldiers from the frontier and to send them out of Hassan, out of Arabia, back to the shabby places they came from: I beg you to receive Colonel Masterman back into your confidence, as befits the friendship of our two nations.

'That is my earnest desire, to which I commend Your Highness.'

It sounded flat and unconvincing in English and the Agent had little hope that he would get other than a neutral reply.

Abdullah the Wise, who had joined them, spoke first. 'Major Kennedy's unit is only a part of the Emir's bodyguard, responsible to the Captain; it is not within British jurisdiction.'

It was like Abdullah to suppose that something he had mastered with difficulty would be unclear to others. The Agent simply nodded. He did not wish to stand upon the letter of the Anglo–Hassani agreement, under which the employment of mercenaries was clearly disallowed; such distinctions carried small weight in the present forum.

Traditionally the Emir gave his judgements at once and without reflection, and his rulings were beyond appeal. But in this hall of audience, which was also a place of casual discussion, it was just possible the Emir would speak without prejudice. 'I have heard the opinion of Mr Peachy,' he said with ancient courtesy, keeping his eyes on the floor.

He did not continue immediately. For once, he seemed to be

149

giving a political matter his full mind—an attention as deep
as that he had given the murderer an hour ago—and Peachy
allowed himself to hope that something might be gained, even
as he knew such hope to be absurd. The gentle hubbub of
voices continued in the hall as the Emir squatted in silence at
Peachy's side. On the frontier thirty miles away Major
Kennedy and his bastard army were in search of fresh lives
in fulfilment of their contract. They could be brought back;
war could be averted; it needed only the whispered agreement
of the King, for a decision made at the Emir's majlis was as
solid as anything in Arabia.

'His Highness has heard Mr Peachy,' said Abdullah the
Wise.

The Emir kept the polite inflection in his voice. 'The man
Hamid was an Hadraifi agent,' he said.

(O God, would the misdeeds of that wretched soldier have
no end? Peachy thought desperately. Hamid, what did you
do?)

By custom, the petitioner was allowed to argue his case,
heatedly if he chose. Peachy said now, speaking in Arabic,
'He was not an agent. He was a man on his own, following
where his heart led——'

'It was not so. He was an enemy of the state, just as Captain
Sloan was a friend.'

The Agent despaired: the Emir's opinion was fixed, and
even in this softly-spoken exchange, where he might have
relaxed into sanity, his mind was not open to persuasion.
Peachy tried once more, claiming the full right of the
petitioner to open his heart to the King. 'My Lord Emir, these
are shadows in your imagination! Hamid was a crazy soldier
who fired a bullet in a moment of madness and then ran into
the desert. This was pure bedouin, as Your Highness will
know. Captain Sloan had a love of Arabia but a strange, unnatural loyalty. Do not let your fear of Hadraif turn these
soldiers into symbols of enemy and friend. Do not let the same
fear turn you from those who are your true servants.'

He might as well not have spoken; the Emir had not heard.
Hajji Kassim continued now in the same frank voice he had
used all morning, speaking the truth as he saw it. 'Colonel
Masterman gave the Sheikh of Hadraif the opportunity for

war with Hassan by taking an armoured vehicle over the frontier. It was a calculated act——'

'Your Highness——'

'He did not stop there. Captain Sloan was opposed to these designs. This officer had shown his loyalty to Hassan by punishing an Hadraifi agent when Colonel Masterman would not do so, and he knew of the Colonel's allegiance to Hadraif.'

'Your Highness, you are giving meaning to things that have no meaning. These are dangerous thoughts——'

'There was only one thing the Colonel could do. He had to rid himself of Captain Sloan. And he did it in the only effective way he knew: he killed him. There were soldiers in the Levy who supported the Colonel, chief of whom was Sergeant Major Ramadi, himself a servant of Hadraif; and there were those whose loyalty was to Captain Sloan and Hassan. The latter rebelled in the name of the Emir as they were opposed to the Colonel's Hadraifi connection, but they were put down by the strategems of the Colonel and his lap dog, Ramadi. It is in these circumstances, Mr Peachy, that I have been obliged to employ the services of Major Kennedy to protect the state from an Hadraifi invasion, as I could no longer rely upon the Levy to do so.'

The Emir had not yet answered the petition. He said now, 'Accordingly, while I have respect for your opinion, I cannot withdraw Major Kennedy from the frontier, nor can I extend my affection to an enemy of the state, as you have asked me to do.'

The Ruler had given his judgement; there was nothing more to be said. He moved to the next petitioner, a boy from the southern desert who had lost his donkey, and Peachy sat looking into the palms of his hands. The Agent's mind filled with a sick dismay. He watched the Emir's small figure as he gave his rapt attention to the boy; he asked his questions clearly, he delivered his finding in a few admirable words: he would give the boy another donkey because the original had been lost in Hassan.

Hajji Kassim, what must be done with you? The varied possibilities swam through the Agent's mind as he sat with his back against the wall, his knees raised to his chin. A king was a king by right, and the right ended only in death or the dissolution of the state. In a country of bold realities the answer was plain to see: Hajji Kassim must die, he must no longer disfigure the state with his cruelties. But a civil servant, though skilled in manipulation, had not the strength to impose a violent solution—he had no business in that extreme region which lay beyond diplomacy: here he had no power to act, and he must turn to him whose region it was: he must turn to the soldier.

The soldier.

He could not wait another day: the Emir was mad.

He stopped in the market on his return from the palace and sent the car away. He walked between the stalls and underneath the rush screens where the sunlight fell like soft rain and the smell of the fruit was sharp and stronger even than the strench from the creek. The stall-holders greeted him and he raised his hand in reply. When he did not go away, they paid him no further attention, conferring upon him the blessing only Asia gave, that of anonymity—he stood still in the shadows, himself, invisible. Across the narrow alley the quilt-maker continued his work, the material falling in a bright swathe from his table. Somewhere a donkey brayed and a burst of voices disclosed that a cart had overturned. Then, a minute later, the epic stillness of Asia was resumed and the sparrows hopped to within inches of his feet. Here, in a remote, lost quarter of Islam, two thousand miles from the edge of Christendom—from the place where the awful chatter of the Christians was stopped by the desert; where the peremptory voices, the terrible rectitude of the learned societies, the bald assumptions of the priesthood were alike dispersed by the sunlight—here, in this bitter dust, he might be himself. He would rather stay here dead than leave here alive. To Islam, then, the last laugh; for Islam, where there were no professors and no priests, where the heart responded in the fullness of its love or its wrath, was a golden country too precious to describe.

17

The Levy was at dinner. The Colonel sat at the head of the long table with his guest, the Political Agent, on his right hand. The officers in their mess kit, their faces just illuminated by the candlelight, stretched into the shadows. The servants had cleared the debris of dinner before the Toast, leaving only the mess silver down the centre of the table and a glass before each place. There was a throb of well-mannered conversation broken now and then by the eager voices of the younger officers. The Colonel had directed that no speeches should be given; the Levy was simply enjoying its own company at dinner, together with a friend.

The Colonel filled Mr Peachy's port glass, slightly increased the level in his own, and passed the decanter to his left. He gave the Agent a cigar from the silver case and took one himself. The candles had burned down half their length and now the warmth of the desert evening bent their stalks until they lost their alignment. The Colonel loved a dinner night; the ritual, the restraint, the fellowship, these gave him a deep satisfaction no matter that, in Hassan, they were obliged to take Australian wines and it was too hot for comfort.

The servants withdrew. The pitch of the voices lifted. The Colonel spoke of other dinners he remembered, in India, in Singapore, and of the outrageous things that happened there. Mr Peachy, who had drunk too much, spilled cigar ash down his dinner jacket and spoke from his own recollections. The Colonel recalled a general who had marched on the tables, a major of the cavalry who had marched on the ceiling; Mr Peachy spoke of the rajahs and sultans who had kept a thousand wives and swallowed rubies as a cure for impotence. The port came round a second time; the candlelight flickered on the ceiling; at the foot of the table the younger officers exploded in laughter.

The Colonel rose from his chair and sat down again, which meant the officers might leave if they wished. The doors were opened; the candles shivered; the number in the room was reduced until only the Colonel, his guest and the vice-president at the foot of the table were left. His personal servant brought him a whisky, and he ordered brandy for Mr Peachy. In the farther shadows, the vice-president, the most junior officer in the mess, was almost invisible to him.

Peachy struggled back to consciousness with an effort. 'They've gone?' he asked sharply. 'The officers have gone?'

'They're in the ante-room—up to no good, I expect.'

'And the servants have withdrawn?'

'Yes.'

Peachy put his finger in the spilled wine and traced a pattern on the table. He said reflectively, 'I am your guest, and guests should not be provocative. But I have a question to ask. Would your officers—supposing the matter was presented to them satisfactorily—follow you in an operation contrary to their tradition?'

'I'm afraid I don't understand.'

The Agent slumped into lethargy; then he straightened, waved away the alcoholic vapours with the back of his hand, and said, 'I want you to listen to me. Don't tell me I'm a prick till I've finished. You'd better have another whisky.'

The Colonel didn't want one. 'Please go on,' he said.

Peachy drew breath enough to last him, let it go, then began on a low note. 'I'm not given to treason, arson or bank robbery; neither, I take it, are you.'

'I'm not,' the Colonel said.

'We were born to work within the tradition of restraint.'

'Quite; it is our strength.'

'We were born to work within a system of law which has proved of benefit to millions of people with less amiable habits than our own.'

'As you say, Peachy.'

'Yet there are times when our restraint can prove a weakness.'

The Colonel was silent. He had respect for the Political Agent whose mind he believed to be more fluent, more perceptive than his own.

'There are times when we must throw off the burden of tradition and find ourselves at one with the sneak-thief and the assassin—when we must act not with decorum but with with vulgarity, not with restraint but with cheap sensationalism, like whores.'

'I will try to behave like a whore if that is what you wish,' the Colonel said politely.

The Agent stopped as if he had been clubbed. 'God,' he said; 'merciful God, what am I asking?' He took up his glass, looked at the brandy with a fierce eye, and put it down again. 'Listen, Colonel—listen, old friend—if you insist upon it, I'll shut up, no matter what it costs. I can't ask you to listen to the ravings of a drunken diplomat if you find it too much to bear.'

'I think you'd better tell me what you have in mind.'

'Believe me, it's unnatural stuff.'

'Never mind. I'm not easily startled.'

'Then have another whisky, I beg you.'

The Colonel called for a second whisky, more to please the Agent than for want of it. 'Now tell me what you mean,' he said.

Peachy rolled his head from side to side as if to rid himself of ugly dreams. 'The Emir,' he said slowly, as if he had to compress his argument into a single sentence, 'is mad.'

'I won't contradict you.'

'Dangerously mad.'

'Well?'

'He begins to see his friends as enemies; he has taken a course that may destroy the state.'

The Colonel thought so too; but he could not see why the Agent should open the subject so late in the evening. There was nothing they could do about the Emir's madness: it was a natural force, like a tropical storm.

'The use of mercenaries can mean war with Hadraif and the destruction of one sheikhdom or the other. The Levy may become involved.'

'I will not fight an artificial war, I assure you.'

'You may find it difficult to avoid. If the Hadraifis invade Hassan, the Levy would be employed in the defence of the Emirate.'

The Colonel had thought of this possibility, but he had put it from him as too shocking to be likely.

'In addition—this is not beyond possibility—you may have to fight the mercenaries, if only to put an end to their murders.'

The Colonel had nothing to say; the Agent was giving form to his darkest visions. After a while Masterman said weakly, 'I don't see what I can do about it. The Emir is all-powerful and it would be wrong for me to intercede in political matters.'

Peachy took a mouthful of brandy, rolled it round his tongue, and swallowed noisily. 'Only you *can* do something about it,' he said defiantly, brutally.

The Colonel was surprised but not angered. 'Me? I am a soldier; nothing more than that.'

'You have the force behind you.'

'But it can't be used in support of politics.'

'It can, if necessary.'

'To what end, sir? What are you asking me to do?'

The Agent no longer troubled to subdue his voice. 'Colonel, I am asking you to get rid of Hajji Kassim, one way or another. I am asking you to act in defiance of your training and instinct. I am asking you to do the one thing you will think impossible. I am asking you to commit regicide.'

Although Colonel Masterman was deeply shocked, he did not show it; he simply nodded at the Agent's point, raised his head and spoke to the young vice-president down the length of the table. 'Mr Vice, I do not think we need trouble you further. Will you please thank the chef for our dinner and wait for me in the ante-room.'

When the young officer had withdrawn, the Colonel turned again to the Political Agent. He was distressed and humiliated, but also humble. He said awkwardly, 'I think you had better explain more fully. I really do not understand you.'

Even when he was far from sober, Peachy's mind worked with speed and accuracy. He looked now at the Colonel's strong face, from which the candlelight had rubbed all expression but for a grave melancholy, and he knew he had to make an impression upon him in the next minutes if the

Colonel's mind was not to close upon him. He had only a slim chance of success, but he must take it. He prayed for lucidity, for the words that might move a soldier, for only the Colonel had the means to save them.

'Look, my friend, I know that politics are distasteful to you. I know that you are a practical soldier who has never thought in political terms. No one would deny the strength of the Army lies in its disinterest, and only a lunatic would want to change this tradition. I can imagine your opinion of the political colonels of the Third World—the mountebanks in their fantasy uniforms who are greedy for power and clumsy in its exercise: they will disgust you, of course. Indeed, the Colonels' revolt has become a cliché of the mid-century, just as the strong man who is strong in weapons but not in acumen or charity is a vulgar bi-product of these terrible decades, whom any true soldier will despise.'

The Colonel smiled wistfully. 'I am bound to agree with you so far, Mr Peachy.'

'Yet the fault may not always lie with the colonel.' Peachy was anxious to be fair, to find the exact truth. 'Believe me, the fault may not be his, even when we see some strutting peacock, jaw extended, hamming the part of saviour, whose object is personal decoration and the accumulation of wealth.'

'I see,' said the Colonel quietly. 'I would have thought that it was.'

Peachy waved away the cigar smoke with a fussy hand, supposing this also dispelled their confusion of thought. 'The fault lies in the system, in the concentration of power in lunatic hands, in customs which do not allow for a change of ruler even when the ruler is incompetent or paranoid: in this situation only the army commander has the power to effect a change in the government. Now he *must* take the sorry scheme of things into his disciplined hand and shake it into order.'

The Colonel had listened patiently. He said now, with no alteration in the level of his voice, 'In my recollection, the soldier usually makes a worse mess of it than his predecessor. I am totally opposed to military intrusion in civil Government. I cannot remember that a soldier has ever ruled successfully following a seizure of power.'

'Cromwell,' said Peachy abruptly. 'Napoleon.'

'It may be so; but I am neither of these. I do not understand politics.'

'You understand the employment of force. That *is* politics in Arabia. In any case, I am not asking you to rule, only to rid us of Hajji Kassim and then to keep order for a few days.'

The Colonel laid down his glass and turned to the Agent 'Mr Peachy, I am a regular officer on secondment. I am still on the active list, with loyalties to my service and its traditions. I have spent a lifetime in maintaining the political decisions of others—those appointed or destined to rule by whatever the local process may have been—and I have never, that I can remember, entered the political field other than to give advice on military matters.'

He looked into the shadows, the better to read the past. 'I have tried to behave reasonably. I have contained a riot in Malaya by thumping the ringleaders with rubber batons. I have relieved famine and distress in Bengal by bringing up food and medicine. I have shot people when I couldn't do anything else, and I have dug latrines.' He contrived a wan smile then. 'I can assure you, Mr Peachy, that the latrines made by the Army are the best anywhere because the Army understands the requirement and the method. I have dealt with the human need as I have seen it, and I believe I have done some good. Politics are beyond all this and above my head.'

Peachy snorted. He removed his cigar and belched. He said with morose conviction, 'Colonel, there comes a time—sadly, there comes a time—when it's all one, when everything merges into a single necessity and no one can claim to be outside politics.'

'And it is now?' the Colonel asked.

In the ante-room the officers were playing football with the cushions. Peachy's glass shook ever so slightly at the sound of their voices.

'Yes,' he said softly, 'it is now.'

As ever, a conspiracy could only be made in whispers.

'What exactly do you want?'

'That you should remove the ruler from power, to some place where he can do no further harm.'

'You mean I should kill him.'

'That is the Arabian method, and it is permanently effective.

But I'm not asking for that.'

'I couldn't be a party to his murder.'

'He was almost a party to yours.'

'It makes no difference; his methods are not mine.'

'I know, I know,' the Agent said. 'Overcome the bodyguard, transport him across the frontier and make certain he doesn't come back.'

'And what would result? Anarchy, needless to say. The tribes would murder and pillage. Someone would have to assume power.'

'Yourself, of course. You would command the only effective power in the state.'

'I won't do it.'

'For a few days only, until the political scene has hardened.'

'It's absurd. British officers don't behave like this.'

'The next ruler will appear very quickly, obliged to act just as you will have been obliged to act, and he'll be better than the old one.'

'I suppose you mean Saud, a Marxist. What good can that do?'

'No, not Saud. He won't act. He's a political dilettante, given to a study of theories; he's not concerned with the realities of opportunity. Nor Abdullah the Wise, who's too close to Hajji Kassim. It'll be Abdullah the Wicked.'

'I don't believe it.'

'There's nobody else. And he's harmless, with a generous impulse.'

'A madcap, Mr Peachy, interested only in pleasure.'

'There are worse rulers in Arabia.'

'Listen, Peachy, listen! I can't think like this. The Emir is my master, no matter what his faults may be.'

'A wicked, cruel man, vicious and unnatural, who would have taken your life——'

'I can't help that. He is the ruler by right of succession.'

'He killed his predecessor, more likely than not.'

'He is head of state, commander-in-chief, and chief justice. Authority stems from him. You can't ask me to put my hand against the established authority.'

'Not even when that authority rests in a diseased mind and is seen to have a diabolical purpose?'

'Not even then.'

The Colonel's face was firm. As ever, he had issued his decision from a perfect repose.

The candles burnt down towards their sockets. In the neighbouring room, the officers were still playing the lively games the Army had played for a century. The Agent put down his glass.

'One minute more, one last word. . . .'

The Agent held the Colonel by the arm and obliged him to listen. They had moved on to the mess roof, under the clear stars. In the rooms below, from which the light spilled out to illuminate the grey sands, the eager voices of the officers continued. The Colonel did not feel able to deny Mr Peachy this last indulgence.

'Colonel, you would agree that a soldier's first duty is to his troops.'

'I can think of no more compelling duty, if that is what you mean.'

'Their safety, their comfort—these must be his first concern.'

'Of course.'

'And he would place this duty above his responsibility to a superior authority.'

'That doesn't follow. Discipline depends upon the acceptance of authority at each level. A soldier must often risk the safety of his troops at the direction of his superior.'

'Where his orders are reasonable within the context of the situation, of course, I agree with you: however, when those orders are plainly absurd, and would needlessly destroy the troops under his command, then surely the soldier must think first of his troops and their safety.'

'Mr Peachy, you are not thinking in a military way. A soldier can't decide which of his orders he will accept, which he will ignore.'

The Agent paused, looking at the stars. Then he said with slow gravity, 'I want you to ask yourself this question: can you conceive a situation where an officer in independent command would be bound to place the safety of his soldiers above his respect for authority?'

The Colonel tried to consider the matter fairly. 'It would be a mess,' he said at last, unable to think of anything better.

'I am bound to say that, in his present mood, the Emir may try to destroy the Levy by one means or another.'

'He would? He would try to do that?' The Colonel tried not to show his concern. 'Surely, if that were the case, he would simply dismiss me and the other officers and disband the companies.'

'No, sir, no. He's Al Farahid, a descendant of Kabina. He would prefer to kill you than to dismiss you, because death is the only form of dismissal he understands. He would prefer to see the Levy destroyed in battle than dispersed. Certainly, whichever way it went, he would contrive the deaths of Ramadi and the other soldiers who have taken your part.'

'I am obliged to take this seriously?'

'It would be as well. Moreover, in the darkest part of his mind, the Emir has a task for the mercenaries other than defence: he intends to use them against the Levy, to destroy the object of his loathing.'

'What a mess,' the Colonel said, and sighed. He was at a loss, his heart heavy with dismay, because he could not see the cardinals of discipline, a willing obedience given to a just authority. His next thought, which contained a private horror, would not fall exactly into words. He struggled to find his meaning. 'I believe that disobedience leads to madness, to the disintegration not only of the individual soldier but of the army itself, which turns into a mad animal. It becomes an awful, an unnatural thing.'

Peachy laid a hand on his arm, not in patronage but in private sympathy. At the moment he had nothing to say.

With greater strength, the Colonel said, 'I can't believe that the best interests of Hassan will be served by my disobedience —or, worse than that, by my seizure of power. In any case, you were a British official and I am a seconded regular, and I can't think the home government would approve of our taking independent action of this kind.'

The Agent raised his shoulders in hopelessness. 'Only we know how things are. You can't expect a civil servant sitting in Whitehall to understand the mind of Hajji Kassim. We have to act alone.'

'I see. It's a damnable mess. I don't know what to do.'

They were alone on the roof with their terrible responsibility.

Peachy said then, 'No matter what you decide, you must send Ramadi away. I can't vouch for his safety, as the Emir believes him to have been your partner in conspiracy. His tribe, the Rashkir, is somewhere in the southern desert.'

'Ramadi? He's just a soldier. All right, I'll let him go.'

Of a sudden the Colonel was bitterly angry. 'Lord God, why should we be faced with this? Why should we have to expect the murder of a soldier? It wasn't like this in the old days; then there was some sort of courtesy. Even at the end in India we kept traces of dignity and pride, and our opponents didn't dislike us personally. There was a sanity, a charm of manner, an affection even. I don't know what's happened now. I accept that imperial government had to go, but for the life of me I can't see that this new world is the better for it. It's mad, mad!'

Peachy did not respond, and the Colonel was ashamed of this outburst which did nothing to solve their problem.

'I can't give you an answer, Peachy. I'll have to think about it.'

'Don't think too long.'

'I won't. It's an awful thing you're asking.'

The Agent turned to go down, having no reply, but a single thought brought him back.

He said, 'I know what I'm asking. I know what this means to you. I know that it's not your way. But there's nothing else that we can do.'

He disappeared, to play rugby with a sofa downstairs, and the Colonel remained at the parapet.

A dog's breakfast, he thought. I've never seen anything like it in all my life.

18

The Colonel's long experience had taught him to verify the facts before reaching a judgement. Accordingly, next morning at first light, he took the armoured car on to the southern road so that he might patrol the Hadraifi frontier and, if possible, learn what business the mercenaries had there. So far he had ignored Major Kennedy and his men because, to his mind, they were an obscenity he did not wish to recognize; however, if he were to take Peachy seriously, he must now judge for himself what danger they represented. The armoured vehicle ran down the unsurfaced road dragging a cloud of dust behind it.

Sergeant Major Ramadi, in bedouin robes, occupied the second seat behind the driver. With reluctance, the Colonel had signed his discharge from military service and had agreed to take him part of the way to the southern desert where his tribe, the Rashkir, were believed to be grazing their animals. He felt the loss of Ramadi so keenly he had been unable to speak to him that morning; and now, while they occupied the small interior of the vehicle, he kept his eyes from the stocky figure in the unfamiliar robes in case he should show his distress. Instead, the Colonel watched the turns and gradients of the hill road as they made rapid progress towards the Maledifah desert where the Hadraifi frontier lay by right if not by usage.

After an hour they came to the camel track which would take Ramadi in the direction of his people. The Colonel swung the turret through a complete revolution to make certain it was safe for them to leave the vehicle. At a distance of a mile a Land-Rover without markings had stopped near to the track, but Masterman could not see if it was occupied or not; almost certainly it belonged to the oil men who pursued their unattractive product in all parts of the interior. He stood with his head and shoulders outside the turret and examined it through his binoculars. The lack of military markings and of screens over the windows suggested an innocent purpose and he jumped down into the road. Ramadi followed him, carrying his possessions in a cloth bundle.

The Colonel could not find his voice. Finally he said in simple Arabic, 'Go and find your people, Ramadi. Our soldiering is over. I will not forget you.'

The Sergeant Major nodded. He had something to say. He was looking for the words.

'What is it, Ramadi?'

'The Colonel will come with me?'

Colonel Masterman laughed, used as he was to the exaggerations of the bedouin. 'I would like to come with you and meet your people, but I don't know the ways of the desert.'

Ramadi spoke abruptly, which the Colonel put down to his lack of ease at parting. 'The Colonel will come with the bedouin. At this season they will be moving southward towards the mountains. In three months we will reach the Jebel Hajarek and the Colonel, if he wishes, can then go on to the coast, where there are people of all types and he can find a boat to take him to India. The Colonel will come with Ramadi!'

Masterman was moved; he had not expected this invitation. 'And what would I do in the desert, friend?'

'Hunt, talk, take mutton and coffee.'

'You are kind, Ramadi, but I cannot leave the soldiers.'

The Sergeant Major had been a soldier too long to argue with his commanding officer. He took up his bundle and, too distressed to say good-bye, started along the camel track away from the vehicle. When he had gone twenty paces, he stopped and turned back. For a time he stood looking at the Colonel, his figure clearly defined in the desert light.

'With the bedouin, the Colonel will be safe; they care nothing for politics.'

'I know, old friend, but I cannot come.'

'They will harm you.'

'Maybe. I have to stay.'

Ramadi resumed his long walk to the southern desert and Masterman watched him until the haze blurred the edges of his figure. Then he climbed back into the turret and told the driver to continue along the main road towards the frontier.

Inside the jolting vehicle, Masterman tried not to look at the empty seat behind the driver because he did not want to be reminded of the absent soldier. He took his map from the case and identified the place where the Hadraifis had been killed and where he would probably find traces of the mercenaries. Leaving the road, he directed the driver along a series of intersecting tracks until he reached the village of Bir N'jef, which was a poor place even by the modest standards of the Rub al Khali—a mosque, a pen, a few mud hovels, chiefly in ruin, and a dry well. All around him the sunlight consumed the fine detail, leaving only the blazing sand and the rocks.

Under the arches of the mosque some ragged tribesmen were resting. They wore black robes and seemed to be Kadafs from the Maledifah, the poorest among tribes where the mean was poverty, and though the Colonel spoke to them, asking for news of the foreign soldiers, they would not speak to him, nor would they raise their eyes from the dust. He left them to whatever dreams they had.

He told the driver to skirt the Surahdin escarpment northward towards the limit of the Hadraifi coastal plain; here some grazing was in perpetual dispute and the Awali of the district had reported firing by day. This tip of land was hit by the south-west winds blowing off the Indian Ocean; the desert imperceptibly gave way to a ground scattered with thorn, and succulent, and finally to a bank of palms growing along the coast. The village of Razpat, nothing more than the house of the Awali, a well where the bucket was lifted by a donkey treading a wheel, a ruined fort built centuries ago by merchant Christians, a heap of refuse and a sense of unalterable boredom and decay—the village lay at the point where the desert tracks joined the trade route leading into Hadraif and the Arabian Horn. A caravan was halted in the broken light under the palms, the camels kneeling, the bales off-loaded, the traders sleeping upon rush mats.

The Awali, an elderly man nearly blind with trachoma, had heard the sustained firing of light weapons in the frontier region two days earlier. He had seen no one, identified no one; he pointed in proof to his weak and guttering eyes. But he was lying; he was stiff with the fear of Hajji Kassim and his irregular soldiers.

The Colonel followed a track in the direction shown, coming at length into broken hills where the wind had blown the rocks into strange convolutions. The frontier lay some miles to the eastward, on lower ground. It was from these hills that Kabina and her sons were said to have raided the plains in the dark century when Hassan was founded: indeed, the defensive advantage of these rocks, which rose three hundred feet from the plain, would be obvious to anyone with the instinct of a soldier or a bandit—or of a modern mercenary paid to kill effectively.

The mercenary camp lay in flat ground where a cliff afforded some shadow; it was not guarded. The Colonel noted this lack of security with surprise, supposing the mercenaries to despise all traditional methods. The tents, cut on modish lines, were in the bright colours favoured by the makers of holiday equipment, and to the Colonel they looked unsuitable for a campaign in desert conditions where the predominant colours were grey, dun and a lambent rose.

He left his vehicle by the track and went in search of Major Kennedy. The mercenaries at rest in the camp grinned at the regular uniform, the campaign ribbons, the erect and deliberate carriage of the visitor as he inquired after their commander: they themselves were in loose camouflaged overalls, the berets and soft suede boots of the world's irregular forces, a uniform the Colonel found odious in its indiscipline. Major Kennedy received him in the mess tent. He had a round pale face in which the eyes were set far apart, and the nose and tiny mouth were both small and indistinct, with the anonymity of babyhood. His face was as soft and obscene as a buttock. He showed only mild surprise at the Colonel's visit: his face was cleaned of expression, as if he were freed from commitment, from the restraints of custom and living again amid the infinite possibilities of childhood. He did not smile; he simply opened his eyes more widely and drew his mouth into a little oval. When he spoke his manner was familiar, his accent that of the American eastern seaboard.

'I heard you were in the district, Colonel. They told me you left Warboys at daybreak, taking the Bir N'jef road, and that you carried a passenger as far as the second intersection—tiresome, no doubt, to have your movements monitored, but an armoured vehicle is not exactly inconspicuous. So?'

He laughed, but his face did not respond. He called a second officer into the tent, an Australian with broken features and an eye that twitched in the semblance of a wink. 'This is Duke, my second-in-command. We're pretty informal in this outfit. Duke, this is Colonel Masterman, of the regular force.'

'Hi, Colonel,' said the Australian.

'How do you do,' said Masterman.

'Hell, sit down,' said Kennedy. 'What do they call you? Clive, isn't it? Well, Clive, I don't expect you to approve of an irregular outfit. It's not your style, I agree; too easy-going, too independent; but I see no reason why we should get fouled up with the regulars. In a place like Hassan there's hardly room for two armies, but provided we accept we each have a job to do, then I expect we can rub along. Don't you agree, soldier? Isn't that so.'

'It was about your job that I wished to speak to you,' the Colonel said.

'Our job,' Duke repeated. 'Hell in this heat, Clive.'

'Oh, our job,' Kennedy said. 'Don't you worry about it, Clive. We'll keep out of your sight; we won't compete in ceremonial or things like that; and I'll let you know if you're treading on my toes. Sure.'

The Colonel decided to speak his mind. 'Major Kennedy, you are right in supposing that I don't approve of irregular forces and that I have misgivings about your present employment. The duplication of forces without a common command or policy is obviously dangerous, particularly in a country where motives are often confused. You have no natural loyalty to the Emir. Your force is not responsible to any international agency. However, it would help me if I could know —on a confidential basis—just what it is you have been directed to do.'

'That I don't doubt, Clive. I've got what you might call an open-ended commitment. My style, if you understand me— very little bull, very little ceremonial, just a directive to sit around and now and again give the dissidents a lesson in caution.'

'Hell in this heat, Clive,' Duke said, winking.

'It won't upset the regulars one bit. Sure,' said Kennedy.

Masterman again spoke firmly. 'I would prefer an exact account of your directive. The possibility of an Hadraifi invasion cannot be discounted. My own position as the commander of the Emir's army would then become very difficult.'

'Now then, that's true. As my old friend Colonel Svenson said, yours is a command with distinct problems. The Hadraifis might be inclined to invade, or at least to occupy tribal territory in the Emirate, and that could lead to conflict.'

'Bang, bang,' said Duke.

Kennedy said, 'And I can't guess how the Levy will behave in action. Now then, can you? Morale hasn't been too good since the demise of Captain Sloan. We'll help out, of course. Soldiers should certainly help one another. You can count on the irregulars to impose the whip every once in a while in the interests of regimental discipline.'

The Colonel contained his anger; he would not be drawn on the subject of Captain Sloan. Instead, controlling the level of his voice, he said, 'You must understand, Major Kennedy, that on no account will I accept outside interference in the discipline of the Levy. I have already declined to surrender my powers of punishment to the civil court, and as far as I know your unit is not recognized by any agreement or charter which might confer upon it the right to inflict punishment.'

Kennedy gave a slow, wintry smile. 'Very well put, Clive. I'd say you were right. But just what difference does it make in this rum desert where they haven't read the books and wouldn't abide by them if they had?'

'I will not tolerate any interference in the affairs of the Levy. I will resist you, by force if necessary.'

'Well now, there's a thing,' Kennedy said. He looked at his watch, as if they had already gone beyond the point in time where the Colonel's objection could be met. 'As it happens. . . .'

Duke grinned, put on an expression of mock gravity, and said, 'Funny you should say that, sport.'

'What are you telling me?' the Colonel asked.

'Nothing you need worry about,' the Major said.

'You must explain what you mean. I cannot accept your silence.'

'Military security,' said Duke.

'If you have taken any action against my soldiers, no matter what it may be, I shall hold you to account for it.'

The Colonel sat on the edge of the mess table in deep distress. He was in a country where he no longer knew the landmarks. The mercenary officers were wholly relaxed, wholly neutral; they were creatures from the new world, from the future, from whom restraint had been withdrawn leaving nothing but a motiveless expediency. When the argument ended, the mercenaries were left. He recognized nothing in their manner but their contempt.

He could no longer contain his anger. He said with guarded fury, 'Major Kennedy, I will not waste your time or my own, but I want you to understand my mind. The presence of mercenary forces in Hassan disgusts me.'

They were not offended. They lived in a world without passion. 'That's not very nice, Clive,' Kennedy said.

'I condemn the motives of all officers who undertake military service without a fixed loyalty. They seem to me morally outcast and dangerous. Only with an abiding respect for a country, and that country's purposes, can one use the methods of war and be free from guilt.'

Why should the mercenaries care? They simply laughed.

'Moreover, I tell you this: I command a force of greater size, skill and training than your own, and I have a warrant to use it in whatever seems to me the best interests of the state. If I think you are going beyond the bounds of legitimate defence, or if I think your actions are likely to provoke disorder or war, or if you in any way interfere in the business of the Levy, then I shall not hesitate to use my force to correct the situation, no matter that such an action may bring me into conflict with you. I shan't even hesitate if I find myself in conflict with the Emir. You don't frighten me, Major Kennedy. You disgust me. I hope I am clear to you, because I will not repeat myself now or in the future.'

He left the camp abruptly, resumed his seat in the armoured

car, and ordered the driver to make his best pace out of the district.

He sat hunched up in the turret not bothering to watch the road. When his anger passed, he felt simply tired and sick. The smooth countenance of Major Kennedy stayed before his mind's eye, an emblem of those new forces, clad in sloppy overalls, which had spread into this theatre now that the imperial armies had gone. In weakness, he allowed his imagination to show him the lost armies, their flourish and discipline; he saw the long columns under the steep Indian sunlight as they moved up to the frontier in support of an old, familiar order; he recalled the endless days of the British peace which had been marked by calm and sanity. The armoured car continued its violent passage out of the hills and towards Razpat. He welcomed the movement and noise which shut out the memory of Major Kennedy and his mercenaries.

He had no answer for Mr Peachy. His disgust with the mercenaries did not amount to an argument for revolution; in fact he was confirmed in his belief that a break in discipline could lead to nothing but total madness when the last restraint would be gone. His mind would not adapt to revolution: he did not even think the possibility through, listing the measures that would be necessary for an assumption of power: the matter lay outside the range of his mind.

He saw telegraph wires crossing the turret hatch above his head and he knew they were passing through Razpat and taking the track along the face of the escarpment towards Bir N'jef. Two hours, perhaps, to Warboys.

Then his thought lost all form in the shuddering movement of the vehicle. Sloan; it came back to Sloan. As if in sickness, single images from the past weeks occupied his mind, each drawn in more savage lines than they had been in reality: he saw Sloan at the edge of the roof, telling him Hamid had deserted; he saw Sloan taken to court martial under escort, charged with an assault upon Hamid; he saw Sloan living, speaking; he saw him lying in his chair, his throat open, perhaps ten minutes dead—ten minutes into a long oblivion while behind him the consequences of his action multiplied. Sloan had brought the mercenaries into Hassan. What on earth had been the matter with Sloan?

He was jolted awake as the vehicle came to a halt on the desert road. His soldier's mind, which continued along an even course of assessment and decision no matter that he was awake or asleep, told him they were beyond Bir N'jef and somewhere close to the main road into Bir-el-Shama, an area where there was seldom trouble. He could see nothing through the turret sight to represent a danger. He called to the driver, asking what had happened, but he could not hear the reply above the beat of the engine. Following his instinct to examine things for himself, he raised himself through the open hatch and stood on the upper plating of the vehicle. In the afternoon light the dunes were violet and backed in shadow, the hills on the seaward side were softened in outline, the sky was marked with cirrus at a great height. They had stopped at the intersection of two tracks; the Colonel did not know why.

He jumped down on to the road and walked to the front of the vehicle where he could talk to the driver through the open port. 'What is it?' he asked.

The driver said nothing but pointed up the road, and the Colonel turned to follow the direction of his finger, knowing in the instant that some fresh cruelty would be shown to him, that the tragedy continued, that there was nothing he could do. At a distance of thirty paces, and just visible round a screen of rocks, the body of a man had been planted upright in the middle of the road, held by a pole; the tilt of the body was towards him, the right hand was fastened to the eyebrow in a parody of a salute, the face was smashed by the exit wound of a bullet. The Colonel's military reflex compelled him first to examine the rocks on either side of the road for signs of ambush. When he saw none, he went quickly forward to the dead man, instructing the soldiers in the vehicle to follow him. With as much gentleness as he could contrive, he lowered the body into the road, withdrew the pole from the clothing and turned the man over for identification. But he did not need to examine the broken features: he knew from the stocky figure and bedouin robes that the man was Ramadi.

Ramadi.

The driver whistled in horror.

'Be quiet,' the Colonel said.

Oh Ramadi—who was it, why was it done? By long habit, the Colonel closed his mind to the dead soldier while there was still danger. He told the driver to bring sacking from the vehicle, and together they bound the body of Ramadi and lashed it to the flat plating forward of the turret where it could ride back to Warboys and decent burial. Only when they were safe behind the armour and the vehicle resumed its journey did the Colonel's mind tumble into rage and despair. Ramadi, Ramadi.... He remembered the Land-Rover beside the track where the Sergeant Major had alighted, and in a fury he blamed himself for not having examined it more closely. Beyond doubt this was mercenary work; the bullet through the back of the head was the approved method of execution in the irregular armies, which they had learned from the totalitarians; and it was only in the erection of the body where he was bound to find it, and in the attitude in which it had been arranged, that this murder was distinguished from the commonplace. Another killing in the Third World; it didn't add much to the tally of the dead.

The Colonel sat with his head in his hands, his eyes smarting with tears, his heart filled with a dull, shapeless anger, seeing nothing but the broken face of Ramadi.

19

The vast area to the east of Suez, where Colonel Masterman had spent his working life, was no longer a place of British interest. The maps were put away; the tactical problems were relegated to the pages of regimental history; the theatre was left to its own savage devices. British frigates no longer cut white paths into the gulfs and inlets of the Indian ocean. The pink mountains of the Middle Eastern Barrier and the olive jungles of Malaya were no longer crossed by the shadows of British military aircraft. The regular battalions had all withdrawn. It was over and done with, the task accomplished, with nothing much left to show but the empty lines and the telegraph poles planted with precision between one decaying cantonment and another. Once amid the foliage of Penang the shouts of the non-commissioned officers had put the orioles to flight, and at Barrackpore the singing in the soldiers' mess had disturbed the bats which hung in the casuarina trees. It was not so now; the establishments filled with litter, and the officers' mess collapsed in a cloud of yellow dust; the ressaldar, the subahdar had stood down. Across the whole theatre there was a movement to erase the imperial past as though it had never been.

In Arabia the movement was not yet complete.

Following the murder of Ramadi, Colonel Masterman could not think plainly; he felt dull, hurt, no longer able to trust his own judgement or to assess what his next action should be. He had hardly the strength for revolt; but neither was he still secure in his own opinions, believing in the overriding importance of the military virtue; it did not seem to matter what he did. He supposed the old values to have been withdrawn with the armies, leaving only a bitter cynicism which swept like a hard wind over the area once controlled by the British. In this demented land, did it matter what obligations were broken?

He began to think, idly and without using his best mind, of the means he might use to shift Hajji Kassim from his office if that should be the only method of keeping the peace in Hassan and saving the lives of his soldiers. Once he had overcome his objection to thinking in these terms, the main lines of the operation fell into place; it was simply a tactical problem presenting no difficulty to an officer of experience. He did not know if he had the resolution to carry it through, nor could he be sure if the situation would improve if he did; he saw the whole thing in the half light of exhaustion, with no firm conviction of what he should do.

He paced the balcony outside his office at Warboys from where he could see the familiar outlines of the camp. The setting, and his measured footsteps, were enough to put thoughts of mutiny out of his mind, but again and again he remembered the need for action, as he might have remembered a sick dream, and he wondered how it came about that a colonel of infantry should be faced with this decision.

Major Tillotson, with his nose for the disagreeable, came to him on the second day. 'Frankly, Colonel, you'd better tell me where we stand. It's clear we are faced with a crisis of some sort, and it's not difficult to see that it must arise from a failure of confidence between the Ruler and yourself. It's rumoured —I can't say with what truth—that the Emir may have attempted to dismiss you from the Levy.'

The Colonel smiled weakly. 'Something of the sort,' he said.

'As second in command, who would have to take over in your absence, I think I should know your complete mind.'

It was like Tillotson to want so much. His complete mind? He did not know it himself. And even in better days he would have been disinclined to share anything with the officious Major, let alone his most intimate motives.

'I'm sorry, Tillotson; there's nothing I can tell you at the moment.'

He could not involve his officers in conspiracy. The decision must be his, just as the responsibility for failure could only rest with him. If necessary, he would simply tell the officers of his intention, and they would then (he did not doubt, do as he asked them; the wretched politics he must keep to himself.

He didn't know at which moment he made the decision.

Perhaps he didn't make it at all. He was sitting at his desk, spinning the paperweight, when he realized the decision was in the past and that he was thinking of the operation as something he intended to mount. His mind had dismissed all other possibilities and left him with only one course of action. His training did not allow him to do nothing. God, he thought, it's a damnable business, but they shouldn't have killed Ramadi. He felt sick; he felt the featureless misery which is treason. He walked sharply up to the officers' mess and ordered a double whisky which he took on the veranda looking out at the desert hills.

Well, he thought after a while, what's one colonel more or less? Who am I to have principles? All that sort of thing came to an end when the soldiers went home. But it's a bugger's muddle, none the less.

'Sarita,' Peachy called in the dark garden. 'There are only a few days more.'

'We have those days, then.'

'I could meet you in Tehran.'

'Go away. Stop bullying. What would I do in Tehran?'

The Agent said, 'Have you seen how the vines look when the light shines through them? You can't see how brown and thin they are.' It was true; the vines looked luxuriant with the light from the kitchen window behind them. 'And the lawn—you can imagine it covered with grass. This is a lovely garden!'

'It's only dust. Nothing else.'

'You could leave tomorrow by the plane from D'jeb-Hej.'

'Dust and convolvulus, like all desert gardens. The grass doesn't grow.'

'Oh, but it's full of beautiful flowers—marigolds, lupins, night-scented dandelions. Where are you, my darling?'

'Nowhere. Just here. I'm not going.'

They collided at the corner of the house, by accident, which was the only way they ever met. His memory sketched her face, which was too close for him to see; her breath played across his cheek and then stilled. He counted the seconds until the number was meaningless.

'Terrible, terrible incest,' he said.

'Yes.'

'It can't come to anything.'

'It *is* something.'

'You'd better go away.'

'No.'

'The Colonel will have to act. Poor man, he can't avoid it. I can't say what will happen then.'

'I don't mind. I want this one thing.'

She ran away to the end of the garden, leaving her ghost behind as fragile company. He could not move from the place where he stood. A dew—the strangest thing in Arabia—brushed his cheek where the girl's had lain and spread into the corners of his eyes.

'Go to bed,' he called.

'No.'

'Don't, then. Stay just there. Where I can see you.'

'All right.'

She was in his sight, just, a shape by the farther wall.

'I can't tell how long this will last,' he said.

How long would it last?

After the burial of Ramadi in the military cemetery at Warboys Camp, the Agent invited Colonel and Mrs Masterman to tea in the Agency garden. He also invited Abdullah the Wicked and Sheikh Saud. He had no clear idea of what might happen, and he was aware that his invitations were provocative, but he saw a need to bring together those of his acquaintances who might contribute to a solution in Hassan. The servants erected a coloured awning over the terrace and set a table with the Agency silver. They brought sandwiches and chocolate biscuits on dishes lined with paper doilies. It did not look a proper place in which to plan a revolution.

Sheikh Saud, with what relevance the Agent could not say, treated the tea party to his view of the Arabian past. 'A story of unrelieved darkness,' he said with satisfaction, flicking crumbs from his robe. 'I have been long convinced that madness is the natural condition of Arabia with only occasional visitations of sanity. It is less vexing to regard the nation as mad than to find explanations for each departure from sense; then, in contrast, the periods of our lucidity seem to be times of extraordinary light. That the Arab nation has chosen to live in an arid waste land in itself shows a lack of sense amounting to defectiveness. An interesting point arises: why is it, Mr Peachy, that so many English gentlemen—men of unquestionable sanity, of the most awesome probity—choose to devote their lives and talents to a people manifestly out of their minds. I can only suppose that the restraints of wisdom and logic grow wearisome, that there is some part of an Englishman's make-up that responds to absurdity as to a heady drink.'

'As always, Your Excellency paints a vivid picture,' Peachy said.

'Are the servants to listen to our talk?' asked Mrs Masterman. 'Is that what you intend, Mr Peachy?'

The Agent sent the servants away.

'I find it extraordinarily difficult to think in these terms,' the Colonel said.

'I do not,' said Saud; 'but then, my heritage is different.'

'Will somebody tell me what it is we do?' asked Abdullah the Wicked. 'We blow something up? Yes?'

Colonel Masterman had changed very little, the Agent noted: he gave no less attention to the comfort of the ladies, and his smile, which had always been remote, came no less frequently; his cheek was perhaps more drawn, his mind more difficult to arrest, but these changes would only have been apparent to one who knew him well. The Agent was nonplussed: it looked a very ordinary tea party.

'The plates are beautifully arranged,' Mrs Masterman said. 'I detect a lady's hand. Miss Peachy, I think you must have cut these sandwiches, as I cannot believe the house boy could have managed these scalloped edges.'

'Sandwiches,' said Abdullah, holding one up between thick fingers. 'What is this thing sandwiches?'

Saud the Fat managed his tea cup with composure. He held the saucer balanced on the crown of his stomach, and when he raised the cup to his lips, his eyebrows lifted in appreciation, his head inclined forward no farther than was necessary, and certainly not to a vulgar level—it was an achievement of skill and observation but one which, the Agent realized, did nothing to help them in their present business.

'Mr Peachy,' the Sheikh said brightly, 'you must tell us the purpose of this delightful tea party. Well, perhaps not.'

Without lowering his voice to the approved level, Abdullah said, 'It is necessary always to curtail the work of the post office. It must go up, into fragments, into vapour.'

Merciful God, thought Peachy.

'I cannot assent to any plan dependent upon bloodshed,' the Colonel said firmly. 'If this thing is to be arranged, then it must be done without violence. In any case, I do not think bloodshed is necessary.'

'Was there ever a revolution without bloodshed?' Mrs Masterman asked.

'This is not a revolution, my dear; it is simply an enforced transfer of power.'

'Certainly it is not a revolution,' said Saud, with the delicate precision of one whose only interest is in the use of words. 'It is not rooted in the struggle of one class against another, or against an entrenched privilege. It is, more correctly, a *coup*.'

'I would prefer not to use that word,' Masterman said; 'it has distasteful overtones.'

Peachy saw the need for a definition of their purpose. 'We are asking only that Colonel Masterman should use his force to remove the present ruler from the palace, and to transfer him across the frontier; then he can receive treatment for his malady. A council of elders will appoint a successor.'

'Which will be Sheikh Abdullah, I assume,' said Mrs Masterman. 'I mean to say, there will be no other choice.'

'That will be nice,' said Sarita, a plate in each hand.

'Saud,' said Abdullah moodily. 'They say it will be Saud.'

Sheikh Saud was dismayed; he actually trembled, so that Peachy could hear the rattle of the tea-cup. The Agent felt a trace of sympathy for him, knowing how distressing it could be when an ambition was translated into fact, and he said decisively, 'I cannot say who will be chosen. Certainly no one will be required to serve against his will.'

Cheered by this assurance, the Sheikh renewed his smile. 'There are many possibilities,' he said. 'Abdullah has administrative experience in the Department of Sanitation.'

'What is that?' asked Abdullah. 'What is that you say?'

'I think it would be unwise for Sheikh Abdullah to play any part in the arrest,' Peachy said reflectively. 'Or you, Sheikh Saud. It is necessary for the Colonel to act alone and to hold all the state offices for a few days. Only in that way can the transfer appear orderly and in the best interests of the state.'

'I have no wish to govern,' the Colonel said, and it was plain from his voice that this was the truth.

'My dear, you must,' said Mrs Masterman.

'I shall not govern. I have no right, no skill, and no wish to do so. I will simply administer the state until the next Emir is appointed. Then I shall stand down and resign my appointment in the Levy and, if necessary, my commission in the Army. I do not believe in military government.'

Well, there it was, the assurance that had been given a hundred times as the precursor of brutal dictatorship; but this time Peachy was disposed to believe it, for after all this was an English colonel. 'We are running too far ahead,' he said rapidly. 'I have no doubt the people of Hassan will be grateful to Colonel Masterman for his benevolent, and temporary, intervention.'

'There must be a band,' said Abdullah, 'playing tunes.'

'I'm sure it can be arranged. Colonel, I know this will be irksome to you, but I think it essential you occupy the palace and make your headquarters there.'

'Quite,' said Saud. 'A *coup* is a drama, a theatrical production; it has to be convincing in terms of human symbolism. The Colonel must sit on the Emir's stool, with the apes and tigers.'

A twitch in the Colonel's cheek was the only evidence of his displeasure. 'Mr Peachy—and Your Excellencies—let me tell you this. That I am bound to act in these circumstances I count an extreme personal misfortune. I would prefer anything to an action of this kind, which cuts against the things I have stood for. If I must do it, I will; but I am not going to adopt the antics of a power-crazy colonel. I shall behave as I have always behaved, and if that's not good enough I am prepared to abandon the operation now, come what may. I shall occupy the palace because it will be necessary to disarm the bodyguard but for no other reason. If we must have a *coup*— if that is the word for it—then I shall conduct it without vulgarity and with as much dignity as I can manage. I am opposed to the band on these grounds. Certainly I shall do all that I can to prevent bloodshed.'

'There is always bloodshed,' said Mrs Masterman. 'I do not see why it should be different this time. These people are given to disorderly behaviour.'

The Colonel said, 'I give you my word, gentlemen, that this operation will be carried out with discipline, restraint, and a respect for the dignity of the departing ruler.'

It sounded a proper manner in which to conduct a revolution and the Agent was well pleased. 'I am certain we may leave these things to the Colonel,' he said.

'It is a pity we have no band,' said Abdullah the Wicked. 'Last time I think we had a band.'

'It is not required in any doctrinal sense,' said Saud.

The Agent's mind was adrift from the small details of revolution. The sunlight was catching a bed of marigolds on the far side of the lawn, lighting it gently, like a happy omen. He allowed himself a dream of success: the Emir would surrender himself gracefully, and the alternative government would assume power with sober attention to the needs and safety of the state. He listened to the chink of the tea-cups; he observed the restraint and sanity of Colonel Masterman as he stirred his tea with an apostle spoon and listened with courtesy to Abdullah's views on the need for symbolic violence. In his hands, might it not go well, with the relaxed good humour of the county regiments? A revolution with style? A change in government had never been made under these auspices before, and the Agent had a vision of the perfect *coup*, one handled with swift decorum and leading to a stable future. He was conscious of his weakness in thinking so: he was making no allowance for the unpredictable mind of Hajji Kassim, nor for the violence of the mercenaries. The dream turned sour as he dragged his mind back into reality.

'There are two diplomatic moves which I shall make to ensure the strength of our position,' he said; but he knew even as he spoke that his mention of them would reveal their weakness. 'I shall, on behalf of the transitional government, send a message to Major Kennedy assuring him that his fee will continue to be paid for the time being by whatever government succeeds. It may be as well to increase their pay to make certain of their loyalty. This will ensure that the mercenaries keep out of the matter.' It would do nothing of the sort, of course; they might try to reinstate their champion with a view to their indefinite employment, or they might seek a job with the enemies of Hassan. 'And I shall inform the oil company that their concession will not be revoked, which will secure the state royalties for the future.' Again, this was by no means certain; often enough the companies, frightened by revolution, had cut down their working or closed their wells.

'I am certain we can leave the politics to Mr Peachy,' said the Colonel. 'These I do not understand.'

'Of course, yes,' agreed Saud. 'Mr Peachy will conduct the politics very nicely. When placed in Arab hands, politics tend to become incoherent, one might even say reversed in their object; we had far better leave these matters to a British official, even if at present he should not be conducting Hassanite affairs.'

'Your Excellency does me much honour,' said the Agent.

The Colonel said, 'It's better like that, Peachy. I believe in each man doing his own job. I wouldn't ask you to do the soldiering, and I really wouldn't want to do the politics.' He said it as if he were declining the job of garbage attendant; Peachy alone was to move between the miasmas of political necessity.

'Naturally, all matters of politics are for Mr Peachy to decide,' Mrs Masterman said dismissively.

Well, Peachy would do it, he would foul his hands with these matters, because that was his bent. 'Will you take some more tea, Colonel Masterman?' he asked. 'Sarita, my dear—the Colonel's cup.'

'I am convinced everything is in good order,' Saud assured them. 'We are lucky in being able to place our little *coup* in such trustworthy hands. The Levy, I imagine, will follow the Colonel.'

'Why should they not?' asked Abdullah. 'He blows the pants off them if there is monkey business.'

'Since the murder of Ramadi, the Levy has hardened in its dislike of the mercenaries and, it follows, of the Ruler's policies,' Colonel Masterman told them. 'There are many of

Ramadi's tribe, the Rashkir, in the companies, and I will use them in the operation against the palace. They are bedouin whose natural grounds are as much outside the state as in, and they have never been concerned in urban politics. I can trust them, I am sure, as their discipline has always been good.'

'Hamid, of course, was not of that tribe.'

The Agent was surprised by his own voice. He had spoken without thought, recalling only that Hamid had not been amenable to discipline; and at once he regretted his mention of that unhappy soldier whose antics had given rise to such trouble.

The Colonel was distressed. 'I judge Hamid to be dead by now, Peachy, just as his tormentor is dead. That wretched business came to an end with Sloan's suicide. I suggest we don't let our minds dwell on the past in dealing with the future. There's really no connection between Hamid and the problems now facing us.'

'No. Of course.' Peachy was dismayed at his own lack of delicacy. It couldn't do them any good to remember the chain of events which had led to the terrible present; their only concern was with the future. 'I am sure we can look forward to an humane and successful transfer of power,' he said in recompense, hiding himself behind his tea-cup.

So it might be; but he knew that, were it so, it would be the first in history.

At this time, Colonel Masterman found comfort in the manner of life at Warboys Camp. Nothing here was changed; the routine had continued unbroken during his recent trials, and indeed it simply carried forward the pattern of life he had known since he first came east of Suez thirty years earlier. More and more his mind turned to the past, which he knew to be an indulgence, and he recalled the order and wisdom of the regiments which had seemed likely to go on endlessly into the future. He was inclined to believe that good order was the gift of the regiments alone and that, when they were withdrawn, disorder was bound to follow. Liberty contained a fierce destructiveness.

He wanted the unit clean, he wanted the unit bright. He

ordered a day of camp cleaning and he chased the officers unmercifully to ensure that Warboys was brought to a high standard of order before his act of unparalleled indiscipline. The non-commissioned officers went through the native lines and tidied every wayward blanket. The roads were swept, the windows cleaned, the gateposts had their paint renewed. Then the Colonel went through the unit with a fierce eye, conferring summary punishments where the standards did not meet his own.

I suppose it will have to do, he thought.

He wrote down no part of his plan; he would rely upon a verbal briefing of the officers an hour before the start of the operation. Nevertheless he felt the need to leave some record of his extraordinary conduct in explanation if not in defence; and so, in the late afternoon of the day before the operation to put an end to Hajji Kassim, he went into his office, locked the door and took out a sheet of writing paper. He wrote quickly and without reflection:

Warboys Camp
Hassan

For the attention of the British Military Authorities
As I believe war to be imminent in the Emirate, either with Hadraif, or between the two wings of the Ruler's forces —war which I have no power to prevent—I have taken it upon myself to remove the Emir, His Highness Hajji Kassim bin Mahomet Al Farahid, from his office and from the country in order that he may be replaced by someone who can reverse the present state policies. This action I believe to be necessary to protect the lives of my soldiers and for the peace of the country.

I am aware that, in doing so, I am departing from the terms of my engagement as Commander of the Hassanite Levy, and from the usual practice of British officers on secondment, but I can see no alternative.

Clive Masterman
Colonel

He placed the letter in his safe and locked it. He ordered

an officers' briefing for two hours before dawn. He could think of nothing else he needed to do; so he sat behind his desk and played with the paperweight, thinking of Ramadi.

Very well, he said to himself later, pulling his bush jacket straight; if we must have a *coup* we'll have a bloody good one. No shilly-shally, each man in his place, slappity-bang, umpity-poo. Then, my lords and masters, you can have my resignation and my blessing.

He was still sitting at his desk an hour later when an orderly came to close the shutters.

20

Colonel Masterman kept his briefing simple; he did not believe in flamboyant speeches before action. The Ruler was unfit to govern—therefore, the Colonel told his officers, he would be unseated and taken to a place outside Hassan. He did not tell them where the idea originated; he allowed them to think the operation had official approval, in this way not only ensuring their co-operation but, should things go amiss, their innocence of conspiracy.

'We shall move in one hour and take up our positions before first light. "A" Company, in which the Rashkir predominate, will undertake the operation against the palace; "B" Company will cover the southern road beyond Bir-el-Shama and prevent the return of Major Kennedy and his force. A platoon of "C" Company is to contain the rest of the mercenary force in the Arabian Hotel.

'I shall command "A" Company personally; "B" Company will be under the command of Major Tillotson. "A" Company should have no difficulty in entering the palace as the external guard is mounted by the Levy. Captain Lovelace will simply withdraw this guard a few minutes before our arrival. Once into the courtyard, the company will divide, a platoon under Captain Barrie entering the hall where the bodyguard rest when they are off duty and disarming them; a second platoon commanded by myself will overcome the bodyguard on duty and arrest the Ruler in his bedroom. Detachments working simultaneously under junior officers will take over the communications room and the office of the Chamberlain. If the leopards give trouble, they are to be clubbed.

'I shall rejoin "A" Company in the courtyard as soon as I have the Emir in custody. He will then be conveyed by Land-Rover, with an escort of two armoured cars, to the airstrip at D'jeb-Hej, from where a light aircraft provided by the Agency will take him to an oasis outside the country and at a distance sufficient to prevent his return. As a courtesy, he will be allowed to take his favourite concubine, two slaves, and at least one member of his personal staff. This part of the operation will be under the control of Captain Lovelace, who will also accompany the Emir as far as D'jeb-Hej and treat him with the deference due to his rank.

'Are there any questions?'

There were none that mattered: the concept was familiar enough.

Once out on the dust road leading to the palace, in the moist morning air, smelling the bitter scent of the desert, the Colonel was nearly happy. He knew he had devised the best plan he could and that the limits of his task, for the moment, were precisely set. The company moved in silence behind him. By now Tillotson and the second company would be beyond Bir-el-Shama and forming the essential screen to prevent the mercenaries from returning to the capital, and Peachy's messenger would have told them their wages were safe.

The desert hills were just visible in the starlight. A mile ahead of them, breaking the skyline, the sharp outlines of the palace were showing. The Colonel felt a quiet pride in the discipline of his troops; they moved forward without speaking, holding the broken step (which to highly drilled soldiers was more difficult to keep than the march), trailing their arms so that the slings did not rattle, climbing the slight incline towards the palace gate in perfect order.

It was a still and windless morning, the only sounds the muted footfall and the long soft sibilant as the men took their breath on the incline. The Colonel found pleasure in action; the problems of his command were reduced to a single hazard, and his mind quickened to a new pitch of excitement. He relied upon the soldiers' instinct for obedience, and the anger of the Rashkir at the death of Ramadi, to carry them through the next half hour. They followed him on the long hill. They obeyed the order for silence. They advanced in their loose formation up to the walls of the palace, where Captain Lovelace was waiting.

The palace guard had been withdrawn half a mile. Only the personal bodyguard now lay between themselves and the

Emir, and the Colonel knew these askaris to be poorly trained, dull-minded and without leadership. Earlier in the night the Captain of the Bodyguard, the Yemeni, whose devotion to duty was less than absolute, had been seen at a drab establishment in Bir-el-Shama, and Charles Peachy had sent a message to the proprietress begging her to keep him there with special favours. The Colonel accepted that in the Middle East a device of this sort might be acceptable if it lessened the risk to his soldiers.

He looked at his watch: five minutes to the moment of arrest. It was enough.

Lovelace, his face blackened, came out of the shadows to report the palace quiet, but in the slave quarters there had been voices and movement.

'It doesn't matter,' Masterman said. 'Slaves have no mind for action.'

'Colonel, Colonel....'

The Colonel turned his ear to the Adjutant with reluctance. He didn't like Lovelace, nor his stupid grin.

'This is Arabia, sir. The method you have planned may not serve the purpose.'

'What do you mean?'

'You may have to blast his head off.'

'I shall do no such thing. You are to follow your instructions, without question.'

He left Lovelace smiling into the darkness and took his company into the first courtyard. The Adjutant would now bring the guard back into position on the walls and embrasures, but this time the soldiers would have their arms turned inward. In the starlight, the Colonel saw the courtyard to be empty but for some sleeping beggars; they would not interfere in revolution; he left them lying there and passed through the screen into the second court, where he concentrated the company around him.

Three minutes to the arrest. So far they hadn't awakened the palace.

He detached a party under Captain Barrie to enter the guardroom and armoury and subdue those of the bodyguard not on duty. He directed two junior officers and their troops towards the communications room and the state offices. This was pointless, he knew, because the radios didn't work and a guard in the council chambers would have only a symbolic purpose. The men vanished without sound.

My word, the Colonel thought; I'm enjoying this more than I ought.

He took his party of twenty soldiers towards the Emir's quarters. He relied upon the slackness of the guard to give him a few seconds of advantage. At the entrance there was no leopard, although a ring-bolt and chain showed where the creature usually lay, and the door was unlocked. It's really too easy, the Colonel told himself, passing into the scented interior. How careless of the Ruler to invite the assassin and the predatory colonel into his apartments!

Take it easy, he thought. Don't count any chickens.

He passed down a long corridor and up a stairway, guided by flashlight. The walls were hung with carpets and the place smelled of cheap scent. No doubt that Kabina was ancestress here. A door opened and a girl looked at them, and she laughed at the sight of so many soldiers with blackened faces. The Colonel continued fast in the direction he had been told would take him to the Emir's chamber.

Wake up, Hajji Kassim, he said inwardly as he approached the door. We're here to get you.

Never trust a colonel, not even an infantryman.

This is it, my Lord and King....

The bodyguard gave no trouble. Of the two men at the Emir's door, one rose stiffly to his feet and saluted, the other did not wake. They were quickly disarmed, the Colonel thanking God for Arab laxity.

'Take them away,' he said sharply. 'Open the door.'

He thrust his way into the Emir's bedchamber, his pistol in his hand. Hajji Kassim, disturbed by the noise outside, was pulling a robe over his head, and when two soldiers caught him and threw him to the carpet he could not see whom his assailants were.

'Who is it?' he asked in Arabic.

'It is I, Colonel Masterman.'

'What do you want?'

'I am obliged to arrest you.'

The soldiers raised him to his feet and freed his head from the robe. He recognized the inevitable conspiracy of the soldiers.

'This is treason,' he said, and spat.

In his bed a girl was crying.

'You will not be harmed, sir.'

'You cannot replace me. In my lifetime I must rule in Hassan.'

'I have no alternative.' Now that the danger had passed, the Colonel was struck with embarrassment. What was he doing in the Emir's bedroom, a pistol in his hand? 'That I must subject you to this indignity, I regret. Will you please dress immediately and accompany me out of the palace. I am obliged to act to prevent the state from being destroyed.'

The shabby platitude convinced neither of them. Despite his lack of height, the Emir was a master of disdain.

'You will not succeed, Colonel. The people will kill you.'

But already the Colonel had lost heart in the operation; he was sickened by the vulgarity of revolution. He leant against the wall, letting the seconds pass, knowing he had still to enforce a soldierly solution. He struggled upright. With as much strength as he could manage, he said, 'Will somebody take that girl away and comfort her. Call the Emir's attendants and see that he gets dressed. His luggage must be prepared. At once, do you hear?'

As he went out of the room, he turned once more to Hajji Kassim.

'Your Highness, I regret the necessity for this action.'

The Emir spat in his face.

In the corridor outside he collided with Mr Peachy, who had arrived from the Agency.

'This is wrong, Peachy; quite wrong.'

'It was inevitable.'

'It is wrong and cannot succeed.'

He took a seat in a small ante-chamber. Everywhere girls were laughing, crying.

'God, will somebody take the girls away,' he bellowed. 'This is bedlam. Fetch the Chamberlain.'

When the Chamberlain came, shuffling in slippers, frightened for his life, the Colonel told him to prepare the Emir's luggage and a small retinue: a secretary, two slaves and a favourite.

Meanwhile, the Colonel sat with his head in his hands, alone. He wondered what his regiment would think of him. Would they laugh at his indiscipline? Would they say that he lost his head? He heard voices in every part of the Emir's palace as the soldiers took over the state rooms and the military government began. There did not seem to be resistance; no doubt the palace was totally surprised.

In a while the Chamberlain was back, cringing.

'The former ruler desires two favourites, if the Colonel pleases.'

'One only,' the Colonel snapped, 'and be quick about it.'

'Then it will be Mrs Jason-Caldicott.'

'Very well. See that she is informed. Whom did you say? Never mind; it doesn't make the slightest difference which woman he takes with him.'

He went down to the courtyard to take the reports from his officers. The bodyguard had surrendered and were now secured in their mess hall, from where they had asked for coffee and gramophone records. Their Captain had been arrested as he stumbled up the road towards the palace, too wearied to resist. The palace had fallen too easily; the employment of force against weakness was obscene, and the Colonel felt a sharp distaste at the way things had gone. Across the desert the light grew slowly.

The soldiers reassembled in the courtyard. The violence done to the Ruler excited them and they whispered within the ranks as they took their company order.

'Silence!' the Colonel roared. 'I won't have a bear garden of any sort.'

The NCOs kept the ranks quiet with difficulty. Captain Lovelace brought up the Land-Rover and the two armoured cars which would take Hajji Kassim to D'jeb-Hej, and he placed them with their engines running facing the entrance.

'There will be a guard stationed between the doorway and the vehicles,' the Colonel said. 'Not a guard of honour, you understand, as that would be inappropriate, but three ranks of soldiers who will come to attention when the Emir leaves the palace. We will show him that measure of respect. There will be no talking of any kind. The officers will salute.'

He fretted in the courtyard waiting for Peachy to bring down the departing ruler. He wished the wretched business over. In the dawn light the courtyard was an unfamiliar place filled with shadows. The beggars who slept under the arches had not wakened; in the morning they would open their eyes to a new government, composed of the military, who had seized power by the oldest of means while they slept, but it was unlikely they would be much concerned.

Why doesn't he come? the Colonel wondered.

While the Ruler remained in the palace he was still Emir. Masterman wanted him gone, stripped of his office, sent far outside the state where he could no longer assert his kingship. Of course, to have killed him the moment he burst into his bedroom, in the manner of the country, would have served better, but this remedy was beyond the Colonel. Now they must get rid of Hajji Kassim as quickly as possible and build something new and honest in the state of Hassan.

He must go where he could do no further harm.

He must go.

Peachy led the small party into the courtyard. The Emir's favourite wore a fur coat and seemed very much at ease. The Emir himself was composed, containing his anger, looking small and vulnerable now that he was deposed from authority. A secretary carried a box of papers; the slaves brought out a number of matching suitcases, a monkey, two dogs and a bird in a cage.

The King was leaving with light baggage. The King was leaving in the face of revolution.

An Arabian revolution, which could have only one ending.

As the Colonel saluted, there was a disturbance in the guard and a rifle shot sounded, the report much magnified in the courtyard. The Emir's party halted as if in astonishment; then Hajji Kassim slid to the ground like a robe falling off a peg and lay there, a little white bundle on the flag-stones. The revolution, the transfer of power, was complete. A beggar raised his head.

'That does it,' said Lovelace.

I should have known, the Colonel thought.

The soldier who fired the shot lowered his rifle and stood at attention. The guard still showed their respect for the person of Hajji Kassim.

The Colonel found his voice. 'The man is to be arrested and placed in confinement. Captain Lovelace, the unit medical officer is with the support party; bring him here immediately with the ambulance.'

Who killed Hajji Kassim? Just a soldier, it seemed, who had fired for no purpose.

The Colonel approached the guard, showing his fury. 'Why did he do it?' he asked in Arabic. 'Why?'

It was Ramadi's brother, they said.

His father.

His uncle.

His second son.

God, I should have known! the Colonel raged in his mind. The bedouin always avenged a killing, and these men were Rashkir, Ramadi's people. He approached the guilty soldier, who now stood quite still, and struck him across the face with the force of his arm. The soldier fell to the ground.

'You have killed the Emir,' the Colonel said with hopeless anger.

No, not the Emir, the Rashkir replied. The Colonel had dismissed the Emir and turned him out of the palace. The man lying on the stones was no one of consequence.

'It is the Emir,' the Colonel insisted, 'the King.'

The Rashkir kept their discipline; they would not argue with their Colonel even when they thought him wrong.

Is there no end? the Colonel thought.

The ambulance turned into the courtyard and the orderlies jumped down, but the Colonel gave them no attention. Hajji Kassim was dead; Arabia had contrived the proper ending. He crossed the courtyard to Mr Peachy, who was comforting the Emir's favourite, the monkey, the dogs, the macaw in the cage.

'You see what happens, Mr Peachy. This was inevitable from the start. I should never have agreed to the operation.'

'You could not have foreseen how the soldier would act.'

'It was bound to happen.'

'It was chance, chance.'

'I don't think so.'

'Colonel, you can't blame yourself for this.'

'I can, and do.'

He went to take the doctor's report, which was concise enough: the former ruler was dead, shot through the heart. The Colonel ordered the body raised from the flag-stones and taken to the mortuary at Warboys Camp. A grave was to be prepared at once in the cemetery. Living or dead, Hajji Kassim had to be removed from here and into some place where his name would diminish.

'See to it,' he said to Lovelace.

When the ambulance had left with the Emir's body, and his murderer had been taken into close arrest, the Colonel approached the Levy. The soldiers came to attention; some 'presented' their arms, awkwardly but with deliberation.

'Why do they do it?' Masterman asked the sergeant in charge. 'What do they mean?'

The sergeant would not say.

'The movement is inappropriate. Bring them to the "order".'

But the soldiers held the 'present', the mark of utmost respect, despite the shouting of the sergeant.

'I don't understand it,' the Colonel said to Mr Peachy. 'What has come over them?'

Peachy shook his head, reluctant to tell the truth.

The Colonel was humiliated; he spoke with a sob. 'It is entirely inappropriate. I am nothing, just the commander of the Emir's army. I have no wish to rule in Hassan.' And when Peachy did not speak, he continued violently, 'It is a savage custom, the mark of a medieval people, to believe that the succession can be decided in this way. To kill a king confers no rights upon the killer. It is a terrible thing——'

Mr Peachy took the Colonel's arm and guided him firmly into the second court. Here in the great hall the slaves stared in panic at the conspirators; for all they knew there would be further killings in the palace. Peachy clapped his hands and sent them scurrying away. By habit, the Colonel had recovered his composure.

'Look, sir, the damage is done,' Peachy said urgently. 'The

Emir is dead; he was the victim of a tribal vendetta, of a type commonplace enough among the bedouin; you cannot blame yourself for that, as it had nothing to do with the transfer of power.'

Masterman stood erect, as only an infantryman can. 'You cannot expect me to believe that. No bedouin would kill a king. The soldier killed a discredited ruler, a man like himself, and it was I who brought him to this state.'

'It is absurd to blame yourself for something you didn't intend.'

'It was inherent in the situation. I should have known it.'

'That isn't true.'

'Mr Peachy, you don't understand force; I do. Only a soldier knows the workings of violence. There is no such thing as a bloodless revolution. You cannot depose a king without killing him. You cannot employ force without cruelty. Here you must accept a soldier's word.'

'Hajji Kassim had to go.'

'Quite; and he has gone in the only manner possible.'

'The soldier killed him for reasons of his own.'

'I suspect that I killed him.'

'We're in this together, sir.'

'You're not in it at all. Only the soldier with the force behind him can be held responsible.'

'None the less, we must decide together what is best for the country now that we have dismissed the Emir. You will have to assume power temporarily——'

'I do not have to assume it, Mr Peachy. I *have* it, regardless of my will. The soldiers acknowledge my authority. There is only one way to go in a revolution.'

'That may not be wholly true.'

'It is. The killer replaces the ruler killed.'

'You will have to try the guilty soldier for murder.'

'I will not.'

'If you don't, there will seem to have been collusion.'

'There was.'

'I cannot argue with you when you're so determined.'

'You cannot argue with the truth.'

'We must plan a course of action to save the country, sir.'

'The country cannot be saved. It will be destroyed. We have killed the King.'

In the great palace there was movement, alarm and some laughter. Word of the Emir's death passed through the kitchens no sooner than it happened, and the donkey boys plundered the larders, stealing cakes and spiced fruits. The slave master, a eunuch from Riyadh, a man of subtle cruelty, was attacked by the Sudanese boys and beaten with split bamboos until he died; then the boys threw his body down a well and ran away into the gardens. Members of the Chamberlain's staff, the only literates in the palace, whose tastes had been formed in the universities of Iran, stole up the side stairways and entered the quarters of the Emir's concubines—they took with them wine, perfume and books of poetry, and they found a delighted welcome in the silk-walled bedrooms of the widowed favourites. Others in the retinue broke open the strong-room where the Emir had kept his pictures, potions and obscene devices, and these they took up to a high tower and threw down into the forecourt below. The Somali freedmen, whose wages had instructed them in the use of money, and with an avarice unknown in the slave quarters, combed the palace upon tiptoe, looking for jewels and porcelain, and they took them to the merchants who were already knocking at the rear entrances.

Even before it was light, word of the killing passed down the soukh in Bir-el-Shama. The Emir was dead, the Colonel had occupied the palace. The traders in gold and silver put up their shutters, barred their windows, and went upstairs in fear for their lives. A money-lender in the market place, too slow in his movements, too heavy from over-eating, could not escape the assault of his debtors who beat him to death with his cash box, overturned his booth and scattered his records in the dust. The brothels closed: they would open again to increased profit when the new government announced a public holiday. Along the gutters, the sellers of sweets and ginger folded their bundles and crept away. Soon only the dogs and the blind beggars moved in the streets. The town was quiet, waiting for the first dangerous hours to pass, waiting to applaud the new ruler. The festival of revolution opened no differently today from any other time.

Colonel Masterman asked Peachy to summon a council of sheikhs that morning. In his view a successor to Hajji Kassim had to be appointed as soon as possible. Peachy expected delay, as the Sheikhs did not like to make up their minds too quickly: they needed time to bribe, to threaten, to hear the evidence of informers.

'I can't help that,' Masterman said. 'The Sheikhs are to meet this morning and make their decision. After that, I intend to resign my commission.'

'I shouldn't be too hasty.'

'I can do nothing else. I have behaved inexcusably.'

He wanted to wash, to rest, to bring some order into his mind. A slave took him upstairs to a large light room opening on a roof garden, and he brought towels, oils and scents. The Colonel took a shower, washing himself vigorously, as if he could rub away the smell of revolution; the oils and pefumes he set aside. He asked for a robe, but they brought him an affair in silk and brocade which he threw into a corner. He resumed his uniform. He watched the sunrise from the roof garden.

An hour later the Chamberlain came, tapping on the door with extreme caution.

'What is it?' the Colonel asked. Indeed, what news could follow that of revolution?

The Chamberlain, an elderly, womanish Bahraini, was shaking in terror. He took three paces across the carpet and abased himself.

'Get up at once,' said Masterman in horror.

The old man did not stir. He invited the Colonel to place a foot upon his neck.

'I will not have it,' the Colonel said. Then, harshly, 'I wish it known that while I am in the palace I'm to be shown no considerations other than those due to a colonel. This sort of thing is ridiculous. I wish business conducted upon military lines with no idiotic abasements of any kind. Certainly there must be no extravagance, no levity. I expect you to keep a proper account of all expenditure which we will show to the new ruler when he is appointed. Now, for heaven's sake get up off the floor.'

The Chamberlain rose, but his English, never sound, had deserted him and he spoke in Arabic. 'My Lord will take fruit——?'

'Cheese and biscuits, if you please, and a little iced water.'

'The kitchens have prepared a breakfast.'

'I don't want it. You may take the tray to Mr Peachy, if it's likely to be wasted.'

'They have killed twelve sheep.'

'God, has no one any sense of proportion? There is to be no feasting. This is a solemn and tragic occasion in which a human being has died.'

At the mention of Hajji Kassim, the Chamberlain shook his head dismissively. 'A man of cruel practices——'

'Very likely; I don't wish to hear.'

'——lustful and heartless——'

'Kindly remember you are speaking of an eminent Sheikh, lately dead.'

'——whom My Lord has dispatched——'

'Be quiet,' the Colonel ordered. 'I will not have the Emir disparaged. He will be buried at Warboys, with a decent monument.'

The Chamberlain went away to fetch cheese and biscuits and the Colonel walked on the roof under the pergolas and in the fretted sunshine. Three hours had passed since Hajji Kassim died. In the council chamber the Sheikhs were in conference to decide the succession but so far he had received no message from them.

A black boy brought cheese and biscuits on a silver tray; he was accompanied by twin Kashmiri girls who bore between them a basket of fruit, the support of which took them to the limit of their strength.

'Put it down, put it down,' said the Colonel in despair; 'you'll hurt yourselves if you don't.'

He took the tray to a table in the roof garden. The girls sat beside him, so closely they were touching him; the Colonel sent them away gently.

He had not finished when the Chamberlain returned with Mrs Jason-Caldicott. The lady had changed her dress; she was marvellously composed. 'My dear Colonel, I must speak with you——' she said in a voice of shuddering personal entreaty.

'I cannot believe it necessary at the moment, madam.'

'I can be of help to you, I am sure.'

In Arabic, the Chamberlain said, 'My lady is very obliging.'

'Thank you, but I do not need help. I suggest that you return to London, Mrs Jason-Caldicott, as I may have difficulty in guaranteeing your safety in Hassan. You must understand that in the first days of the new government those close to the late Emir may be in danger if there are demonstrations in favour of the new ruler.'

The lady went away in golden displeasure.

Peachy came then, his arm round a Syrian dancer; he was not yet wholly drunk. 'The Sheikhs have decided in favour of Colonel Masterman,' he said. 'The decision was unanimous, enthusiastic, and accompanied by the discharge of fire-arms. I am bound to communicate their decision, if only as a preliminary to serious consideration.'

'Very well. You know my answer.'

'It is in the negative, I assume. The Sheikhs will be disappointed. They are not in a mood for further effort.'

The Colonel said, 'The Sheikhs are to be kept in conference until they have made a sensible decision. They are not to leave the palace, nor are they to receive entertainment of any kind. They may have food and refreshment at army scales, but nothing more.'

'You will address them?'

'I will not.'

'They won't enjoy bread and jam.'

'I cannot help that.'

'Come, daughter of delight,' said Peachy to his companion, 'we have business to transact.'

In the afternoon, demonstrations were reported from Bir-el-Shama. They had carried a banner through the town upon which the Colonel's likeness had been roughly painted. Cards with the name 'Masterman' had appeared in the shop windows, from which every photograph of Hajji Kassim had been removed. Two youths had died from rough handling in the crowd.

'It must be stopped,' the Colonel told Lovelace. 'I shall impose a curfew from nightfall. I want Tillotson to take a company into the town and remove any placard, banner or effigy that seems to relate to me. I find such sycophancy disgusting and politically absurd. Who ever heard of a British officer assuming the title of Emir? Please waste no time.'

Peachy came back to the roof garden as it was growing dark. He was sober and alone. 'The Sheikhs have no answer,' he said with low spirit. 'There has been some disagreement. Abdullah the Wise has suffered an injury. I cannot recommend they be retained, as they have no gift for committee. I suggest we let them go until attitudes harden one way or another.'

'It will mean factional hostility, trouble in the tribes, perhaps violence.'

'It's the way of the country, of course.'

'Damn it, they *must* decide. Nothing else is acceptable in the present crisis.'

'At the moment they are simply deepening the divisions between themselves.'

'Very well, let them go; but they must reassemble tomorrow morning at nine-thirty in the council chamber.'

'I doubt if they will.'

'They *shall*. It is their duty.'

'I can't expect a decision in less than a week. They will need to judge the dangers of each nomination, and this can only be done if they consult informers, which takes time. Meanwhile, we should issue a statement saying that military government will last only until a successor is appointed.'

Masterman realized the need for a ruling. 'I will give them three days. I dare say I can hold the position that long. However, in three days' time they are to meet here prepared to appoint the new Emir or they will forfeit their right of election. If they don't turn up, the soldiers will fetch them. I won't stand for delay in this vital matter. You can be as rough as you like.'

Peachy managed a small, quickening smile. 'I will do what I can. I know how much today has distressed you.'

The Colonel did not answer, having nothing to say, and Peachy went downstairs to chide the Sheikhs and issue the Colonel's warning.

The darkness covered the desert. The nearer hills merged one into another until only the skyline could be seen against the fading sky. From the roof garden the Colonel watched the last of the light touching the horizon, then vanishing as if daylight would never be renewed. Even now, with the long day behind him, he found it hard to remember that Hajji Kassim was dead; with his weaker mind he saw the death of the Emir as a sentence upon himself which still might be removed; he had died so quickly, so easily, giving the illusion of pretence. Wicked kings did not slip from life with such a lack of display. Yet Hajji Kassim was dead, shot by the Rashkir, sent to whatever darkness awaited the infamous ruler, and even now the consequences of his fall from authority were multiplying in the state, surrounding his successor with their destructive energies.

He stood at the edge of the roof, quite still. He laughed without humour. He reminded himself that the events of the morning had indeed taken place and that—for the time being at least—he ruled in Hassan. He felt a deep, irreducible shame.

Well, there's no way back, he thought. I can only go forward.

God forgive me, forgive me!

21

Colonel Masterman had forbidden his wife to join him at the palace, and he allowed only a few members of his staff and one company of the Levy to take up residence there; he did not want his occupation of the palace to seem other than temporary. The gardens apart, he disliked the Ruler's home with its vulgar decoration and resident menagerie. Certainly the outside elevations had an enchantment when caught by the rays of the setting sun; at such a time the arcaded courts, the domes and minarets, had a harmony of form and colour which the later architects, who had combined the styles of Mamluk, Mogul and Ottoman, had done their best to destroy; but the Colonel was oppressed by the place and could find no comfort there. The gardens with their fountains and fish pools were more to his taste and he spent much of his time walking there.

On the second day after the *coup*, Peachy brought him news from the Agency. The world Press had noted the fall of the Emir but had published no details; a violent change of government in a country so small that even its name was unfamiliar did not rate much coverage in a world given to brutal readjustments of this sort; only the most sober of the British papers had drawn attention to the manner of the Ruler's death and the nature of the provisional government. Peachy's former department in London had sent a telegram of urgent inquiry which he had undertaken to satisfy with a formula of his own; a full reply would be sent only when a new Emir, given to peace, progress and the correction of wrong, had been appointed. Meanwhile the Sheikhs had called in their advisers and clairvoyants and embarked on the process of decision. Riders went in search of the tribes to canvass or extort an opinion. Shots were fired across the nearer dunes. The mercenaries had made no move, keeping to their camp on the Hadraifi border; those confined to the Arabian Hotel had not tried to leave. Should they attempt to negotiate an alternative contract, Peachy felt sure he would get wind of it from one source or another—from palace or brothel, where the traffic in news was usually brisk—and that the Colonel could then redeploy the Levy in time to meet the threat. The soukh in Bir-el-Shama remained closed. At night the curfew was broken only by the cats.

Colonel Masterman was pleased to see Sarita in the garden on the afternoon of the second day.

He said, 'My dear, I hope you took care in coming here.'

'I walked up the road.'

'That wasn't wise; there are madmen about.'

He tried without discourtesy to look beyond her, avoiding the image that distressed him; he didn't want the past brought back so abruptly.

'Why do you do that?' Sarita asked.

She was too close, too swift. He felt a moment's sharp embarrassment. 'I beg your pardon?' he said.

'You know what I mean.' Her voice was all complaint. Then she said softly, 'Whatever you like. I don't mind.'

'It was nice of you to come.'

'You knew that I would come, didn't you?' The terrible respectability of the Eurasian cancelled the first thought almost before she had spoken it, and she went on shrilly, 'I was just taking an afternoon walk. How surprising to find you here, Colonel Masterman! I came to pick flowers for the Agency drawing-room.'

Masterman said nothing, his thought in suspense. The girl wore formality like clothing. 'I will help you pick the flowers, and then I will find an escort to take you home,' he said stiffly.

'Is it bad?' she asked suddenly. 'I want to know if it's bad.'

'I think so.'

'Are you in danger?'

'I don't know. Perhaps.'

'This thing——' she began, breaking the restraint, trembling; 'this thing I have—whatever it is——'

The Colonel said, 'Yes?'

She was concerned, curious, moved by a generous impulse; but she retreated at once into good manners. 'I do think flowers make life so much more pleasant, don't you, Colonel Masterman?'

The Colonel murmured agreement. 'You were going to ask me something, Sarita?'

She opened her palm, as if her question had flown from it like a bird. 'It doesn't matter. Another time. You have important things to do.'

'I think you'd better tell me.' He was risking injury, but it seemed necessary to put things straight with this girl, who carried the past with her, while there was still time.

'I didn't like it at first,' Sarita said. 'I didn't want this thing I had.'

Masterman nodded.

'You were looking at somebody else. I wasn't there. I was angry.'

He cleared his throat. 'I'm sorry; it was impolite of me.' He wondered if he could speak to her further. After all, his life was in ruin, he had nothing more to lose; but in fact he could speak of the past no more readily than before. He said, 'It happened ages ago, before you were born.'

'And I am like her?'

'Not completely; but there is something in your face that reminds me of her.' There was more to it than that, but he couldn't find the words; it alarmed him even to have spoken of the past. Sarita brought the earlier girl into the present so sharply she dissolved the time between. He raised his head. With the experience of revolution behind him he could make a better effort. 'Sometimes, I think, I have supposed you were Sarah.'

He could get no nearer to it than that. He dropped his head again, dismayed. He had added the pain of a private disloyalty to that of mutiny and regicide, and he could not guess which way his life was leading him.

The girl said brightly, 'You're so intriguing, Colonel Masterman.' More intimately, she continued, 'I needed to know what it was.'

'I believe—though I have not allowed myself to think about it—that I wanted you to know.' The Colonel had a further point to make, but it stuck in his throat. 'You understand, I wasn't seeking anything from you.'

'It wouldn't be your way, would it?'

'No.'

In the Emir's garden they picked flowers for the Agency drawing-room. The Colonel believed that, in telling the girl of the past, he had destroyed it, but the last three days had put an end to so much he couldn't see that it mattered. He gathered the flowers together and put them in Sarita's arm.

She said in her simplest voice, 'I'm frightened. I don't know what's happening.'

'It may not be too bad.'

'What is it you've done?'

'I intervened, when I couldn't do anything else. I didn't want to.'

'I can't believe you would do anything wrong.'

'I did, I think.'

'But it's not possible. You're not like that.' She was crying now. 'It doesn't make sense. You were the one person who was always the same. I could always think that, no matter what, you were there and things would go on the same. And now——'

'My dear, I'm so sorry.' Her sobs distressed him more than anything in the last terrible days. 'If I have done anything to upset you, I regret it deeply.'

He conducted her to a garden seat where once the Emir had sat to watch the fountains and, with solicitude, bent over her as she sat with her head in her hands, crying. An aide came with a message but the Colonel waved him away.

'I wish you wouldn't cry,' he said gently. 'I assure you I am unchanged and that your safety, and that of everyone else, is still my first concern.'

'I'm not bothered about my safety: *that* doesn't matter.' She spoke with a vast petulance, as though he should have known her better. 'It's just that, for once, I couldn't understand you, and then I knew I'd lost something I had to have.'

'It hurts me you should think I've changed.'

'Why should you bother?' she asked, suddenly full of miseries. 'Why should you concern yourself with me?'

The Colonel tried to find the truth. 'I suppose because you're all that's left of something that once mattered to me.'

Perhaps this pleased her. She turned her face upward and moved her head in an arc from side to side, as if she followed the flight of a bird—in acknowledgement, it seemed, of strangeness, of things in which she played a part but did not understand.

'Really, Colonel Masterman, you're sometimes very mysterious,' she said, wearing her most carefully managed face.

'I don't think so,' he said.

He sent for a soldier to escort her back to the Agency, and he watched them going down the steps between the urns of hydrangeas towards the gateway. She did not look back although he hoped she would. She vanished under the arch, taking with her the only part of himself which, had he thought about it, he might have wished to preserve, and for the sake of which he might have contrived to live.

That evening after dark he heard voices speaking English under the roof garden; there were visitors at the palace who, from their manner, had faith in the future. He heard the strident orders given to the guard and, yes, the sound of laughter, as if his guests had determined at all costs to be cheerful. He did not welcome this intrusion, but he passed word that the visitors were to be allowed up. They came out into the soft light of the roof garden; he saw the robed figures of Saud the Fat and Abdullah the Wicked; he saw his wife in evening dress, Peachy, Lovelace and Tillotson in dinner jackets. Their faces showed confidence; plainly they had come, in their own thought, to lend 'moral support' to the provisional ruler. They had brought champagne in an ice bucket.

'My dear Colonel, your trials are nearly at an end,' said Sheikh Saud. 'I have been out and about among the Sheikhs, banging their heads together, compelling the entertainment of thought where no thought has dwelt before—a tedious process, but I think productive. The Sheikhs will decide tomorrow.'

Peachy lowered his voice and said, 'It's true; he's a good friend. He has bludgeoned the Sheikhs towards some kind of agreement. Of course, he will do anything to avoid personal election, but his motive has also been generous. Almost certainly the next Emir will be Abdullah the Wicked.'

'I am not a candidate for election,' said Saud with emphasis. 'I have high blood pressure, an enlarged prostate, and disorderly bowels. It is also a melancholy truth that, after any distance, my knee tends to hinge in the direction opposite from normal, which would make it impossible for me to review troops or to open public buildings with any semblance of dignity.'

The Colonel said, loud enough for them all to hear, using his authority as ruler, 'I insist upon a decision tomorrow, as the present situation cannot be tolerated any longer.'

'Of course,' said Peachy quickly. 'The Sheikhs must give their decision tomorrow.'

Captain Lovelace carried round the champagne on a silver tray; and together, although no toast was spoken, they drank to the frail hope that the Sheikhs would conclude their business in the morning.

'I don't want to be forced into a position where I am obliged to nominate the next ruler,' Masterman said curtly. 'It would make his task more difficult. Indeed, I shall not do it.'

The roof garden opened on the desert, where no lights were showing, where in the foreshortening darkness the sand-hills were brought close to them, adding their sombre influence to the champagne party. The guests spoke brightly together. Plainly they saw the need to cheer the provisional ruler, who had such awesome responsibilities.

'Things are much improved in the state,' Saud told them, his bulk giving his words force and conviction.

Abdullah looked up sharply. 'It is true. The water is back in the taps. Sometime they stop shooting in the desert.'

Swayed by this optimism, Peachy said, 'The wells are producing again. The oil men have expressed their willingness to co-operate with the provisional government. The first tanker arrives at Faleh-la tomorrow and there are others in the Strait.'

'It is kind of you to bring me this good news,' the Colonel said without warmth.

'Needless to say, there are domestic difficulties,' said Mrs Masterman, acknowledging that forces must bear in every direction. 'Prices have risen and the servants are inattentive.'

'Oh, *servants*,' said Abdullah with contempt. 'Mine hid in vases, their legs in the air. I beat their rear parts with bamboos.'

The Colonel was unmoved by their goodwill; it barely touched him; but he allowed the party to continue in the soft light of the roof garden even though he was aware—like every soldier, every ruler in the eastern theatre—that they should not let the lamps shine upon them when they were faced by a darkened landscape, that they could be seen by persons they could not themselves see; and with half his mind he felt a ruler's unease at their prominence on the palace roof.

'When it's over,' Saud said, in a voice that suggested it some-time would be, '—when it's all over, my dear Colonel, you must take a holiday. East Africa is lovely at this time of year. You could hunt something there.'

'Tigers,' said Sheikh Abdullah, but he hadn't listened closely.

Mrs Masterman said in her firmest voice, 'There are no tigers in Africa, Sheikh Abdullah; only in Asia. I would certainly welcome some relief from Hassan, which has been trying in recent weeks.'

Peachy held his glass in front of his eyes, as if the answer to their problems could be read there. 'I see no reason why a holiday should be impossible,' he said slowly. 'In Arabia, a crisis subsides as quickly as it arises, and there should be a period of stability following the appointment of the next Emir.' And he added with a new bitterness, 'I mean, a new ruler is regarded as a blessing, notwithstanding his credentials, and it takes a little time for his mismanagement, or his mal-practice, to become widely recognized.'

'In politics, as in love, things are better at the beginning.' Sheikh Saud beamed at Colonel Masterman across the lighted roof. 'You should take a long spell of ease, dear sir, for which —in view of your recent services—the Hassanite government will be proud to accept all expense.'

'I need hardly tell you,' Masterman said, barely containing his displeasure, 'that I shall on no account accept any pay-ment or gratuity for my intervention in the government of the state.'

'Come now, it would be most unusual, even eccentric, to

decline a reasonable reward after the pains you have taken. In kind, perhaps——'

'Stones, metals, intimate services——' said Abdullah.

The Colonel spoke next as the Ruler, the Emir, and they were obliged to listen, as his words had the force of edict. 'I shall be obliged if you will not mention such a thing again, Sheikh Saud. I decline to profit from my recent action, and neither shall any of my officers or it'll be the worse for them.' He was trembling, possessed by the anger of total sovereignty.

'I see, I apologize.' Saud lost a little of his bulk and confidence. 'I shall make it clear to the minor Sheikhs that they are to offer no tribute or entertainments.'

'On no account are they to do so.'

'A child was born yesterday to the Sheikh of Jehaz, whom he named Colonel Masterman. I shall ask him to reconsider his choice.'

'I have already instructed that I am not to be honoured in any way. The Sheikh is disobedient of my wish, and subject to penalty.'

Saud bent his head. 'It was in any case a girl child,' he said.

'I shall tolerate no departure from the provisional regulations. If necessary, I shall convene a military court to hear charges, or I shall deal with them summarily myself. The people are not to revere me in any way whatever.'

'Er—no,' Saud responded.

'It wouldn't be appropriate, nor indeed constitutional, in the case of a foreign national,' Peachy said. He still dwelt in a little cloud of bitterness.

Abdullah the Wicked lounged in a chair. He said moodily, 'Yet, if you behave like a Sheikh, the people will call you their master.'

'I forbid it absolutely,' the Colonel rapped. He strode the length of the roof garden and stood at the rail. His guests were quiet, diminished in stature, admitting his right to anger. 'If I rule in this country, no matter that it is only for a few days, I shall have it my way.'

They nodded; they didn't say anything; his was the only voice in Hassan backed by authority. He had assumed the rights of absolute monarchy. For this minute in time, standing at the rail, glaring at his guests, he was Emir, with all the power of an ancient nobility behind him. He was Sheikh in Hassan. He was the sheikh of sheikhs. His word was beyond argument. He commanded their silence in a moment of supreme authority. But he had also accepted the hazard of kingship, the risk of injury run by those whose authority can be challenged only by secret means. He heard a crack like the breaking of a stick which he knew to be the sound of a bullet near the end of its flight and passing at a distance of perhaps three feet from his head. His judgement told him it had been fired from a point at least six hundred yards away, from somewhere in the dunes facing him, from somewhere in the unrelieved shadows of the desert.

He ordered his visitors back into the palace. He was angered, hurt, dismayed by the vulgarity of assassination. Tillotson turned off the lights.

The Colonel said, 'It was a shot, intended for me.'

'Are you sure?'

'Perfectly. I should not have exposed myself to this risk.'

'There could be other explanations.'

'Don't argue. I want you to take out a search party and comb the area from which the shot came. The line of flight was roughly north-west, so you should search along the reciprocal. If you find the gunman, you may use your arms, but I suspect you'll find nothing.'

Tillotson disappeared, and the Colonel went inside with Lovelace. He said, 'O God, can't they see that I tried? Don't they know that Hajji Kassim was a murderous tyrant?' He put that thought aside and rejoined his visitors in the hall below. 'A madman, no doubt. I apologize for the incident.'

His guests, treating the matter as a social misdemeanour better ignored, took a last drink in a reception room downstairs. Tillotson returned before they left. He had seen footprints leading into hard ground and beside the tracks he had found a spent cartridge case.

The Colonel held the case to his nostrils, smelling the bitter scent of a bullet recently discharged. The figures round the percussion cap showed the cartridge to be of British make.

'Hamid,' he said. 'I had thought so.'

'We cannot be sure,' Tillotson said.

'I am certain of it.'

Peachy said earnestly, 'The chances are that Hamid died weeks ago. There is ammunition of all nationalities in the desert. You can't identify your assailant on the evidence of his cartridge case.'

'Hamid had a grievance against the Emir.'

'What of it? That was the former ruler.'

'Against the Emir,' the Colonel said bitterly, with the vision of experience, 'the *Emir*—he who assumes the titles, who accepts the guilt of his predecessor as a charge upon himself.'

'Really, this Hamid is a most tiresome soldier,' Saud complained. 'We never hear the last of him.'

'It would have been better if Captain Sloan had beaten him to death in the first place,' Mrs Masterman said with total confidence.

'Sloan, Sloan,' the Colonel whispered.

He was indignant at the shot, even though the bullet had travelled so far wide of him it could have been loosed in playfulness, in a jest recognizably bedouin; a trained rifleman should have managed better than that. None the less he was concerned that a man could menace the palace and escape unmolested. 'When it's daylight, we'll search every wadi for ten miles,' he said fiercely. 'If it's the last thing I do in Hassan, I'll get that wretched soldier. If it hadn't been for Hamid——' He paused, exhausted by his own anger. 'I'm sorry, ladies and gentlemen. Please forgive me. It is unpardonable to discuss military affairs at a gathering of this kind.'

His guests took their leave of him soon afterwards. Abdullah bowed nearly to the ground, without mockery. The Colonel drew Peachy into an ante-chamber by the main entrance.

'I'm not made for this,' he said. 'I'm beginning to mistrust my judgement.'

'I can't believe you'll do anything inappropriate.'

'I don't know what to do. My anger is a substitute for action.'

'Do nothing, sir. Hold the position. Wait for developments.'

'But is that enough? Something may happen. We have created a violent situation which must develop violently.'

'I suggest, whenever a decision is needed, you trust your soldier's instinct; it's unlikely you'll be far wrong.'

'I'm no longer a soldier, Peachy. I'm something else, something I don't understand. I wish I'd studied politics in the past.'

'You've studied the principles of war, and politics are not much different. You've had plenty of experience in dangerous situations. There was India, the Far East.'

'But there I had always a clear directive, and it was obvious what needed doing. Now there are no rules, no plain necessities.'

'Look: you have spent a lifetime in establishing order in a firm and humane manner. You've learned how to distinguish practical possibilities in a shifting situation. The service you come from is the best in the world in this kind of work. You can manage, if anyone can.'

Masterman sighed. 'I would agree with you, Peachy, if I were still an infantryman and the problem was one of infantry tactics. But neither applies: all this is new and different. I no longer know what I am or how to act for the best.'

The guests were calling from the courtyard. Peachy touched his arm in sympathy, in trust, and went out to join them.

It was late, but the Colonel could not rest. He walked through the corridors of the Emir's palace and along the paths of the garden. He wanted to walk in the desert, which he always enjoyed by night, but the presence there of Hamid, or whichever ill-intentioned spirit it was, kept him inside the palace wall, in shadow. Voices continued in the slave quarters, but when he came to the lighted gateway, and the lamplight showed them who it was, the voices stopped abruptly and there were murmurs of awe and fear.

See, little ones, the Ruler! The parents directed their children's eyes towards the gate, where the Colonel stood.

The children stared, and ran away. Masterman was disgusted.

He went up to the wall, where there was a gunstep, and he stood looking across the desert. He enjoyed the small risk that Hamid might see him. If the soldier were to use his rifle, what then? Nothing but the fierce impact of the bullet, the enclosing darkness, the merging of his person with the dead regiments. In the absolution of death he would be freed from his act of mutiny; he would be simply another dead soldier, whose name would soon lapse from memory but who would none the less share in the common tribute. He raised his shoulders above the parapet, increasing the risk, inviting the swift solution that Hamid might provide. Go on, he cried inwardly, with the imperative of senior rank. Shoot, man, shoot! But there was nothing in the desert, not a shot, not a voice, just the empty sand-hills covered by darkness. He shook his head in contempt for Hamid, stepped down below the wall, and went back into the palace.

22

A little while after eight o'clock the following morning, news
reached the Agency that the mercenary company had left the
Arabian Hotel overnight and joined Major Kennedy's force
on the frontier. Peachy told Colonel Masterman on the telephone. The shepherd boy bringing the message thought the
united force had then moved eastward.

'Into Hadraif, of course,' the Colonel said; 'I might have
known it. No doubt the Sheikh has offered them better
terms.'

The tactical situation had worsened at a stroke. With the
mercenaries in Hadraifi pay, he had a powerful and mischiev-
ous force on his eastern flank.

'They may not invade Hassan,' Peachy said.

'I must assume they will,' the Colonel replied.

He called the senior officers into the communications room.
'I had expected this,' he told them. 'They are treacherous
people, without scruple. It is arguable I should have increased
their pay to prevent them accepting an alternative offer. This
device, I admit, was suggested to me by the Agent, but I
declined; I could not bring myself to trade with them in this
manner. Now of course the military situation is much altered
and we must secure the Hadraifi frontier at once. If Major
Kennedy attacks me, I shall give him a bloody nose. I doubt
if he understands desert warfare as well as I do, and those
shabby Germans and Swedes will be no match for the bedouin.
He'll double off, I shouldn't wonder.' He was cheered by this
reflection; and indeed he felt confident that in open conflict
the Levy, with its superior training, equipment and discipline,
could deal quickly with Kennedy, whose skill was in assassination and the exploitation of weakness.

Tillotson said, 'He's unlikely to fight in the open, Colonel.'

'You never know,' Masterman said.

Obedient to the Colonel's wish, the Sheikhs came to the palace at ten o'clock to decide the succession. They did not look a very cohesive gathering and Peachy, who accompanied them, wore a long face. 'They are unresponsive, nettled and suspicious,' he said. 'I can't believe they'll respond to the needs of committee. The Sheikh of Jubehya has passed the time with his concubines; the Sheikh of Kadir has wandered in the desert in some sort of trance. The others have done nothing but gossip. However, Saud is chairman for this session and it may be he can get something out of them. I suggest they are disarmed before they enter the council chamber.'

In the desert kingdoms, to deprive a sheikh of his kunji and bodyguard was to give grave offence, but the Colonel was in no mood for courtesy: the Sheikhs surrendered their weapons in an ante-room and sat in a circle on the chamber floor, disarmed. Masterman, not caring to squat, addressed them standing.

'Lords, you have a duty to perform, one which you may not ignore and which is necessary for the future of your country.' He spoke in simple Arabic, using the same voice in which he had spoken to the soldiers at Warboys. 'I ask you to put aside all thought of the past and let your minds dwell only on the future. I ask you to forget old enmities, old scores and instead to consider the desperate need for one of you to assume the headship of the Hassanite people, so that they may continue their lives in peace. This is a duty imposed on you by your exalted stations; together you are the suzerains of every tribesman, every townsman in the Emirate, whether they are the bedouin of the southern desert, the shepherds of the coast, or the merchants and stall-holders of the towns and trade routes. I am only a soldier and I cannot rule your country. The Sheikhs must decide whom to trust with the Emirate, and then they must look to him as their ruler, acknowledging his wisdom and giving their assent to his laws and judgements. Your decision will be brought to me as soon as it is made and I will announce it to the state. The new ruler may count upon my loyalty, and that of the Levy, in establishing himself as Emir in all parts of the country.

'Lords, you have to decide. Your failure cannot be tolerated. I leave you now to your conversations.'

What a shower! the Colonel thought, as he made his exit from the chamber.

At midday an informer with connections in Ras Al Hadraif called to see Peachy, following which the Agent sought the Colonel in the garden. He did not soften his message in any way.

'It's as we expected. Kennedy has entered the service of the Sheikh of Hadraif, having been offered a large inducement; his force is now concentrated on the Hadraifi side of the frontier. The Sheikh has reasserted his claim to Hassan and his intention of uniting the two countries. They have of course a vague historical unity under the house of Al Farahid, of which the Sheikh is an undoubted member; but he has no title to Hassan that would convince any fair-minded jurist. I think it likely he will employ Kennedy to substantiate his bid for this country.'

The Colonel nodded and walked a dozen yards between the vines before speaking. 'At least matters are clear,' he said, and laughed without warmth. 'I shan't object to fighting that wretched fellow Kennedy. Of course, we need a strong ruler in Hassan.'

As if summoned by his expressed wish, a secretary came then from the council chamber to bring him news of the Sheikhs' decision: they had chosen Sheikh Mahmud bin Ahmed, a boy of five years old.

The Colonel spoke wearily, his words underlined by anger. 'Tell their Excellencies I cannot accept their choice. They are to continue in council until they have appointed an adult ruler. They are not to leave the chamber, nor are they to receive refreshment. They must give a decision in one hour.'

He went next to the communications room and from there ordered a company of the Levy to occupy the high ground overlooking the Hadraifi frontier and to close the road at the escarpment. 'I can't believe the devil will attack me frontally,' he told Peachy, not unhappily now, with the beginnings of enthusiasm; 'he has only soft-skinned vehicles and light weapons. The best he can hope for from the Sheikh's retinue will be a few askaris of poor discipline and perhaps fifty armed police. Despite his duplicity, I don't count Kennedy a fool, and he has some experience of Guevara-type tactics in Latin

America; I think it certain he will attempt to infiltrate Hassan by the camel tracks and to provoke an uprising of the tribesmen in favour of his new master. He will employ murder and intimidation in this cause. Our job will be to prevent his entry where possible, and to seek him out inside the state where it is not.' He rose on the balls of his feet, eager to take part in these operations.

Peachy spoke slowly, thoughtfully. 'It is true, is it not, that an opponent employing guerrilla tactics is the most difficult of all to defeat?'

'Perfectly true. You can't see them, find them. They vanish into the landscape.'

'And there is nothing you can do to protect the people from the cruellest exploitation?'

'Very little, I'm afraid.'

'And it is also true—tell me if I'm wrong, but I don't think I am—that a war of this kind has never been won other than by the guerrillas?'

The Colonel was silent, honestly reflective. 'I think, in principle, you are right,' he said after a while. 'But that should not deflect us from our purpose if we believe it to be a just one. This time it could be different.'

'Can you give me one good reason why it should be?'

'Well, Kennedy is moved by money, not by loyalty to a political ideal. And the people of Hassan will not be in sympathy with Hadraifi aims. They will consolidate around their new ruler.'

The Agent expelled his breath in a long, shuddering draught. 'Precisely, dear Colonel—our new ruler, at present in painful gestation. We need a warrior-king and it's likely we'll get an amiable buffoon. There's only one ruler able to save the state.'

The secretary returned at that moment to tell them of the Sheikhs' latest notion: they proposed a council of three, to rule by majority decision: it had the mark of Saud. The Colonel was nonplussed, such a thing being outside his experience by a wide margin.

Peachy said angrily, 'A stupid, copy-book solution—the work of a theorist without reference to political realities.' He stormed out of the communications room into the rose garden, Masterman at his heels; he was consumed with contempt for the Sheikhs. 'Can you imagine such a thing? A triumvirate has never worked in Europe, let alone in Arabia; they'd cut each other's throats in the first week. It's an expedient to avoid a decision, a divisive measure when we need the unity of true leadership. There must be a single ruler, someone whom the people can see, a man of strength, a sheikh of sheikhs....'

'You won't produce him by shouting,' the Colonel said. He turned to the secretary. 'Tell their Excellencies they are to continue in council until they had elected a single ruler.'

'It's a balls-up,' Peachy said, and sulked.

'Very likely. It doesn't help to use the language of the barrack room. We'll simply have to wait and see.'

They stood waiting in the rose garden, the Colonel silent, Peachy kicking stones in the path.

After a time the Agent said, speaking to the landscape, addressing a world he expected to ignore him, 'It comes back to Kennedy. Once he infiltrates his forces into Hassan we'll never find him. He'll intimidate the tribesmen and torment the townsfolk. There'll be murder and mutilation. He's an evil that should be destroyed.'

'Quite, but I do not see how,' Masterman said.

'By any means available.'

'There are none at present.'

'You have guns, soldiers.'

'My dear fellow, he's across the frontier, in sovereign territory.'

'So what, sir? Hassan, Hadraif—it's all a part of the corrupt and mindless kingdom of the Al Farahid. The people are the same lousy shower of bedouin. It's all the same rank desert. The frontier was drawn by a dull-minded official and has no reality in human or geographical terms. I should ignore it, just as the Hadraifis will; I should destroy Kennedy and his followers while they are still concentrated. They're an excrescence that deserves nothing better than extinction. No government will acknowledge them or call you to account for their destruction. No decent human being will lament their passage out of the world. You will have put an end to something rotten and cruel and cynical and Arabia will be the better for it.'

Colonel Masterman was moved to anger but he kept his voice under control. 'That is hardly the opinion of a diplomat trained in the traditions of sanity.'

'Of course not. It's the wisdom of Arabia.'

'I have no right to declare war on behalf of the Hassanite nation. I will fight Kennedy if he crosses the frontier. Not otherwise. The new ruler may do as he thinks best, but this is clearly a decision for him, not for me.'

In fact, in the matter of the succession, it seemed as if the council of sheikhs had made a decision of some sort, if only a negative one; at that moment a shuttered window of the council chamber burst open as a result of intolerable pressures on the inside and a robed figure fell out into the garden.

'Plainly they have rejected the Sheikh of Kadir,' Masterman said.

Sheikh Saud joined them in the garden a moment later. He was breathless and ashamed. 'The council is not unanimous; there are still wide differences between us. Our sole progress is the elimination of two candidates. One of these lies by the window, as you can see; the other is secured under a heavy piece of furniture. I apologize for the Arab inability to make rational decisions when they are needed. I have pressed my colleagues as far as I can, but I am afraid there is no hope of choosing a ruler other than by some sort of tournament, in which the survivor gains the appointment, and that I'm sure you won't tolerate.' He said then, with genuine contrition, 'It is of sadness to me that, as a people, we should be so inept in politics.'

Peachy took the Colonel aside and spoke urgently. 'Listen, sir, I beg you. I'm an old political hand and I know a crisis when I see one. We are not going to get a ruler out of the Sheikhs, certainly not the strong, imperious nature we need.' He dropped his hand from the Colonel's sleeve and spoke slowly, painfully. 'It's the unalterable truth that you are the only effective ruler in a country on the brink of war and that you must make a violent political decision in defiance of your instinct. You must destroy Kennedy. At once.'

Masterman said nothing; he was embarrassed, distressed. 'I cannot give you an answer now, Mr Peachy.'

He must see for himself, examine the ground, assess the

difficulty of invading Hadraif. He had never made a decision without a careful appreciation of the factors involved. He knew he was finding excuses for delay and that this was a weakness in a soldier, but none the less he would better understand the problem if he looked at the shape of the land and the strength of Kennedy's position; then, perhaps, the decision would become plain.

'I must go to the frontier. I must see where he is. You'd better come with me, if you're so keen on war.'

They reached the frontier half an hour before sundown, travelling in a Land-Rover. Men of the first company were deployed in the rocks at the foot of the mountain road where they could command the frontier post a thousand yards ahead of them across the dun-coloured sand. The Colonel took his binoculars and map case and with the Agent climbed into the high rocks behind the road where they could look deep into Hadraif. He knew the bearing on which to search for Kennedy, and it took him only a moment to find the mercenary camp, where moving vehicles disturbed clouds of dust. Kennedy had placed his camp about five miles inside the frontier.

The Agent was breathless from the climb; he hadn't the Colonel's fitness. 'I see, I see. The devil's over there in a shallow wadi. It will surely be a simple matter to destroy him.'

Simple enough; but Masterman said nothing. He could without difficulty attack the position with troops covered by armoured vehicles and kill or capture Kennedy's rotten army —indeed, he could not at first imagine why Kennedy had adopted such a vulerable posutre.

'I urge you to attack him while he is still concentrated,' Peachy said, struggling for breath. 'Heavens, man, he's left himself wide open; you'll never get another chance like this!'

'The frontier lies between us.'

'Where is it? What is it? There's only empty desert between you and him.'

Colonel Masterman lowered his binoculars. He had not made up his mind, he could speak only from a private conviction of rightness. 'Mr Peachy, I believe in respect for agreements; I believe in fighting from a position of moral strength, not from a position of illegality and moral weakness.'

It did not sound convincing in the hard, remorseless desert, and Peachy said nothing, no doubt allowing the landscape to offer its own contradiction.

'I believe that no lasting benefit can come from an act of treachery, no matter that one's opponent may himself be treacherous.'

He paused again, conscious of irrelevance, conscious of the opposition of the desert.

'You are asking me to put aside thirty years of experience. You are asking me to deny that which I most believe in.'

Peachy nodded; perhaps, at this moment, he did not have the courage to speak aloud.

'I'm sorry, Mr Peachy, but I cannot do it. If Kennedy attempts to invade Hassan, I'll fight him at the frontier or anywhere else I can find him inside the country. To attack him now is beyond me. He knows it, of course; otherwise he would not have placed his camp where I can see it and in such an obviously weak position. That is his humour, his impertinence. I regret that I am unable to do what you ask me.'

Peachy found breath enough for a last, hopeless attempt at persuasion. 'Sir: we act, or we fail.'

The Colonel smiled wearily. 'My dear chap, we've failed already. Our mistake is in the past. And for the time remaining to me I propose to act in accordance with my own beliefs. I refuse entirely to invade Hadraif.'

Peachy looked at him suddenly, with deep personal concern. 'Then it will be worse, sir. It can only be worse.'

'I dare say,' said Colonel Masterman.

23

Following the failure of the Sheikhs to appoint a successor to Hajji Kassim, the Colonel moved out of the palace, taking his staff with him. If he must fight the Hadraifis, he preferred to do so from his own headquarters at Warboys instead of from a vulgar palace where he did not feel at home. He left the Chamberlain to feed the menagerie and to care for the hundreds of servants and slaves. He left the state to its own devices; and as there was no administration, no permanent record, it was not likely this failure in attention would make much difference to the manner of life in Hassan. In Bir-el-Shama the market reopened with no less than its usual liveliness. In the yards behind the magistrate's court the thieves and lechers received their terrible penalties—no matter they were mutilated in the name of no one in particular. The first company kept watch on the frontier, or as much of it as they could see from the escarpment, while behind them the Levy was in readiness with appropriate scales of ammunition, fuel and water.

The Colonel resumed his watch of the nightfall from the roof of his quarter on the evening of his return. He sat listening as the sounds of the camp overlaid the silence of the desert. His gin and tonic grew warm on the table beside him. His mind went back to his early service, as it always did at this time; he recalled the places in which he had taken greatest pleasure.

'Do you remember Orissa, Dorothy? Do you remember the long empty sands of the east coast where you could walk all morning and never see a soul? The jungle was so thick it bulged over the beach, and you could stand in the sunlight looking into the dim interior, listening to the rustle of the animals and the screaming of the birds. And the upper Ganges, where the islands were? In the early morning the mist lay along the river so thickly the boatmen seemed to be floating in air.'

He slapped the arm of the chair, moved by another powerful reflection. 'Malacca! I remember Malacca! I recall how there the fishermen tied lanterns over the gunwales to draw the fish at night-time. The lights stretched so far out to sea you couldn't tell where the boats ended and the stars began.'

And he had loved the palm forests of Selangor where he could look between the white trunks, into the dull shadows, and see at a distance the brilliant robes of the villagers as they moved here and there in some quiet occupation and, though he couldn't see it, he knew the kampong must be near because he could smell the wood-smoke and the sweet stench of the rotting coconuts.

'It's been a good time,' he said. 'I wouldn't have changed it. A pity it has to go.'

The Levy did not catch Kennedy's soldiers at the frontier, nor at the intersections of any of the camel tracks; they did not even see them. Indeed, Masterman had no evidence that Kennedy was active until, two days later, travellers from the Maledifah reported the murder of tribesmen who seemed to be Rashkirs and Khadifas, men of the nearer desert.

He could not say what gain might accrue to Hadraif from these random killings; but Kennedy's next endeavour made the matter more plain. Three women of the Rashkir were killed with a light machine-gun, following which fourteen soldiers from that tribe left the lines and vanished.

'I should have known it,' the Colonel said. 'He's attacking the tribes of the nearer desert, from whom the Levy is mainly recruited, and they'll leave to defend their families. The men don't realize their best means of retaliation is to remain in the Levy.' He sent patrols into the areas where deaths were reported but they found nothing beyond the shallow graves and, occasionally, the vanishing tracks of the light vehicles from which the operations had been mounted.

Another tribe, no doubt impelled by threats, moved out of their traditional area and into the grounds of the Khadifas, where they came into conflict with that tribe; and there were many Khadifas in the Levy. The Colonel waited for the absentee report with failing courage and an outward show of cheerfulness: twenty-seven men, all Khadifa, did not attend the first working parade and were presumed to have deserted.

He did not know which part of the Levy he could trust. For some reason of his own, Kennedy did not attack the Afarhid, the largest tribe in Hassan and the most numerous in the Levy. But they were moody, inattentive and dirty in barracks, obviously troubled and given to squabbling. Hamid with all his oddities had been pure Afarhid. Only fifty or so grim-faced Jamirs, the 'crows of the desert', who for generations had been at issue with every other tribe and who roamed the sour outer deserts with ferocious independence, seemed disposed to continue their soldiering.

Bit by bit the Colonel learned the argument in use: Hassan was a bastard country, ruled by a cruel usurper who had killed the Sheikh and opposed the union of the Hadraifi and Hassanite peoples; he lived upon mutton and cream and the silver dollars rightfully the property of the tribes; he was an infidel sheikh, king of the hyenas and prince of the running dogs.

One night, unseen by the sentries, an atrocious spirit passed through the camp and with a bold hand daubed the walls with the new slogans, in English and Arabic: *Masterman Out ... Union with Hadraif ... Death to all Capitalist Jackals.* The last comment, with its echo of the imbecile Left, was no more than the Colonel expected. Another inscription, which might have been the work of a different hand, appeared only once but caused him greater disquiet. It said simply, *Sloan.*

While the Levy decayed, opposition to the Colonel's assumption of office in Hassan was growing in another quarter. Mr Peachy could no longer ignore the signals of inquiry reaching the Agency from London, nor could he overlook the imperative tone in which he was asked to report the circumstances surrounding the death of the Emir and the involvement of a British seconded officer. His subsequent account of the incident at the palace, reinforced by his view that the Colonel's appointment in Hassan carried with it the right to independent action, plainly convinced no one, and he was informed with chilly courtesy that a senior official would visit

Hassan as soon as communications allowed.

Sloan: they had not forgotten Sloan. The families of the Afarhid, who occupied the biggest single territory inside Hassan, and from whom the Levy was largely recruited, revered his name, recalled his death, and were unsatisfied. Hamid, that erstwhile son of the Afarhid, whom Sloan had whipped unmercifully, had likewise remembered Sloan and no doubt did still if he had survived the cruel sunlight of the desert. The tribal Afarhid were restless; they changed their ground, ignored their boundaries, drank at wells traditionally not their own and bore the consequences of their folly. The Colonel did not know what method Kennedy used with the Afarhid, what combination of inducement and suggestion to perpetuate the Captain's name, and to blacken the name of the man who had killed him, but plainly the tribe carried his memory like an emblem.

Kennedy had learned his trade in the turbulent savannahs of South America; he knew that fighting his opponent by direct means was the most costly form of warfare. He used cheap methods, the expedients of the commercial soldier who must make his warfare pay. He played upon the Afarhid with the utmost subtlety. And Colonel Masterman, with his instinct for a changing tactical situation, knew that Kennedy's chance to employ his army with small fear of loss had come to him when it was reported by the Awali of Kairej, the official closest to the Afarhid, that the tribe had risen against the usurper Masterman.

24

Colonel Masterman and his officers conferred in the map room at Warboys Camp. The lamp was pulled low over a large-scale chart of the Razpat region. The frontier with Hadraif ran through this area on a line never agreed between the two states, but Kennedy's army had advanced along the coastal plain to a point unmistakably in Hassan. The speed and direction of his thrust would take him to Bir-el-Shama in a matter of hours. While the route he had chosen was longer than the Maledifah road, it was free from natural obstacles, there was cover in the dry wadis and the groves of palm trees, and the Colonel knew he would have chosen the same line of advance if the appreciation had been his to make. Of course, it was impertinent: the mercenary captain had pushed his force to a point where the Colonel was bound to attack him; it was a challenge to a force superior in strength and equipment which no commanding officer could fail to take up. If only the Levy was in better heart....

Masterman did not need to consider the situation deeply. 'He's left himself plenty of room to manoeuvre, gentlemen. Note how gently the hills rise from the plain at this point; that will enable him to use the Afarhid on his flank, to harass me from the high ground inland. The untrained bedouin would be uncontrollable on the plain, but they'll be excellent value in these shallow dunes. His own personnel and the Hadraifi regulars will advance towards me on either side of the camel track which is at least a mile from the sea and where the broken ground will give him cover. If only I had a sea-borne force to put behind him, and some aircraft! However, I must fight with what I have, there's no point in wishing things different.... I will aim to stop him *here*, gentlemen, at the Wadi Amriz, which I can supply from Bir-el-Shama without risk to the transport. Of course, the devil knows I can't use my armoured vehicles on this ground, but my guns will do him some damage, and I am confident I can prevent him from reaching the capital. None the less, I could wish I were not so weakened in numbers and spirit.'

Major Tillotson's strength lay in his devotion to unpalatable truths; now he wore his most sombre face. 'Are you proposing to use the Afarhid in this engagement, Colonel? I mean to say, with the tribe in open rebellion against you——'

'My dear Major, without the Afarhid and their tributaries there would not be many soldiers left in the Levy: the Jamirs perhaps, and some Rashkirs who remember Ramadi.'

'Even so, I would not trust the Afarhid. They will not fight their own people.'

'Come now, they're in uniform with months of disciplinary training behind them. I decline to take a pessimistic view of our situation. I trust the Levy to fight as we have taught them, as a corporate body without private loyalties.'

'At least they'll be as good as the mercenaries,' Lovelace said cheerfully; but as Masterman never took account of the Captain's opinion he could not be much comforted.

'They have no sheikh, no rallying point,' Tillotson continued; 'I must believe they will revert to their tribal loyalty when faced with a clear choice.'

The Colonel also believed it likely, but his task did not allow him to be other than optimistic in the face of danger. 'I'm certain you are mistaken, Tony. In any case, I have no other force to use.'

When the Levy fell in on the parade ground to await transport to Wadi Amriz, the soldiers carried themselves with something like regimental dignity and Colonel Masterman was heartened. The recent desertions had left the companies at low strength, but the men held themselves erect for his inspection, each as taut as a bow pulled to the point of release, and as he completed his swift tour of the ranks he felt more confident the Levy would turn Major Kennedy and drive his poorly disciplined troops out of Hassan.

He stood in the centre of the parade ground watching the Levy file away and mount the lorries. The sunlight burned in the dust all around him, giving no shadow; the shabby buildings on the far side of the road, drenched with light, were hardly distinguishable from the rising desert beyond. The lorries started, the men gave their usual cheer; the convoy wheeled away from the parade ground throwing up a cloud of dust and disappeared towards Bir-el-Shama. The Colonel had seen it all before. He stood in reflection after the lorries had gone from sight, declining to think of defeat. Then he turned smartly about and marched off the square.

He spoke with buoyant good humour to the waiting officers. 'We'll give him a bloody nose, gentlemen. Those lousy Swedes and Germans will never stand up to Johnny Bedouin. They're not trained for open warfare, and I suspect they'll run away if we biff them hard enough.'

The Colonel went up to his office to fetch his belt and revolver. He was hardly surprised to find Sheikh Saud and Sheikh Abdullah occupying his armchairs. Saud was at his most affable.

'A temporary liberty, Colonel, which I trust you'll overlook. Needless to say, in the present situation neither the palace nor my own home is entirely convenient. At a time of shifting political allegiance—one might almost say political mayhem —the only place one can relax in comfort is a British military establishment.' It seemed the Sheikhs had taken up residence at Warboys when Kennedy crossed the Hadraifi frontier.

'I think you'd be more comfortable in the mess,' the Colonel suggested.

'It's all one,' said Abdullah, who lay in his chair as if in his grave.

'I must tell you—it's really very funny—I had a surprising communication from the Sheikh of Hadraif.' Saud spoke with continued good fellowship. 'That gentleman has actually invited me to join a federal government of the two states as a sort of grand vizier. An astonishing impertinence, when I come to think of it. The message was couched in a mixture of Arabian courtesy and Maoist jargon which I found disturbing. I must believe the present situation is Maoist in origin. I declined, of course; I was really deeply shocked.'

'Gentlemen, I am unable to discuss these matters at present,' Masterman said. 'My job is to keep the Hadraifi army out of Hassan; nothing more than that. Please make yourselves at home. There will be a decision before nightfall.'

'Ah, yes.' Saud bent to the Colonel's will. 'We must not keep you from your task; you will have much to keep you occupied.'

The Colonel had no further time for the Sheikhs. He pushed his revolver into the holster, gave a short bow to his guests, and went out to the waiting Land-Rover. He could think of nothing but the shape of the terrain at Wadi Amriz, where he would meet the rat Kennedy and his army of mercenaries.

The car was a mile beyond Bir-el-Shama, on the coastal plain, when a new thought struck him. He said, 'Return to the Political Agency, as quickly as you can.'

The Land-Rover followed its own tracks back into the capital and drove violently into the Agency garden. The Colonel hammered on the door several times before it was opened by Zamil.

'Get the Agent,' the Colonel said.

Zamil did nothing; he moved his weight from foot to foot.

'At once, do you hear?'

'The Colonel is planning a battle?' Zamil asked. From somewhere he had obtained a brief, vicious daring. 'The Colonel is going to fight the armies of the federated socialist state?'

'You can keep that rubbish to yourself, Zamil,' said Masterman, who was not impressed by this cessation from cowardice. 'I wish to see Mr Peachy. Jump to it, man! I've no time to waste.'

At once Zamil lapsed into obsequiousness. He walked backwards from the door. 'Of course, Colonel Masterman. I'm sorry to have detained you with my stupid prattle. I will fetch the Agent, who is looking to the window fastenings.'

Peachy came immediately, Sarita at his shoulder. Through an open door at the end of the hall the Colonel saw Zamil resume his desk and bend over his books.

The Colonel did not soften his words: he wanted Sarita saved. 'Kennedy is advancing along the coastal plain. I aim to stop him at Wadi Amriz, but I cannot be certain of the outcome. I suggest, Mr Peachy, that you take Sarita to Warboys, as the town is full of madmen and I cannot guarantee her safety here.'

Masterman had often been surprised by the Agent's readiness to wear a radiant face at a time of danger. This morning, as the mercenaries cut deeply into Hassan, he was beaming. 'My dear Colonel, we'll do no such thing! We're very happy here. I'm certain you'll send the blighters packing. If necessary, I'll put a chain across the main gate and bring in a second watchman.'

'You don't understand me. If the Levy should fail, there may be lawlessness in Bir-el-Shama. Foreign diplomats and their families are always vulnerable on occasions of this sort. I'd be happier if she went to Warboys, where I can provide an effective guard.'

'Oh, stuff and nonsense! You won't fail. I've every confidence in you.'

From beyond the office door, without looking up, Zamil said, 'There will be a victory at Wadi Amriz. There will be peace in Arabia.'

'Of course; it stands to reason,' the Agent said.

'She should not stay here.' He wanted this one thing: that Sarita, and the fragments of the past she carried, should survive the day.

'I won't go,' the girl said. 'Did you think I would?' She took the Colonel's arm and kissed him on the cheek. 'It was nice of you to think of me.'

'I cannot approve your decision.'

The Agent and his daughter smiled; the Colonel had never seen them so happy.

'We have the best defence we could ask for,' Peachy said. 'Who'd ask for more? Now, dear Colonel, don't give another thought to us; we'll wait here until you've finished with Kennedy—in which undertaking, our utter blessing! Things will improve in Hassan after your victory.'

'After the victory,' said the clerk from beyond the office door. 'After the death and bloody dismemberment of every vile oppressor.'

'As you wish,' the Colonel said, and left.

He took his Land-Rover as far as he dared towards Wadi Amriz and left it under the ridge of the shallow hill that lay between himself and Kennedy's reported position. Taking his binoculars, he climbed the remaining height to the observation post that had been established in the rocks on the crest of the hill. Lovelace was there with Major Graves and Major Kirkbride. The first company had taken up defensive positions along the nearer bank of the wadi, which was here several hundred yards wide; the rest of the Levy had deployed in neutral ground to the rear. He could not see Kennedy but a pall of dust hanging over the rocks and thorns on the far side of the declivity gave a clear indication of his position. Nothing lay between the two forces but the broken ground in the bed of the wadi and the brutal sunlight that whitened the rocks and threw a thin band of mirage across the farther desert. Inland from the position the ground rose into low sand-hills perhaps two hundred feet high and corrugated on the windward side.

'An excellent place to stop him,' the Colonel said. He told Major Graves to occupy the high ground on his right hand with a platoon. He didn't think Kennedy would try to outflank him to seaward.

His orders were relayed to the reserve companies and, a while later, he watched the platoon climbing the sheltered side of the sand-hills carrying a light machine-gun; their figures hardened on the skyline and disappeared.

He instructed the gunners who had unlimbered behind him to open fire upon Kennedy's position; and within a minute he heard the discharge of the first gun followed by the crump 'of the impacting shell beyond the wadi.

'I wouldn't have missed this for worlds,' he told Lovelace. He loved the sound of the guns, the sight of the Levy deployed in the rocks, the gleam of the sun in the gun-metal. The problems of his command had resolved into a single engagement of the main forces; the political ambiguities had dispersed, driven away by a clean wind; he was refreshed and happy. He turned his nostrils in the direction of the guns hoping to catch the bitter smell of the discharge. Go on, lads, he silently urged the gunners. Let them have it! Drive the rascals out of Hassan!

He wanted to see Kennedy, to judge the level of his courage, to invest him with the character of hero.

'They don't seem to be advancing,' Lovelace said from the field telephone.

'What a pity he's not a better soldier,' the Colonel replied, speaking his full mind; 'we could have made something of this if he were. Tell me when he moves.'

He went down to the rocks where the first company was lying in cover as he had taught them. Tillotson met him there.

'A very good day to you, Major. It looks as if we may have to tempt him forward. Can't think what the fellow's doing.'

'He's making a lot of dust. Why would he do that?' Tillotson asked the question as if he already knew the answer.

'He's moving in stories. He means to fight me here.'

The Colonel was not in the mood to worry, nor to give thought to the Major's opinions. He felt the glow of excitement, the thrill of professional mastery.

'Colonel, I'm obliged to suggest that Kennedy has lured us here for some purpose of his own. Do you think he means to attack you frontally?' Again, the question contained its own answer.

'I'm sure of it, Arthur. He has chosen the ground himself and he means to face me here. No matter what else I've said about him, I've never accused him of cowardice.'

'It's not the manner of mercenary troops. They don't fight battles.'

'Well, there's always a first time. Frankly, of all the things Kennedy has done since he came to Hassan, his move today is the one I find least despicable: he is prepared to face me squarely, I'm sure, and take the consequences of his action.'

Tillotson drew in his cheeks until his mouth almost disappeared. He gave a little whistle of astonishment. 'I shouldn't count on it,' he said.

'Damn it, Arthur, I must start from an assumption of some kind.' The Colonel did not mean to have the battle spoilt by uncomfortable argument. 'He knows he must break the Levy if he means to occupy Hassan. We'll move forward if he doesn't show himself soon.'

He walked back to his position of vantage. Now the sun had risen to a height where it cast no shadows and the wadi was losing depth and feature. He studied the farther bank through his binoculars; he thought he could distinguish the grey robes of the Hadraifi askaris in the nearer cover.

'They're there, Lovelace! I'll swear to it.'

He wished they'd fire: he wanted the battle to start, to envelop him in its sound and movement; he wanted the comfort of danger and the imperative to action. Come on, fellows, he thought. Let's see what you're made of!

He was not disappointed. A minute later the concealed enemy opened a broken fire with small arms across the wadi a little to seaward of him. He heard the bullets ricochet from the rocks.

That's better, he thought; and he gave the first company the order to return fire. He was heartened by the crash of the rifles as the Levy directed their fire across the wadi, and he watched with admiration as the stones jumped all along the line of rocks where the askaris lay hidden: this was well-aimed, orderly fire, the product of discipline, and the Colonel was encouraged to think that the Levy was in good heart.

He concealed himself behind the rocks and listened with rapt sympathy to a bullet in flight above his head. 'I do believe the bugger's going to seek a solution here,' he said; and he put from his mind the knowledge that mercenaries didn't fight like this, and that in all their warring centuries the nomadic Afarhid had never fought to gain ground but only to inflict injury.

At midday, when the sun burned in the sand-hills behind Bir-el-Shama, the Afarhid attacked the capital down the old camel track and in no sort of order. Their direction was given them by two German mercenaries; their anger was their own. They came on horseback, camelback and on foot, and when they reached the first of the houses they fired through the doorways and used their knives against the people in the street. Only the dogs resisted them. The sound of their advance carried to the market place where the traders left their merchandise on the paving stones and scattered along the small streets of the soukh. The lazy, the fat, the crippled were overtaken by the horsemen and cut down; so were the children who had run in the direction of danger, as if towards shelter, at the moment of attack. The tribesmen dismounted in the market and ran into the stalls where they used their kunjis in short, swift movements. The cry they uttered was not understood by those that heard it: the word was a rendering of 'Sloan', slurred by repetition into a meaningless sibilant which they spoke with fierce emphasis at each downward thrust of the blade: it sounded more like 'Shlar'. The townsmen who escaped did so mainly by working boats out into the creek, for the tribesmen had no understanding of water and did not even glance across the surface at the retreating small craft. The Afarhid who had entered the town on foot, lagging behind the horsemen, could now cut the throats only of the wounded or the dead, as they were covering the same ground as the mounted men; none the less they worked with greater method, searching corners overlooked till now, running up stairways where there was no bloody footprint, using the same cry of savage retribution.

At length someone brought flame from the baker's oven and fired the stalls and houses nearest the market. By the intercession of what providence no one could say, the three brothels escaped the flames, no matter that the walls were darkened by smoke, but the small buildings of the soukh, where the division between one and the next was no wider than a man's shoulders, ignited one after another with an explosion of flame that burst open the shutters and cracked and crumbled the outer walls. The smoke rose vertically into the dry, still air.

When the Afarhid had spent their anger, some withdrew into the desert, leaving the town as it had been left by Kabina the Whore and a score of other despoilers in the long centuries since its foundation; others lay in exhaustion in the market place and by the creek. The trance faded; they slept as they might have done after a religious festival; they had avenged an old soldier who loved them.

Colonel Masterman received news of the Afarhid attack at Bir-el-Shama some minutes after it had become plain that only a thin force of askaris opposed him at Wadi Amriz, and that Kennedy's army was several miles to the rear, a long way out of gun-shot. No doubt the dust pall had been raised by a small number of vehicles towing brushwood. He knew he had been outmanoeuvred. He felt the sickening shame of defeat.

'I have failed,' he said simply. 'I should have expected something of this sort. Plainly he didn't intend to fight me here. We must return to Bir-el-Shama and see what we can do to repair things. Call in the pickets, please.'

He kept his smile fixed as he walked to where the companies were deployed. 'The bastard got behind us, gentlemen. We'll deal with him presently. The first company is to bring in those askaris and then follow me back into town. Why don't the pickets return?' He shaded his eyes against the glare of the sand-hills where he had placed the platoon and the light machine-gun.

Tillotson said, 'They're not in position. They've gone into the desert.'

Masterman nodded. 'No doubt I've also lost the seaward party. It can't be helped. Don't waste too much time in joining me, Major.'

He directed the remaining companies back to Bir-el-Shama, but many of the troops would not mount the lorries. They stood in silent groups despite the barking of the NCOs.

'I don't think they're going to embus,' said Lovelace. A definition of the obvious had always been his forte. 'Perhaps the Jamirs and Rashkirs——'

The Colonel had no time to waste. He approached the reluctant soldiers and spoke to them in Arabic. 'What is it, men? Where is your loyalty? Are we not comrades sworn to fight together?'

They said nothing; they looked at the ground.

'Have you forgotten your oath? Have you forgotten Radami? For this I could shoot you.'

'They are Afarhid,' said Lovelace.

'Disarm them,' the Colonel ordered. 'Take their belts and pouches. They're no use to me.'

'Perhaps if you were to shoot one or two the others might follow.'

'I've never shot a soldier under my command.'

'You have the right to do so.'

'Let them go,' the Colonel said.

The Afarhid were disarmed, the Jamirs doing the job, and the rifles and accoutrements placed in a lorry. Once relieved of their weapons, the Afarhid simply wandered away without looking back. The Colonel mounted his Land-Rover and led the way into Bir-el-Shama. The lorries followed with the remaining Levy—fifty Jamirs, the 'desert crows', whom everyone despised, and about twenty Rashkirs related to Ramadi.

What a shambles! Masterman thought. He could give the situation no firmer shape in his mind.

They cleared the last of the sand-hills and Bir-el-Shama came into sight. Then the Colonel drew his breath sharply, as if he had been stabbed. 'Make haste,' he said to the driver.

The smoke rose in a column above the roofs and at three hundred feet flattened into a plane which now covered not only the town but the nearer hills and sea. The fires had diminished now, the flames showed only occasionally. In the desert on either side of the road he saw the survivors sitting or walking without point; among them, marked with the same insensibility, were some whose robes showed them to be Afarhid, men who had made the attack but now acknowledged the tragedy with the same sense of anguish and wonder. The convoy stopped by the first houses, the lorries drawing off the road where the men could alight. The Rashkirs wept when they saw the ruined town; the Jamirs stayed silent.

The Colonel forced his mind to keep moving, aware that his responsibility was not yet at an end. He detached a party to arrest any of the Afarhid who remained in the town, another to locate the injured and bring what relief might be possible, a third to congregate the dead. He sent a messenger to Warboys summoning the medical and fire-fighting resources available there. Somehow he had to impose a new discipline upon this maddened place.

That was his job. For the time being he must think of nothing else, no matter that the misery of defeat occupied the innermost parts of his mind. 'Get the soldiers away quickly,' he said.

In two hours they had worked through the town as far as the creek and the Warboys road. The dead had been taken out and assembled for burial near the Shakqui Mosque. The severely wounded had been dealt with by the Jamirs, who showed a terrible mercy; the Colonel did not intercede. With equal consideration the 'crows' had assisted those who could walk to the dressing station set up on the outskirts of the town. The worst of the fires had been put out, the litter from the devastated market had been thrown into the creek, there was a great multiplication of the flies. The Afarhid arrested by the Levy now squatted in the courtyard of the police station, their hands behind their heads, forgetful of the morning's insanity; the Rashkirs stood guard. Once the surviving townsfolk saw the soldiers in the streets they returned to their houses and a pattern of life was resumed in Bir-el-Shama, though one much reduced in scale, in numbers. From the time of Kabina the town had been practised in the resumption of life after disaster. It would recover in a year. It had never been much of a place, anyway.

The Colonel was sickened by the smell of blood and ash. He summoned his Land-Rover and patrolled the streets outside the town which seemed to have escaped the Afarhid. He drove past the Shaqui Mosque, where the desert was being opened by a bulldozer and the dead were aligned with a soldier's rule awaiting their swift burial. At least there was order here. At the palace they had closed the gate, loosed the cheetahs in the garden and gone indoors when the Afarhid made their incursion into Bir-el-Shama, and the Colonel found there an atmosphere of beleaguered gaiety. He reprimanded the Chamberlain, showed the secretaries a furious face, and left abruptly.

'I will go to the Agency,' he told the driver.

The car rattled down the stony hill from the palace. He realized then, which he had not thought of before, that he needed desperately to find Mr Peachy and his daughter alive.

The road outside the Agency looked no different from usual. Children played in the gutter, where the eucalyptus trees cast a mottled shade. Along the walls cats lay with their bellies exposed to the sunlight. He stopped the car by the gate. He wanted to talk to Peachy, to draw some comfort from that generous spirit; he wanted to explain just why he had left the town uncovered, why he had supposed the rebel tribesmen would attack him at Wadi Amriz; he wanted confirmation of the inhuman cruelty of Kennedy and his Hadraifi masters, who had urged the Afarhid to a bloody massacre.

He heard Peachy's voice in the garden. There was that much of mercy in Bir-el-Shama that afternoon.

The Agent himself undid the chains that held the gate. The watchmen had gone. His dismay at the bloodshed was shown only in his clumsy handling of the padlock and his vexation over this small difficulty. 'Come in, come in, dear Colonel! You must be tired. I will get you a drink.... Dear me, I'm really no good with these contrivances.'

'Mr Peachy, you will have heard what happened in the town——'

'A terrible thing, which no one could have foreseen. Such madness! Every once in a while the bedouin takes leave of his senses.'

'I did not think they would do it.'

'Of course not. It was like a freak storm.' He freed the padlock with an effort. 'There now! Come in and rest.'

'I can only stay a few minutes. This was my fault, of course.'

Peachy walked in front of him towards the house. He spoke swiftly, as if the subject had no importance. 'It was no one's fault. It was the Arab temper, exploited by an evil genius. It was an accident of human nature. It was my fault, I think.'

'I really believed Kennedy meant to fight.'

'A fair assumption. He might well have attacked you at Wadi Amriz. You were not to know.'

Masterman said slowly, seeking the exact truth, 'A soldier must appreciate every possibility. He cannot excuse himself because his opponent does something unlikely. I left the town unguarded; that was a cardinal oversight. But I didn't see him using the Afarhid for such a purpose.'

At the doorway Peachy turned a brilliant face upon him, and the Colonel was surprised because he had expected the Agent to be critical, to rebuke him for failure. 'Of *course* you expected no such thing! How could you? Kennedy's mind follows a new and dreadful course which can only be understood by someone of the same nature. He's part of a new barbarism, an ugly phenomenon you will not have seen before.'

For a moment the Colonel was arrested by this idea, but then his mind lapsed into the pain of defeat. 'I don't know about that, Mr Peachy. I don't understand such things. The truth is this—that I allowed a town to be destroyed that I should have protected. Now my soldiers have deserted and I cannot save the state from destruction by the enemy. I have failed totally.'

The Agent led him into the study, saying nothing. With half his mind the Colonel noticed the silence in the house, the absence of voices, footsteps. The Agent gave him a whisky from the decanter; then he said carefully but without particular emphasis, 'Friend, you must see this thing with Arabian eyes. A massacre in the desert is a natural disaster like a tornado. It springs from the nature of the place; it's made with a terrible innocence by people who are not themselves bad; and when it's over all the living can do is continue their lives. If it helps at all, tell yourself that Arabia is mad.'

The Colonel had not followed the argument closely. 'An interesting point, Mr Peachy, but it will not save the state from occupation by Hadraif. The enemy has won. The Sheikh will sit in the palace and the Hassanite people will lose their independence.'

'So what? The bedouin is always independent.'

'It cannot make for stability in the area.'

'Nothing ever does. *Hell*.'

'And into the bargain I've lost my command.'

Peachy said then, with abiding sympathy, 'I know. I'm sorry. I'm truly sorry.'

The silence in the house impressed itself upon the Colonel. He raised his head. 'Sarita?' he asked. 'Where is Sarita?'

'At Warboys. Your wife fetched her.'

'And Zamil?'

'I don't know. He ran out, full of madness. I dare say he was killed.'

'And the clerks, the servants?'

'They're hiding, or absent. The state is demented, each individual out of his wits. Sanity will take some time to return.'

The Colonel had not felt the impact of his defeat until then. He sat at the table, the glass at the extent of his arm, gazing at it as if at a symbol of failure. He sat there a long time in silence. At length he said, 'I'm glad Sarita is safe.'

Peachy said, 'Old friend, you did what you could. This was my fault. I urged you against your will.'

'It was bound to happen,' the Colonel said, without moving the direction of his eyes. 'We were wrong from the beginning.'

In his mind the matter was quite plain. He had killed the King, and then the state had gone mad.

25

Following the engagement at Wadi Amriz, the mercenaries did not attack the Levy at Warboys Camp; they had no need. The strategy of commercial warfare, with its emphasis upon profit, required extraordinary gains from an undertaking of this sort, and as they had reduced the Levy to ineffectiveness by other means an attack upon the camp was superfluous. The Colonel had no longer the force to seek out Kennedy and his soldiers and that afternoon the mercenaries moved freely in the state. At Faleh-la the oil men had closed their gates and continued their evil-smelling business no matter that the state was in turbulence: the company, which pursued its profits in the more desperate segments of the globe, had long since grown used to local anguish. Indeed, the Colonel had forgotten all about the oil men and did not look to them for help. On his return to Warboys, he used the troops remaining to him to man a reduced perimeter containing only the vital elements of the camp. He felt as if he should have informed his superior officer of his defeat, but he did not have one; instead he wrote a short account of the day's action and put it in his safe with his other papers for whomsoever should follow him at Warboys. It had never crossed his mind that there would be a time after defeat when he would be faced with continuing responsibility; he had always supposed he would be dead.

I have lost, he thought. My soldiers are gone. I don't know what to do....

He sat at his desk and waited for something to happen. Matters were in the political field, in realms he did not understand and which he must leave to Mr Peachy; and he did not doubt that, at this particular moment, Mr Peachy was drunk.

Mr Peachy was waiting for Zamil; he had things to say; he

was certainly drunk.

And after nightfall, but before the passage of sleep had brought some return of sanity, when the fires were still glowing in Bir-el-Shama, Zamil returned to the Agency by way of the alleys and the servants' entrance. He fell many times, not from drunkenness but because his mind was affected now and again by the destructive insanity of the Afarhid. The madness was not total; each lapse from rational thought, which sent him staggering across the road as if he had been clubbed, was followed by a slow return to clear-mindedness. After all, Zamil had graduated from a university in Baghdad and the habit of exact behaviour was well established; the intrusion into his mind of an impulse having its origin in the ancient wrath of Islam met the resistance of education. When he entered the servants' courtyard at the Agency he was in a mood of timid subservience; he understood the size of the disaster that had overtaken the country.

He heard the Agent's voice from the balcony above him. Peachy was sitting in his basket chair, plainly drunk, and Zamil, who hated intemperate behaviour, frowned in disgust.

The Agent spoke in Arabic. 'O Zamil, what did you see, what did you do? Where are the townsfolk now?'

'The dead are buried, master. The living are in tears. The soldiers have all run away.' Zamil swayed from foot to foot, as ever uneasy in the presence of his employer.

'Was it well done, Zamil? Did the Maoists blush before they set the crazy Afarhid against the town? Is this the federation you scholars want—the joining of the dead with the guilty in a union of blood and shame? I tell you this: that revolution has a callous heart.'

'As you say, master,' said Zamil, bending his head.

Peachy stood up and tottered to the balcony rail, where he berated Zamil as if from a superior level of authority. 'Count the dead, book-keeper. Count every bundle of rags, my earnest friend. Make your peace with Kabina the Whore. Join every brute and butcher who ever made a killing in the name of cold philosophy. But remember that the dead are all offered at the altar of wickedness.'

Zamil sat on the cobbles, his head in his hands, frightened and ashamed. He burbled revolution between his knees. The aura of madness had entered at the edges of his mind and the rhythm of his breathing broke into chaos. He was affected by the spells of lunacy cast by the Afarhid that morning; he was joined in remote succession with the minds of Kabina and her progeny, with the dark visions of Hajji Kassim, with every mad Al Farahid who had blackened the name of Hassan with his cruelties. He rose upon his knees, swaying with frenzy, holding the sides of his head as if to contain the destructive impulse.

Peachy was descending the stair into the courtyard. He miscounted the steps and fell untidily at the bottom. He spoke from where he lay. 'O Zamil, the townsfolk were rabid and corrupt, and they had powerful diseases, but it was a shame to kill them.'

With the last of his sanity, Zamil said, 'Even so, my master. I will not dissent from your opinion.'

'Still, the whores remain, like sunlight and the ocean. Who saved the whores, Zamil? What power held out his shield and said, "Slay all, slay all, but leave the whores"? Even in this abysmal place, is there still hope?'

The Agent got up from the ground and turned into the garden, where the dust gleamed like dew under the starlight. The clerk could hear his voice though he could not see him.

'It's all the same oblivion in the end, Zamil, but one should choose the manner of one's going. For myself, I just don't care; it might as well be now, with the failure of diplomacy.'

Zamil crossed the courtyard in fitful pursuit. He was blinded by the darkness in the garden and found his direction only by the sound of the Agent's voice.

'Don't think it will be easy, friend. The race that made me does not permit surrender.'

The clerk fell twice in his progress towards the voice that mocked him, but he was carried forward by the strength he drew from Kabina and her issue. He stumbled, cursed, searched in the darkness, while his mind filled with the images of violence and death and his education, achieved with such diligence, offered not the smallest restraint.

I don't know what to do, the Colonel thought, still seated at his desk at Warboys. There is no military solution. Someone else must decide the future.

He was awakened later by Saud, who came across from the mess to where the light was burning. The Sheikh had lost no part of his courtesy. 'The oil men are here, Colonel. They have ideas, contracts, solutions....'

Colonel Masterman had no alternative but to hear them, although he did not care for the oil business or for the men who were pumping the world dry for the sake of gain. They came up to his office, brash executives of shallow courtesy, men of energy and decision who wanted nothing from Arabia but the rotten fluid that underlay the desert and who, so the Colonel supposed, would strike any bargain, reward any scoundrel so long as the wells were safe. He barely listened to them.

They did not want to take part in politics, the executives said; they wanted only to protect their investment; but they were bound to conclude that the war, such as it was, had been won by Hadraif, and that no one in Hassan could now speak from a position of authority.

It was true, and the Colonel did not deny it: in the brief war that morning Hassan had plainly lost.

The oil men spoke quickly, not in embarrassment but because they were dictating terms and time was pressing. They had entered into discussion with the Sheikh of Hadraif, and they had agreed to pay him the combined royalties provided he could show that the union of the two states was complete.

It was complete, the Colonel told them; the Hassanites were dead.

Very well, very good, the oil men said. No doubt the Sheikh would use the revenues for the benefit of the united Emirate. No doubt, the Colonel agreed. Of course, the oil men continued, the Sheikh would insist upon the disbandment of the Levy and the expulsion of the expatriate officers; but he would place the province under the administrative care of a local Sheikh as a token of reconciliation; Sheikh Abdullah was his choice, with Sheikh Saud as his vizier.

So, Hassan was gone, given away by the oil men. Masterman said nothing.

His visitors had one further request—they desired the

Colonel's assurance that he would undertake no further operations against Hadraif. The Company had already offered an ex-gratia payment to Kennedy in return for his promise to leave the state, which reward he had accepted. The Colonel simply nodded his agreement.

Their business done, the oil men left without shaking hands, and he heard their rapid steps on the concrete stairway leading down to the entrance. The car doors slammed, the engine note faded as the visitors drove away toward Faleh-la.

Strange how they remind me of Kennedy, the Colonel thought, and laughed in the desolation.

A mile away across the starlit desert a voice was calling. It alerted the Rashkir sentries standing at the wire. They called the duty officer and he listened at the gate, trying to distinguish the words, but only the angry derision in the voice was clear to him.

Along the wire the Rashkirs returned the insults, but the speaker did not heed them.

The duty officer found the Colonel as he left headquarters and together they went up the outside stair on to the roof. The Colonel listened at the parapet; he could hear the words quite plainly, spoken in the Arabic of the Afarhid.

'Where are the townsfolk? Where are the pedlars and the stall keepers? Where are the children and their mothers? Great soldier, where are they?'

'Hamid,' the Colonel said simply. 'I might have known it.'

He went down abruptly, to collide with Saud and Captain Lovelace in the road outside. They spoke to him in the darkness, in the dull voices everyone had used since the destruction of Bir-el-Shama that morning: the Agent was dead, beaten by an unknown assassin to the point where recognition was a matter of guesswork.

'I see. Poor fellow,' Masterman said. He led them on to the lighted veranda of the officers' mess, where Abdullah joined them. 'Gentlemen, I have been wrong. I accept without reservation that I should not have taken action against the Head of State, as a break in discipline can lead only to disaster.'

244

He had nothing further to say, but he was reminded that the Sheikhs had to continue the government of this poor place no matter that the officers would be expelled. 'Sheikh Abdullah, I suggest you give your loyalty to the Sheikh of Hadraif and do what you can to repair the damage in Hassan. Sheikh Saud, your brother will need your advice.'

He wanted to be left alone, and as they judged his mood correctly the two Sheikhs disappeared from the light and he heard their voices on the dark lawn behind him.

Peachy gone: he adjusted slowly to this news. With unusual sympathy, Lovelace brought a whisky in ice and provided a chair just beyond the light into which the Colonel sank as if at the limit of exhaustion. Peachy gone. This was a brutal thing; and with him was lost the only full account of the Hassan rebellion. Without that lucid mind to explain, no one would understand how an English colonel was compelled to seize power in a foreign state. Masterman himself was forgetting how it happened; even as he sat in the dark the past lost coherence and moved into absurdity, and his own part in it became the more strange. Whoever heard of such a thing? he thought. I must have taken leave of my senses.

Saud returned from the shadows, Abdullah behind him. 'I am sorry about Mr Peachy. A man who loved Arabia. . . .'

The Colonel never discussed casualties: he simply nodded.

The Sheikh continued, with some hesitation, 'Your job here is done, sir. You may leave with an untroubled mind, as you have always acted honestly. The response may not have been what you expected, but that was our fault, not yours.'

'Of course; it is clear; we are quite mad,' Abdullah said.

'Gentlemen, you are kind,' said the Colonel.

They left him finally then. With the loss of his command he was diminished in stature. He did not want to face the officers; he wanted to sit in the dark, as if the night would go on for ever and the sunlight never again disclose the outlines of Warboys Camp. He had nothing more to do but evacuate the British personnel, and the few women, and the adjutant could take care of that.

Nothing more to do.

He became suddenly alert, his mind at once precise and resilient, his limbs attuned to action: he had a job to undertake before surrendering his command, and he could not think why it hadn't occurred to him before. He jumped up, relieved at the prospect of action.

'Captain Lovelace,' he called, 'I'm leaving the unit for a time. I shall be back before dawn.'

He walked swiftly to the Armoury, where he beat upon the door until it was opened to him. He drew a rifle and forty rounds and with the skill of the professional he withdrew the bolt and examined the barrel. Then he pressed the rounds into the magazine, shot one into the chamber and applied the safety-catch. He also drew a Very pistol and cartridges. He slung the rifle at his shoulder and went out into the dark.

The Sheikhs stood on the lighted veranda of the mess and the Colonel called to them good-humouredly. 'Lord Saud, you are wrong; I still have a responsibility to discharge.'

'Forget it, sir. An ignorant soldier——'

'Yet of importance, Excellency.'

'Take care.'

'Naturally. I am a professional.'

He would take care; it was not in his nature to take less than reasonable care, for there was vulgarity in recklessness. He called at the guardroom and enrolled three Jamirs to assist him; he sent a vehicle with three armed men to make a wide detour into the desert and block the camel track leading eastward at a point four miles from the camp. He could trust the Jamirs; they did not care upon whom they drew their sights; they were everyone's enemy. He guided the small party through the gate, where weeks ago Captain Sloan had cruelly whipped the soldier he now pursued, and out into the warm bitter-smelling desert where the sand broke under his feet and his heart responded to the emptiness as it had always done. He walked eastward for half a mile and halted, listening.

Not a sound in the great desert. He thanked God for the taciturnity of the Jamirs which kept them silent. He directed them on a path which would take them at ninety degrees to his own; after a mile they were to turn towards him and beat forward, hopefully driving Hamid in his direction and to a point where the Colonel could cover him with his rifle. If Hamid opened fire, the Colonel would shoot him. If he ran more deeply into the desert the party in the vehicle might catch him. It was a slender chance either way, but the Colonel was thankful for this action.

The Jamirs disappeared soundlessly on his left; and if anyone could catch a crazy Afarhid with a gift for invisibility it was a 'desert crow'. Masterman continued in his direction, at present making no use of cover because Hamid would not be this close to the wire, and in any case there was little cover in these shallow dunes but for the occasional litter of rocks. He held his rifle at the trail with the safety-catch open; he kept his eyes, by now accustomed to the starlight, swinging widely across his front; he walked only in the soft sand so that his boots should not ring on the rocks and betray his presence to an alert bedouin versed in the sounds of the desert by night; he moved forward steadily while the sounds of Warboys Camp, the voices, the hum of the generators, faded behind him and he became disengaged from the trappings of his command, alone and in pursuit of an enemy who had injured him fatally. He fixed his direction upon a clear star just above the rim of the desert and continued another mile.

He stopped. The lights along the wire at Warboys were small and distant. He covered himself behind a shelf of rock which jutted from the side of the dune. Above the desert the stars were brilliant, lighting the vast horizon.

He laid the rifle across the rock and waited in silence, holding his breath. Nothing. A star fell. Yet Hamid was there; his cross-grained spirit was alive in the desert; somewhere he lay in a fold of the rock, watching, laughing, moved by an impulse the Colonel did not understand.

An hour passed. So far he had not heard the Jamirs.

The voice when it came was so close, and so magnified by the darkness, the Colonel started and brought the rifle to his shoulder although he could not see the speaker. He did not know what words were spoken but he recognized the derisive, bantering voice. He moved his line of sight left and right searching for Hamid. Then some words spoken in the old dialect of the Afarhid became clear to him. 'Great soldier, thou art a fool. . . .'

Masterman said, 'Hamid, you must surrender. I have soldiers in the desert.'

'Soldiers, master? Three crows chasing their shadows; a lorry fixed in the sand.'

'Give yourself up to me!'

'Foul thyself.'

A rifle shot and the whine of a ricochet merged into a single violent noise. Hamid's bullet had struck within inches of the Colonel's body. He did not know if the soldier had fired wide deliberately, but none the less he took careful aim into the shadows, at the point from which the voice had spoken, and fired three rounds in rapid succession.

'Thou art a fool, a fool....'

Colonel Masterman lay in the shadow of the rock and worked himself forward on his elbows. He was happy in action. He was fighting a trained soldier who had the surpassing courage of the bedouin, and in this there was an ancient fitness.

Just let me get a crack at him, he thought.

From the veranda of the officers' mess Sheikh Saud could hear the shots quite plainly. The rhythmic pattern of the firing continued for about three minutes; then a pause intervened.

Abdullah, who had taken only casual interest in the shots, said now, 'This Hamid—he has been a nuisance. Yes?'

Saud nodded gravely. 'He cannot forgive the Colonel for killing Captain Sloan,' he said; and he grunted in confirmation of his own opinion.

A single shot sounded next, then another. Saud could not tell which way they had gone, but he supposed them to be Hamid's.

The bedouin soldier left cover, carrying his rifle. He emptied the magazine, eased the firing spring, and crossed the stony ground to where his adversary was lying. A white dawn spread along the dunes giving light enough for him to see. From Warboys Camp he heard the starting of a vehicle, and he saw the headlights—diminished now in the first daylight—pass through the gate and begin to probe into the desert, but he paid no attention. He stood for a time beside Colonel

Masterman, whose body lay face downward with the rifle still extended; then he turned the body with his foot and looked at the face. He laughed. A minute later he sat cross-legged, cradling the head in his arms, crying, while the noise of the vehicle being forced through the lower gears came closer to him, and the light grew in strength to the point where he must soon be seen.

The brash English voices alerted him as the soldiers left the vehicle and continued their search on foot. He did not hesitate then. He stood up quickly, slung his rifle as he had been taught, and vanished into the rocks.